Story By

Thomas Knapp

Based on MegaTokyo: Endgames By

Fred Gallagher

Editor

Ray Kremer

Copyright 2014 Fred Gallagher. MegaTokyo and MegaTokyo: Endgames are registered trademarks of Fredart Studios LLC

Day 1: The Keep by the Sea

Pirogoeth was not fond of walking. Seemed like a fairly silly exercise, all things considered. For the sake of general activity, there were a multitude of more engaging things. For the sake of travel, there were several more effective means.

They had been using one such method to cross the distance through her home in Bakkra, in the Western Free Provinces, to where they were now, but the old man leading her decided just yesterday to drop their horses and take the rest of the travel on foot.

The elderly male had said they were rented horses, and could not be taken off the Great Trade Line, which was believable enough, but didn't make the walk any less of a nuisance.

The cobblestones, well made for a horse's hooves, not so much for human feet, weren't doing her any favors. Even with well fitting boots, her heels were becoming unbearably sore, and she could feel spikes of pain shooting up her shins with each step.

"It is a truly wonderful day. Not too hot, with clear skies and a gentle breeze. These are the perfect days to take a walk in this beautiful world we live in without stressing your thoughts. A long walk is an exercise in resting your mind," her escort offered. He liked such wordplay. Pirogoeth wasn't fond of it. She said nothing, lest she encourage further attempts at banter.

Dominus Socrato, Venerated Citizen of The Imperial Aramathea, one of the most prominent mages of the living world, was *nothing* like what Pirogoeth had expected.

He *looked* the part of an Aramathean elder, that much was true. Bronzed skin, a thin line of silver hair in a half circle around his otherwise bald head, thin withered frame wrapped in a pristine white toga and tied with a golden sash that managed to somehow remain unblemished despite the dusty trade lines they had followed for the last two weeks. A pair of round, sophisticated glasses dangled from a gold chain at his neck, though he had not *used* them, finished the look of a respected, learned sage of the Southern empire.

But that was where it ended. He moved with a vitality that should not have come from a man of such evident years. There was no creaks to his joints, no apparent aches and pains. And there was little in the way of quiet reservation. Socrato was jovial, boisterous, and loud; as quick with biting wit as sage wisdom.

Socrato was undeterred. "You could at least *pretend* to look more enthusiastic, young lady," he commented, bright and cheery despite his advanced age; his voice not reflecting any discomfort despite the sandals on his feet, of all things.

"There are a thousand mages in the world, of varying talent. I have only deemed a handful worthy of my attention," he continued in monologue. "Are you not aware of your opportunity, I wonder?"

Of course Pirogoeth knew. Her first teacher, Torma, had been one of those rare pupils to learn from the Dominus. When Pirogoeth started to exceed what Torma was willing and able to teach, that had led to the summoning of Socrato. Torma had spent the last two weeks before the elder Armathean's arrival in Bakkra telling Pirogoeth all about the honor she was receiving.

Torma had not mentioned anything about a day's hike.

"Still not impressed, are you?" the wizened mage noted, his lips turning downward into something that wasn't an obnoxiously cheery smile for the first time Pirogoeth could note. His gaze drifted off the road, towards the southwest, and he said, "Maybe *this* will stir your spirit."

Socrato then veered off the cobblestone, and onto the dry grass, taking far longer strides than Pirogoeth would have expected for someone his age. She scrambled to keep up with him; while the dry grass was easier on her feet than the road, her boots didn't get quite as good of a grip.

Her path went up a steadily increasing incline, while the road wound south around the rise. Socrato looked down from his position at the top of the hill, beckoning her forward. She clenched her jaw in annoyance, and forced herself up the remaining distance.

Once she reached the summit, huffing with lost breath, she followed Socrato's outstretched hand and the panorama provided by the higher ground, focusing on the southwest, and the heavily walled keep in the distance.

Pirogoeth had certainly *heard* of keeps like the one in front of her. She had even listened to Torma speak of this particular one. But when the largest "city" she had ever experienced was the wood-walled city-state of Wassalm, this was a jolt to the system to see in person.

Below, the hill dropped into a fertile valley at the mouth of a river that emptied into the South Forever Sea. Sitting upon that delta was a double walled keep, the first exterior wall of dark gray stone, with several entrances both from land and from the river as it branched across the delta. Between the first and second walls were colorful awnings of shops and shingled roofs of houses.

This was followed by the second wall, but of a different material that Pirogoeth couldn't quite identify from the distance, only that it was considerably lighter, and shimmered under the sunlight. Then, within that interior wall, was a tower of the same material, reaching to such heights that even with Pirogoeth's vantage point it required her to lift her head to see the top.

The top of the tower more resembled an observation deck, with a copper dome on the top, though the angle made it hard to tell what the dome was for.

A smile of triumph stretched across Socrato's cheeks. "This is Kartage, my domain, and home to the tallest man-made construction short of the Royal Spire in Grand Aramathea."

He puffed out his chest, and said proudly, "This is where you will continue your learning, a place where you can apply your studies without worrying of terrifying villagers with pyroclastic displays. There are no bullies to torment you as you read. No menial chores to waste your time and talents. You will be respected here for the gifts you possess, for this is where magic is expected, and much will be expected in turn."

Pirogoeth tried very hard to sound annoyed, but wasn't successful. "You have managed to impress me. Well done."

Socrato turned about with a bright laugh, and began to retrace his steps back towards the road. "Come along, dear girl. The road is not much longer."

That was more music to Pirogoeth's ears. "Good. I haven't walked this far in my life."

The old sage then abruptly stopped, nearly causing Pirogoeth to run into him. "Unless..." He said thoughtfully, then spun right back about towards the crest of the hill. "You tire of walking, do you?"

Pirogoeth followed as Socrato returned to the road, stopping just shy on the grass. "Yes..." she said warily, deciding that being truthful was the better part of valor.

And at that point, Socrato pushed her onto the decline.

It was a fairly sharp decline at that, and Pirogoeth quickly gathered speed, curling into a tight ball in a potentially vain attempt to avoid serious injury. Fortunately, the earth was much softer than its parched appearance would have implied, with so much give that she barely felt each impact.

The sky and the ground blurred into one incoherent mess in her eyesight, and vertigo began to play tricks with her stomach. She remembered her peers would go rolling down the hills outside of school after classes ended, and that they seemed to have no end of fun doing so.

Now with that experience, Pirogoeth really did not understand the allure at all.

The world didn't stop spinning even after she finally did, splayed out on her back, her hair having come free of its ties, and the longer locks at the back of her head having come to rest over her face.

As her mind finally began to sort itself out, she sensed a shadow fall over her. Pushing her hair out of her eyes, clearing eyesight processed Socrato hovering above, a broad smile again stretching his cheeks. "Enjoy yourself?"

"Are you *insane*, you old bat?" Pirogoeth screeched, quickly scrambling to her feet only to discover that her balance hadn't quite returned and forcing her back gracelessly to her knees. "Are you trying to *kill me*?"

Socrato scoffed at the accusation. "Oh, do not be a dramatic. I assure the Hermian Theatre has plenty of actors already, and does not need any more. I promise you were in no danger, and look! It was so much faster, wasn't it?"

Pirogoeth rubbed dust off her face, and tried to beat it out of her clothes, with less success. "Oh, is that how you travel this path, then?" she snarled in a voice dripping with sarcasm.

The old sage shook his head as if dismayed by the thought. "Oh Coders, no! My frail body couldn't possibly take such a jostling. No, such a method is best reserved for the young. Oh... you dropped these, by the way." Socrato held out his right hand, holding her faded leather hair ties. Pirogoeth crossly ripped them out of his palm, angrily tying back her hair while scowling in disapproval of her new teacher.

The old man regarded Pirogoeth's appearance, and then declared, "We will have to get you some new clothes in Kartage. It simply will not do to have you looking so dirty in my tower."

"*That's because you pushed me down that damned hill!*" Pirogoeth bellowed.

Socrato's jaw dropped with mock astonishment. "Language, young lady! I will not have such an uncouth tongue in my halls!"

It was obvious that Socrato was intentionally prodding her temper, and so Pirogoeth clenched her teeth tightly, forcing back any further words. She doubted it would stop him, ignoring bullying behavior never did, but it didn't do her any good to keep playing his games.

He wasn't wrong, if Pirogoeth was being entirely honest with herself. Even before her tumble, her clothes would hardly have been considered sophisticated or lovely. They were working clothes, designed for a life in the farming community of Bakkra, not the halls of learning in Kartage.

"Come along. It's not even an hour to go, if we do not linger," Socrato announced, gesturing Pirogoeth to follow as he took the shortest path available back to the road. Pirogoeth clenched her eyes, took a calming breath, and fell in step behind him.

She really started to get a sense of just how large Kartage was as they got ever closer. It looked big before, but the full height of its sixty-foot-tall walls didn't sink in until they stood before her, looming and imposing. The only breach through that nigh impenetrable barrier held the promise of two thick metal portcullises, one behind the other, hovering above the entry to block any unwanted sorts. And if that wasn't enough of a dissuasion, the score of Arameathan soldiers, ten to each side, would no doubt offer further pause.

"One wasn't enough?" Pirogoeth asked dryly, pointing to the barricades locked in an open position.

"If you look closely, the second door is solid steel," Socrato corrected. "It's used at this gate in the spring to hold back water after the snows melt in the North and flood the delta."

He then leaned in, and with a conspiratorial note added, "One of the keep's defense mechanisms involve storing water from the high tide, and temporarily flooding the plain in the case of an attack. You'd be amazed at how devastating the power of water can be."

"Hmm," Pirogoeth acknowledged passively.

Socrato clicked his tongue in disappointment. "I would recommend not being so dismissive. I understand Torma allowed you to play with fire nigh exclusively, but as my student, I will expect you to respect and to be versed in all the schools of magic by the time you leave."

Pirogoeth didn't have the desire to explain it was a lack of interest in flood plains rather than a lack of interest in magic. "Yes, Dominus," she said.

Socrato's eyes narrowed suspiciously, but he didn't press the issue further. "Yes, yes. Very good. Now onward."

Getting through the gates was not just a matter of walking right through, to Pirogoeth's surprise. She would have figured the lord of the keep would not be held up.

"Greetings, Dominus," one of the soldiers to the right of the gate, distinguished by three red bands crossing over the chest plate of his bronzed armor, said amiably, even as he lowered his spear in their path. "Papers please."

"Ah! Yes, of course, Captain," Socrato replied with equal cheer, reaching into his clothing no doubt for the documents requested. Pirogoeth couldn't help but find it extremely odd to see such a pleasant exchange while in the presence of drawn weapons.

The documents were taken, examined, and returned, then the captain's spear returned to its rest position, followed with a respectful bow. "Thank you, Dominus. I trust the girl is with you?"

"Yes, Captain, she is. This is Pirogoeth; she will be my pupil for the time being," Socrato declared. "I trust she will have papers drawn up for her as well."

The captain bowed again. "At once, Dominus. I'll have Footman Trius send word to the Registrar immediately."

An official order wasn't necessary, as a member at the rear of the company immediately broke off and retreated into the keep proper. Then the captain addressed Pirogoeth with another respectful bow. "Apprentice Pirogoeth, I welcome you to Kartage. If there is anything you require during your stay, day or night, you need merely ask any of the Phalanx stationed here. If they cannot offer assistance, they will find out who can."

Pirogoeth was not used to such reverence, especially from someone so physically imposing. She could get used to this. "Thank you, Captain..." She let her voice drop off, hoping to bait out a name to go along with the rank.

"Daneid, my lady." The captain correctly offered, earning him a pleasant smile.

Socrato sternly leveled a glare first at the soldier, then at Pirogoeth. "Let's press on, Apprentice," the sage said coldly. "We still have to get you some new clothes before settling you into your quarters."

He stepped forward deliberately, and when he felt Pirogoeth wasn't responding as he liked added gruffly, "Make haste, my girl. You were the one that wanted to get off your feet."

She shuffled off after Socrato, eyes narrowing in annoyance. But before she could demand what had irritated him, he provided the answer.

"Captain Daneid is a decade your senior." He said simply.

Pirogoeth rolled her eyes. "Coders... did you *honestly* think that was what was on my mind?"

"Don't pretend you weren't preening."

She didn't deny it, mostly because the old sage wasn't wrong. "I'm... not used to that sort of attention and respect."

"Some attention isn't worth what you get from it," Socrato grumbled warningly. "Not from the captain there, to be fair. He would most certainly respect your limits. But some men are not nearly so gentlemanly." The old man's eyes narrowed, seeing something ahead as they got closer to the bazaar. "Like this example..."

Two men appeared from the horde of shoppers in the marketplace, leading a pair of long haired, stockily built horses the likes of which Pirogoeth had not seen before, one chestnut brown and the other black with white markings across its snout and flanks.

The men themselves were most certainly *not* Aramathean: They were both far too pale in both skin and hair color to ever be confused for people of the southern lands. The first one caught her eye because of his size; if he wasn't seven feet tall he was close enough for it to not be of much difference, and likely would have looked even taller if not for the slight curve to his back. He had broad, shoulders and impressive bulk, and a mop of black hair pulled pack into a simple, inelegant tail. She had no doubt he was very physically strong, even if his build was not carefully sculpted muscles like the soldiers at the gate.

He was also dressed simply and suitably: light brown trousers and similarly colored sleeveless shirt. If it wasn't for his sheer size, he'd be a perfectly unassuming fellow.

His hands and face carried heavy callouses and scars, with dark stains on his palms. His brown eyes squinted in the sunlight, taking in everything as they darted back and forth nervously. It took Pirogoeth a while to remember where she had seen those sort of traits before. Once she did, it seemed pretty obvious. At some point in time, this man had been a miner. It could not have been a comfortable life, and explained the curve in his back. Mining tunnels were not large.

The other man was nearly everything the first was not. He was long, gangly, and thin, like he had been uncomfortably stretched three inches longer than he was supposed to be. A neatly trimmed mustache and carefully styled hair, mostly hidden under a flamboyantly red feathered hat, and a similarly colored formal suit nearly hid the similar traits he shared with his companion. They were most likely related in some fashion if the eye, hair color and skin tone were any indication.

"Dominus Socrato! Pleasant days to you, my lordship!" the

smaller one declared with a wave, halting his procession. "It is so rare to see you outside your tower this early in the day."

For all the pleasantness the man was trying to project, Socrato was not putting on airs. "If only it were as rare to see you here, Julian."

Julian threw his hand over his heart in dramatic pain. "You wound me, Dominus! My trade only comes through twice a season at best!"

"Which is twice too many as far as I am concerned, charlatan," Socrato said with a dismissive scoff.

Julian lost his joviality, protesting, "That was a *year ago*, and I paid due recompense, with added value, I may add, for those who bought my reptile scale serum! I have not attempted to sell *anything* I have not personally vetted since!"

"And what exactly were you trying to validate when you were cavorting with my magister's daughter last fall, may I ask?"

"She seduced *me!*" Julian countered. "Tell him, Pierre!"

Pirogoeth had expected a simple voice and manner from Julian's larger companion. But rather than follow that cliche, Pierre was soft in tone and well spoken with remarkable enunciation and clarity of voice despite the low volume: "I am not getting involved."

"I remain astonished how your brother got both the size *and* intellect in your family." Socrato said with a polite nod to the larger man. "I trust you are doing your best to keep him out of trouble, Pierre."

A long, tired breath escaped Pierre's lips. "As much as I am able."

During that exchange, Julian caught sight of the girl behind the Dominus. "Hello, hello! Who do we have here?"

Socrato quickly imposed himself between Julian and Pirogoeth. "Someone so far above you that to even *try* to gaze up to her level would break your neck, peddler."

It was only at this point that Julian became visibly cross. "I was asking *her*, Dominus. I didn't think you'd be one to presume to speak for a lady."

"My name is Pirogoeth. I am Socrato's newest apprentice," she finally said, "And I am right here, so I'd appreciate it if you both stopped speaking of me as if I weren't."

"An apprentice?" Julian said, the smarmy grin returning. "Then I would guess the Dominus is right that these are matters beyond me. So with that, I must end this banter. Pierre and I have much ground to cover along the coast if we are to make Reaht by the end of summer."

With that, Socrato's face softened from scorn to mild interest, "Taking a long route this year, are you?"

Julian shrugged. "Some clients back home have a taste for more exotic fare, and when the money is right, I take the long road. I wouldn't think you'd be so bothered to know that I'd be absent until fall at the least."

Pirogoeth sensed there was more to this discussion than the two were letting on, like a secret code only they understood. Socrato's next words didn't change that impression. "I know well how goods from Reaht are received in Aramathea. We tend to not approve of such foreign goods passing through our lands."

"I take all care, as you should well know."

"If only you kept the goods in your trousers as well hidden."

Julian clicked his tongue cheekily, then with a flick of his right hand, beckoned his brother forward, leading their laden horses around Socrato and Pirogoeth. "Oh, I did just deliver some fine linen and silk from Caravel to Lanka's Clothiers. I bet they'd be a welcome change from the rags your apprentice is currently clad in," he said in parting.

"*Thank you, peddler,*" Socrato snarled loudly in annoyance at the retreating pair. "Come along, girl. As obnoxious as the merchant can be, he knows his materials. We'll take his advice."

"Who were they?" Pirogoeth queried as they resumed their own path, though she doubted she'd get a straight answer. "I sense they were more than mere merchants."

"Their names, as you should already know, are Julian and Pierre," Socrato answered. "As for what they do, it depends entirely on who you are. For your sake, you should hope they remain mere merchants. The moment they become more than that, it means trouble."

"I take it they did something bad here?"

Socrato shook his head, and reluctantly grumbled, "No. Not here. And in all honesty, it was trouble I invited upon myself. The only thing they did was exactly what I told them to do. It's my fault I didn't take all the risks into consideration."

"What happened?" she pressed further.

Socrato eyed her warily, and bristled. "I asked them to acquire a very valuable item for me. I did not expect the previous owner to be quite so unreasonable in his price. So when I told them to get it, no matter the cost, I didn't exactly impress to them that the cost needed to be greater than zero."

"They stole it," she surmised.

"In a sense, in the way that merchants 'steal' things," Socrato clarified. "They traded a great many items with highly perceived value that had little real value. When the man they cheated learned of this, he was understandably irate, and came to me with that rage, as I had the item in question. It was... not a pleasant exchange, and I had to get... violent. It was a very important item for me to have, you see. Vital for my research. I will not pretend that I was wholly in the right, but it needed to be done."

"What could be so important?" Pirogoeth said, more wondering out loud than an actual question.

Socrato offered a vague, "You may find out, presuming I find you worthy of that knowledge." He turned right, pointing ahead, and added, "This way. Lanka's is off the center road by more than a handful of strides. She likes it that way... She is not fond of random customers."

The exterior of the shop certainly reflected that desire to not attract walk-ins. It was dingy wood with faded red awnings over windows that had not been cleaned in some time, judging from the layer of dust caked upon them.

Inside, however, was a picture of exquisite luxury. Plush red carpeting was a blessing to Pirogoeth's feet, and the windows to the rear of the store facing away from the road were impeccably clean, casting sunlight through to illuminate the interior. A chandelier of crystal overhead was currently unlit, but Pirogoeth had little doubt it would look spectacular as evening approached.

Waterfalls of velvet, satin, silk, lace... every fabric Pirogoeth knew existed, and many that she didn't, lined the shelves and the walls. A central desk with a satin cover and a stack of books drew her attention as a woman stepped through a curtain on the south side of the building.

The woman was the embodiment of elegance, wearing a long-sleeved violet dress of silk with gold trim, embroidered with what Pirogoeth vaguely recognized as Ancient Aramathean runes across the sleeves and skirt. It highlighted her deep caramel skin and the black hair tied back with a shimmering, thin silver band across her forehead. The woman wasn't exactly young, but she wasn't old either... Resting right at that age where she still had a youthful glow but also possessed an experienced, practiced posture and manner.

She threw her hands out wide, and sang, "Dominus Socrato! It is a pleasure to see you again, my master. It has been far too long!"

Socrato grinned brightly. "Lanka, I keep telling you, if you want to see me more often, you simply must not make such fabulous and indestructible clothing."

"Which is why I am surprised to see you," Lanka retorted. "I can't imagine you need something mended already."

"It is not for me," the Dominus answered, "but for my apprentice here. Pirogoeth, step forward if you may. Lanka does not see distances well."

Pirogoeth complied, shuffling forward in front of Socrato and directly into the line of sight of the clothier.

"Oh my! Such a slight and tiny thing!" Lanka squealed. "You are just so adorable, I could eat you up!"

Pirogoeth was not amused, but tried to hide her annoyance with a thin lipped smile. She hated being reminded of her small stature.

Lanka, however, gave it no further thought, putting her right hand on her chin in appraisal. "You are clearly not Aramathean. Western Free Provinces, I'm guessing." Leaning in closer, the clothier nodded in affirmation. "Indeed, you have the eyes of a Dayne and the complexion of an Avalonian. High cheek bones, consistent with a mixed heritage, though your brows carry a hint of Sparian blood of the old North Aramathea. You are from Wassalm, am I correct?"

Pirogoeth was genuinely surprised by how close the clothier had gotten just from a look at her face. "You came very close. Bakkra, not even two days travel to the west. Though the city-state is so small you might not have ever heard of it."

"I have now," Lanka sang, flipping open the top most book of the central pile on her desk, testing a quill with her tongue before making a quick note. She then pushed that book out of the way before picking up the next three and making another stack with them further down the desk. "Now then, you will no doubt be needing at least two outfits straight away, formal attire and training clothes, am I correct?"

"You are, as always, Lanka." Socrato supplied.

Pirogoeth asked, "What of those times when I'm not at some formal gathering or training?"

"You can get such plain, unremarkable rags anywhere else," Lanka grumped. "I do not do mundane, child. I specialize in the hardy and elegant, the sturdy and the refined." The clothier spun about swiftly, and started rifling through the books she had set aside, making thoughtful sounds as she turned the pages, and stealing occasional glances at Pirogoeth.

"Yes, I do believe I have something which will suit until we can fashion something specifically for her," Lanka at last declared, moving back to the original pile of books and carefully sliding one out from the middle of the stacks. "Hmm... yes... this way, my dear girl. I shall get you dressed for the proper occasion."

Socrato nodded his approval, and said, "I shall wait here for your return."

Pirogoeth obeyed, falling in step behind the taller clothier as they crossed past the curtains into the back room of the shop. "As an apprentice mage under Dominus Socrato, you will be learning and doing things that you likely have never done before. The clothes and gear for your training will need... special traits in order to stand the tests ahead."

The rear section of the shop was set up for efficiency as the front was set up for aesthetics. The shelves were more like cubbies: small compartments where finished items were sorted by type, fabric, and style.

The sets nearest to them were gloves. Lanka found the number she was looking for etched on the front of the compartment, drawing out a pair of brightly polished leather with open fingers and bronze colored trim. "Try those on, and tell me how they fit. You will want them snug and tight, as loose fitting gloves can allow residue both physical and ethereal to linger and potentially cause injury over time."

Pirogoeth complied, though she had never heard of such consequences. "Really?" the apprentice asked as she pulled on the left glove over her hand.

"Dominus Socrato is an accomplished apothecary as well as a mage. He will likely teach you the crafting of such potables as well... the residue of which can be very flammable or reactive when the energy of spell casting flows through you. You would not be the first to severely burn her hand in such a fashion."

"I see," Pirogoeth said thoughtfully. "Then I worry these might be a bit too loose."

Lanka plucked the material to assess for herself, then came to agreement. "Indeed they are. No matter, for there are many other options. Try these..."

From gloves, they moved onto bracers. "By instinct, people tend to cover their faces with their arms. It helps to have some actual protection on those arms, yes?"

Then, leggings... With knee and seat pads. "You might be surprised how often you will find yourself thrown to the ground by an errant spell or concoction. Something sturdy and padded is essential."

A jerkin. "Thin enough for ease of movement, but with added protection in the chest. Feel how the chest is firmly molded and not the same supple leather as the rest? You will likely need a belt for these and your trousers to fit properly. One moment..."

Then boots. "Open toed shoes are *never* a wise choice for an apprentice. Until you have mastered your art, you will no doubt have a lot of stray energy spraying about. Residual embers from magical channeling can and has burned the feet of many a young mage. Now, go try these on in the changing room at the east end."

When Pirogoeth returned five minutes later, she wasn't sure she liked it... "I look more like I'm getting ready to train in swordplay rather than spellcraft."

"Why shouldn't you?" Lanka asked. "Magic is far more dangerous than any steel. And rest assured, whatever learning you had before you came under the Dominus's wing will be nothing compared to what you are to experience." Then with a warm smile, Lanka offered, "But I think you'll find this next part much more fanciful to your eye."

Truth being, it wasn't. Pirogoeth had never been particularly driven to look "pretty" or "cute" or "fancy." She found dressing up to be a chore more than anything. That opinion didn't change when she found herself in a long sleeved pale blue formal gown with silver trim, complete with puffed shoulders and pearl colored high-heeled shoes and matching gloves. Though she did appreciate that it was an Aramathean design rather than some that she had seen from Avalon with the crinoline that flared the skirt to absurd sizes.

Lanka added a belt of similar color to the gown for Pirogoeth's waist, and said, "It will suit for now. I'll have you properly measured and better fitting formal and training attire prepared as soon as I am able."

"So can I change back?" Pirogoeth asked.

Lanka's lips curled in distaste. "Girl, I would sooner *burn* those filthy garments you came in here with before I let you trudge up my store again. I'll package your training gear, and you can wear that out."

Pirogoeth held back a groan, not wanting to insult the shopkeeper. High heels were *not* exactly helping her sore feet.

Lanka offered a silent answer to that concern, presenting a pair of blissfully low heeled tanned moccasins. With a conspiratorial lowered voice, the clothier said, "Perhaps I have *some* plain and unremarkable things in this store. But only shoes, and only because I know what a terror raised heels are."

As Pirogoeth changed shoes, the clothier ordered, "now, return to the Dominus, I will be back with your purchases shortly."

Pirogoeth then reminded herself these were things that had an expectation of being paid for. "How much will all this cost?"

"Never you mind that, apprentice. The price is between the Dominus and myself."

"But..."

Lanka said sharply, "If price were an object, or he expected you to pay, he would not have brought you to me. Now *out!*"

With a startled squeak, Pirogoeth scampered through the curtain and to the sales floor. Socrato seemed quite pleased with her new appearance. "Lanka has an eye for what looks good. Just wait until she has the chance to tailor something for you."

On that prompt, Lanka emerged from behind the curtain with a cloth covered package bound in silk ribbon. In her other hand was a tape measure and a row of pins between her lips. "Come here, girl. Let's get you measured," she ordered between clenched teeth as she laid the bundle down on the desk.

The clothier's skills were readily apparent as she swiftly used the tape and pins to take various measurements at every perceivable angle around Pirogoeth's frame without even so much as a prick from any of the needles, and recording the numbers in still another book at her desk.

"Very good," Lanka declared. "I think I have a good idea of what will look magnificent on her as well, Dominus. I trust money is no object."

"Is it ever?" Socrato answered with a smile.

"I shall have three sets of training and formal clothes available in two weeks time. I will send word the morning they are completed."

Socrato bowed respectfully, which Lanka returned. "Ever gracious. Thank you again, Madam Lanka." He straightened and then spun about with a gesture to Pirogoeth. "Come now, child."

Once outside Lanka's store, Socrato asked, "Would you like to finish shopping, or save that for the next day and instead settle into your new living arrangements?"

"I *really* need to get off my feet," Pirogoeth admitted tiredly.

Socrato nodded. If he were disappointed by her admission of fatigue, he didn't show it. "Understandable. Then come this way, to the tower we go."

But once they stepped back onto the main path, it was as if a thick blanket fell on the bazaar, muffling the ambient noise. Pirogoeth was keenly aware that a considerable amount of attention had turned her way.

"There she is!" someone nearby declared, though Pirogoeth couldn't identify the source of the voice in the crowd. "The girl with the Dominus!"

"Is that the one that Socrato will be teaching?" another asked. "She doesn't much *look* like a Princess."

"If she *is* the Crown Princess of Avalon, she likely would have never seen the court."

Pirogoeth looked up at Socrato and asked, "do you hear that? What are they talking about?"

Socrato kept his eyes forward as if he heard nothing amiss. "Empty gossip. The lands to the west had a violent revolution years ago, and the royal family there was executed. Some believe that one of them escaped into the Free Provinces."

"And they think I might be that person?" Pirogoeth said with a roll of her eyes. "Hate to disappoint them. My family has been mudrakers in Bakkra for generations."

"I am aware. All the more reason not to dignify their flights of fancy with a response," Socrato advised. "There are going to be many assumptions about you due to your association with me, though it will rarely be to your face."

"Wouldn't be the first time people gossiped about me," Pirogoeth replied darkly.

Socrato nodded in somber approval. "No, I suppose it wouldn't. Let's waste no more thought on baseless banter. We are almost to the tower."

As large as it looked earlier, that *still* didn't do the size of the tower justice once she reached its base, its diameter at least five times as wide as the main road through Bakkra. Socrato let the size and scale sink in; then, after he deemed suitable respect was paid, put a hand on Pirogoeth's back to usher her forward.

They passed over the thick stained oak double doors at the main entrance, he instead guiding her along a cobblestone path around the perimeter to the west. As it curved to the south, the path declined, going to a depth of at least fifteen feet by the time they reached the opposite side of the tower. A single, less grandiose iron door appeared over the bend, guarded by two Aramathean soldiers.

"And why are we going this way?" Pirogoeth queried.

Socrato said, "This is a less conspicuous entry. I prefer it so as to avoid too much attention from those waiting in my tower who do not deserve it."

The door swung outward by an invisible hand, but the light from outside offered no illumination of what was across the threshold. "It's a magical defensive mechanism." Socrato assured as he saw Pirogoeth's wary step forward. "If you were an invader, you'd have much to fear. As you are not, there is nothing on the other side that can or will harm you."

A desire to not look like a fearful child overcame being a fearful child. With a quick, irritated glance at Socrato, Pirogoeth took two deliberate steps forward...

... Into a lavish, well-furnished bedroom.

Spinning about back where she came, she discovered not only was the exterior door no longer there, it seemed that there was no reason for it to be there. The wall behind her was, in fact, an interior wall, made from thin wood without even a window, much less a doorway.

The exit was in front of her, and led into a curved hallway that she assumed was an interior hall of Socrato's tower; well maintained and lit with candelabras every five or six feet, though Pirogoeth correctly guessed that is was no normal fire that burned from the unmelted wax sticks.

She took a step back and turned full about again, this time let herself take in what was her new home.

It was indeed exquisite, if a bit too pink for her liking. The carpet beneath her, drapes and bedding were awash in the hue, although it was tolerable considering that she had a genuine *bed*. She was used to the old cot back in Bakkra. While she had never thought it uncomfortable, that opinion changed the minute she threw herself down onto the mattress with her arms thrown out to her sides.

It felt like she was floating on a cloud, a softness she had never experienced before. The mattress surrendered to her every movement, the resistance so gradual that it seemed like she would never stop sinking into it.

"I do apologize if you were disoriented by the travel. Some do not take shifting very well," Socrato said from the doorway, causing Pirogoeth to yelp in surprise and tumble onto her stomach so she could face the venerable sage.

"Shifting?" Pirogoeth asked.

"It's a means of connecting two places together that are not connected. It's a rather complex art that is usually not worth the time invested into it. But useful if you want to get from one place you frequent to another quickly."

"I see," she replied, though she wasn't sure she did.

"Enjoying your accommodations?" Socrato then asked, his eyes perusing the room with what looked to be pride.

"I don't so much like the color," she admitted.

Socrato shrugged. "Easily enough changed," he then said, snapping his fingers... and turning everything that had been pink into a pale blue. "Or would you prefer green?" Another snap, and sure enough, her room was now a light green.

"How are you doing that?"

Socrato grinned. "The art of illusion. The mind is a very powerful thing. What you believe affects what you see, not so much the other way around. Even when you *know* it is a ruse, your eyes will often refuse to believe you."

Out of curiosity, Pirogoeth asked, "then what is the *real* color in this room?"

"What *is* real other than what we perceive to be true?" Socrato answered. "If you see green, and I see orange, which one of us is wrong? How *does* orange look to you, by the way?" A snap followed, and the room changed to an orange cream, which Pirogoeth immediately showed distaste in. "No? How about brown?"

Pirogoeth blinked in the middle of the shift this time, finding her surroundings now a rustic earth tone. "Then allow me to rephrase, what were the colors in this room before you started working your magic?"

A snap, and the room became a very drab and lifeless white. "That one."

Pirogoeth smiled in amusement and said, "I'll take the blue."

With her room the color she preferred, she asked, "So I take it I'll be able to do this sort of thing in time?"

Socrato nodded warily. "I am sure... though not as effortlessly. All mages have their innate talents; we're more naturally skilled in some schools, and less in others. Torma told me you are more attuned to material magics, fire most notably. My talents tend to lie in the ethereal, like the illusions you saw here. While I insist on my students being versed in all schools, you are naturally going to shape your strengths far more than your weaknesses."

He then reached into his toga, and pulled out a narrow tome. "Speaking of which... this is for you."

Pirogoeth hopped out of the bed, and eagerly dashed to the

sage, a broad smile on her face as he handed her the tome. Her first magical book, and it was indeed all hers.

Most mages of the world could cast minor cantrips without channeling anything, and up until now, that was what Torma had had her doing. To do anything beyond a flash of fire or skip a stone across a lake with a thought, a mage needed a much more robust power source.

And that was where tomes came to be. Within the pages of such enchanted books, mages could channel far more complex and powerful techniques. While she doubted anything too incredible would be found in that thin book that was maybe fifty pages if she were being generous, it was still a significant step forward from what she had been able to experience up to that point.

"That is a third edition training manual," Socrato warned. "Do be careful with it."

Pirogoeth nodded, understanding the serious responsibility her new master had given her. Few spells were new and unique at this point. The old enchanters from ages ago had long mastered most of the techniques that would form the backbone of the magical arts. The best that modern mages could do was pass along that knowledge as well as they could.

But there was no such thing as an exact copy. With each iteration, minor flaws would be introduced to the tomes. And while every so often a correction of an older tome would be made that would restore some or most of the old ways potency, or an alteration that actually served to increase the power of the original, a good rule of thumb was that the older the edition, the more powerful the techniques within it were. A third edition was at the very least a century old, and possibly older depending on how well its owners maintained and repaired it. She held it close to her chest and said, "I will, Dominus."

"Study it tonight. Dinner will be provided shortly to your room. I doubt you want to be immersed in tower life on your first night in strange environs."

Socrato then departed, closing the bedroom door behind him. Pirogoeth returned to her bed, sat down, and examined the thin tome more carefully. Some magical books had elaborate covers, but this was not one of them. Plain russet brown leather and an equally unremarkable black binding. It appeared to be a trait of books once owned or possessed by Socrato, as Pirogoeth recalled that many of Torma's tomes had been unremarkable in appearance as well.

The spine creaked warningly as she lifted the cover, and she winced in worry. Quickly examining the binding to make sure she hadn't *already* damaged the tome Socrato left in her care, she determined the sound to be natural to the behavior of older leather, and her nerves calmed. At that point, she allowed herself to drink in the contents of the tome.

That wasn't as much a metaphor as what really happened. To someone without the spark of magic, a tome would look like nothing more than an empty book. They'd see no writing, no runes, no diagrams, or anything other than blank pages from front to back.

To those that *did* possess the gift of magic, what was etched within jumped from the page; energy flowed from the tome, through the body and weaved itself into the memory of the mage. Some spells, like the bulk of those within the book, could be retained and cast at whim with enough repetition. More complex techniques could not be so easily remembered, or had physical components necessary for the spell to be properly channeled.

Like one that Pirogoeth had just come across on the tenth page. An immensely powerful flash of fire, far hotter and more intense than what she would be able to normally channel from this tome... but required an already existing flame as a catalyst.

There were a few spells in the tome which were like that, requiring certain conditions or items on hand to be properly used. No doubt *this* was the measure of a mage: it was more than learning spells, but the circumstances that allowed them to be used to maximum effect.

Then there were the ethereal techniques that Pirogoeth found were as alien to her as Socrato expected they would be. She understood the concept behind the power of the mind, but she was a far more practical sort, and had a hard time wrapping her brain around casting magic that by design wasn't there.

This promised to be *nothing* like the simple spellcraft and study she had had with Torma back home.

Home.

It occurred to her that she hadn't given much thought to her family back in Bakkra since she hopped on the Great Trade Line to The Imperial Aramathea. She hadn't felt at all guilty about that... until she felt guilty for not feeling guilty.

It was silly to feel bad about it, she told herself. It's not like she had much value on the farmland. A diminutive girl with barely any physical strength or wide birthing hips wasn't exactly what would be called an asset, either in the field or as a wife. Life with the other village children her age had not been... pleasant, either. If word of

Pirogoeth's gift hadn't managed to filter to a journeyman mage passing through named Torma...

Pirogoeth *really* didn't want to think about *that*.

But despite the troubles, she didn't think she had grown up unloved. Her father had worked hard to support his family, had never hurt her or even harshly punished her. Her mother the same. They both had accepted what little help Pirogoeth could provide on the farm without expressing shame or disappointment.

They had gladly accepted Torma's aid in assisting Pirogoeth with her awakened talents. They had tearfully accepted Torma's recommendation that Pirogoeth learn from Torma's old master nearly half a continent away.

She missed them both already.

A sharp rap on the door turned Pirogoeth's head from the tome and her thoughts. "Come in," she said.

An Aramathean girl who Pirogoeth approximated was twenty at best pushed a wooden serving cart through the door. The girl herself was unassuming, in a plain white full length toga, lacking any noticeable traits other than it was immaculately clean and a cloth sash dyed brown, and with entirely average features for her country; tanned skin, brown hair and eyes, neither ugly nor beautiful.

The girl did have a very pretty smile, however. Pirogoeth would give her that.

"Greetings, Apprentice," the girl said. "I am Taima. The Dominus told me to send your dinner here."

Pirogoeth sat up, then stood. It seemed more polite to address the delivery in such a fashion rather than inelegantly sprawled across her bed. "Thank you, Taima. I must admit I'm not used to such pampering."

"Oh, I do hope I didn't startle you, Apprentice. I meant not to disturb."

Pirogoeth shook her head animatedly. "You did nothing of the sort. Where I'm from people wouldn't bother knocking, much less bring food with them." She turned her attention to the cart, and asked, "What *do* you have here, if I may ask?"

"Sheep rolls," Taima answered. "They are a common and popular Hermian dish."

Pirogoeth knew what rolls were. They were fluffy appetizers made with yeast and bread dough, topped with butter or jam. This was *not* a roll. She picked one up, and examined it. The bread wasn't light, nor did it have a golden brown texture. It was far thinner, not the slightest bit flaky, and heavy.

She discovered that the weight was because there was something *inside* the bread, identified once Taima sliced one open. Ground meat, though of a drab gray unlike the browned beef that she was familiar with, spinach leaves, yellow maize, and a white crumbly cheese.

Pirogoeth continued to regard the food with considerable apprehension, even as Taima happy showed Pirogoeth how to properly eat one, by slicing it in half with a knife then eating from the open end towards the closed one.

Nervously, she took a bite, and determined it... wasn't bad at all. Unlike anything she was accustomed to, but certainly more than edible. And once it hit her stomach and reminded her how hungry she was, it was little effort to finish that sheep roll and two others.

Taima then reached down to the lower shelf of the cart, pulling out a broad bottom glass carafe, tinted a light purple, that narrowed into a thin neck, and partially filled with a red liquid that was poured into a pair of what Pirogoeth had initially assumed were bowls. Pirogoeth's eyes raised questioningly as a pungent aroma hit her nose. "Wine?"

"Of course," the servant girl answered, demonstrating how to drink, by cupping the bottom of the bowl and gently tipping it forward with short sips. "It's good for you!"

Pirogoeth had seen enough people stumble out of one of Bakkra's three taverns to doubt that claim very much.

Taima gathered the disconnect quickly enough. "This is not the spirits that are drank in the Free Provinces, I assure you. Aramathean wines are cultivated to enhance the mind and body, not to steal it."

Pirogoeth did comply, bracing herself for the biting sting of alcohol on her tongue, only to be surprised when she barely felt a tingle, the tangy flavor of the grapes being the far stronger flavor. While further sips did increasing the alcoholic sting, it would have likely taken that entire carafe and a good deal of a second to intoxicate even her waifish frame.

"And here is some water," Taima announced, setting and filling a more customary glass in front of Pirogoeth from a clear carafe. "Anything that is left over, please include it with the cart and set it outside your door. I will also return before dusk for your clothes, as you will need them washed for the morning."

Pirogoeth watched Taima retreat, then nervously asked, "Is there somewhere you have to be?"

Taima shook her head. "Nothing of immediate need. My orders were to attend to you specifically."

"Would you... care to join me? I certainly won't be able to eat this all myself."

Taima offered as warm of a smile as Pirogoeth had ever seen, astonishingly white teeth and all. "I'd be glad to, my lady."

To have anything resembling normal interaction with a person about her age was a novelty, and one that Pirogoeth found enjoyable. She found the time spent with Taima to be enlightening, though not always in positive ways. Such as when Pirogoeth discovered exactly how indentured servitude worked in The Imperial Aramathea.

"You have to work here *ten more years*?" she gaped in astonishment.

Taima nodded. "That is how it is for the layman. At fifteen, we perform service to a lord for five years to become lower citizens. At the end of those five years, we can offer ten more years of service to attempt to become higher citizens of the empire, including the right to vote and even seek political office. There are some exceptions for those of remarkable talent, but that is the road to full freedom for nearly the whole of the people of the First Empire."

Pirogoeth had a very hard time processing how such a pedantic process was necessary. In Bakkra you became a citizen the moment you were old enough to push a plow and farm your own land. "But why be forced to..."

Taima shook her head rapidly. "Oh no, I am not forced into servant work. I could have very easily followed in my father or mother's footsteps, and become a higher citizen in that way when I turned thirty, provided I had saved enough money to afford a plot of land. But I had no desire to be a smith or a cobbler. This process of servitude allows me to learn a different craft under someone else and make my own path in life."

That made a little more sense, she supposed, but she still found the precise number of years to be an unnecessary stipulation. "So what *is* the path you wish to take?"

"I wish to be a chef," Taima said. "Working with the Dominus's chef here in Kartage was an honor I had not expected. Vargat is in my mind the finest chef in the whole of the First Empire. I've learned so much already and still have so much to learn!"

"And then once you've reached the end of your servitude... what?"

Taima shrugged. "I could open my own restaurant with the

stipend I would be granted by the Dominus after my stay was complete. I could take a position under a venerated citizen, like Vargat has with the Dominus. I haven't decided obviously, but what matters is that I will have my choice and many options available to me."

There was something to be said for that, Pirogoeth supposed. "You probably need these clothes to get them cleaned, don't you? Especially if you actually want some sleep tonight."

Taima stood and offered a polite bow. "That is most generous of you, my lady, I'm sure the linen maids will appreciate the courtesy." She then started wheeling the cart away. "Set your clothes down outside the door once you are ready."

With that, the servant girl left, and Pirogoeth quickly settled her remaining business for the night. It took surprisingly long for her mind to settle itself in the unfamiliar setting, but once it did the comfort of the bed allowed her a deep, restful sleep.

Day 2: When in Kartage...

Her dress from Lanka had been returned to exactly where she had left it the night before, only much more expertly folded and with her undergarments tucked inside the folds rather than resting on top. She quickly grabbed them before anyone could see her while indecent.

Taima arrived with a gentle knock just as Pirogoeth was tying her belt around her waist. When bid to enter, the servant girl said, "Dominus Socrato requests your presence for breakfast in his private dining hall. I am to lead you there."

Slipping into her shoes, Pirogoeth nodded, and said, "Then lead on. I will follow."

Socrato's tower, at least the ground levels, was formed like a spoked wheel, with eight halls corresponding to the main directions of the compass cutting through three halls that flanked the perimeter. At the center of the tower was a spiraling staircase that went up to the higher floors.

They went up three floors in this case, then took the northwest hall to the second ring. Taima stopped at an oak door with a scarlet banner, then opened it and stepped aside for Pirogoeth to enter.

Socrato's private dining room was not as large as she had expected. Maybe twenty feet from end to end and fifteen deep, with only two entrances, the one she had come in from and another that apparently was for the cook to have access with food, as a man in a white smock and folded back hat with a broad brim had just appeared with a plate in his left hand.

"Ah, dear girl. Excellent. Thank you, Taima. I suggest returning to the kitchen, I do believe Vargat wanted you to prepare the sauces for midday."

Pirogoeth turned her head to watch Taima's pleasant bow. "Thank you, Dominus. I shall see you again, my lady."

"Perhaps when my errands today are done?" Pirogoeth offered.

"I'd appreciate that. With your leave."

Taima disappeared, closing the door behind her. Socrato then gestured across the long but narrow table to an empty seat across from him as the servant set down the plate he had been carrying, and retreated back through the side door. "Have a seat, eat, and we'll discuss our business for the day."

The table, like everything else she had seen Socrato possess, was not the least bit extravagant. The surface of the wood was stained and polished. That was the extent of the work done to it. No etching, no sculpted legs or edges, it could not have been more plain and been fit to eat off of.

Her plate was filled on the left side with a fried and scrambled egg topped with white crumbled cheese and a mix of green and red peppers. To her right were two links of an oddly red tinted sausage. Nervously taking a bite of the sausage, having experience that things that color were of considerable heat, she was surprised to find it possessed nothing more than a very light hint of spice. It was also of a much smoother texture than any sausage she had before... having been used to the chunkier and more marbled sausages from the butchers in Bakkra.

Aramathean cuisine was clearly full of surprises.

"So I understand you and Taima made an acquaintance quickly," Socrato noted. "That's good. She's quite a bit younger than much of my serving staff. It will do her good to have someone more her age and friendly."

"By the time she gets out of here, she'll probably be their age." Pirogoeth grumbled, still not quite accepting the path of Aramathean citizenship her new friend was on.

"Pardon?" Socrato asked, hand cupped to an ear he leaned in her direction.

Pirogoeth figured he had heard her perfectly fine, and that there was no sense in lying. "Keep Taima here working as a servant girl until she's thirty. You don't see anything wrong with that?"

Socrato nodded knowingly. "Ah. I see. Yes, the path to high citizenship probably does seem quite alien, doesn't it? For what it is worth, I hope Taima expressed that it was her decision."

"She did," Pirogoeth said with a glower, not even trying to hide her displeasure.

Socrato shrugged. "The Imperial Aramathea has many different levels of freedom. Taima has, admirably or foolishly depending on who you talk to, chosen to seek the highest and most difficult one to attain on a person's own merits."

He took another bite of sausage in the middle of his explanation. "There are two grades of citizen, lower and higher. Lower citizens have the full protection of the law and attain that status upon twenty years of age, so long as they aren't stripped of that privilege due to serious crimes against the Empire. Taima will gain that status in a month's time, at which point she could fully leave my employ without penalty. With her talent, she could very easily become a personal chef to nearly any higher or venerated citizen looking for one."

He drummed the index finger of his left hand on the table in front of him. "Higher citizens have that right, as well as the right to own land, vote for venerated citizens, propose legislation, and seek political office of their own. That requires three things, to be thirty years of age, to be a master of one's chosen craft, as well as to demonstrate undying fealty to the empire... though attaining the first two is almost always deemed sufficient evidence of the third if one is a natural born citizen."

"Why would anyone think seeking such goals is foolish?" Pirogoeth wondered.

Socrato frowned, "When they are lower citizen parents who are insulted that their daughter has decided the life they live isn't good enough for her."

"Oh." Pirogoeth said in surprise. That idea made even less sense than the whole citizenship process. "Why would her parents... *not* want her to have a better life?"

"Not everyone has such supporting and thoughtful parents as you, Apprentice," Socrato said sadly. "I would recommend not pressing Taima on that issue either. Even after five years, I think it is a bit of a sore point."

"Will *I* have to be here until I'm thirty?" Pirogoeth wondered out loud and with no attempt to hide her disdain at the idea.

Socrato shook his head dismissively. "Oh no no no... the training for a mage is more like the Free Provinces and Avalon in methods, which works because there are not as many, and direct one on one instruction is not only common, but I would suggest necessary."

Pirogoeth was much more familiar and comfortable with that idea. You apprenticed under a master until that master deemed you were ready, then you were allowed to explore and broaden your talents as a journeyman, finally settling down, honing your craft until you could be deemed a master in your own right.

He brightened, then pointed to her plate with his fork. "Now finish up. I believe we have to get you some more comfortable clothes yet, then we can begin your lessons."

Pirogoeth didn't take long finishing her breakfast. She was a bit taken aback by the orange juice, not being used to the fruit and finding it a bit too tart for her liking, but had little issue otherwise.

Both she and Socrato stepped away from the table to allow servants to clear and clean it, and left the room for the central stairwell.

Unlike yesterday, the pair left through the main doors. The bazaar up ahead didn't look nearly as busy, nor were the roads nearly as heavily traveled. "Most are still having breakfast or waking up. I like to get an early rise to the day for precisely this reason. If we are quick about it, we can get you your necessities and make our return just after the keep has settled in to their duties."

Pirogoeth fell in step and asked, "You mentioned it earlier, as did Taima last evening. What is a venerated citizen?"

"At fifty, higher citizens are eligible to be venerated by the empire." Socrato answered. "There are two ways to do this; the most common one is to be recognized by other higher citizens for your contributions to the good of the empire. The second is to be honored by the Emperor for exceptional valor in a time of war. The only additional duty a venerated citizen has is that they can elect a new emperor or with a unanimous vote depose the current one."

"You can vote for an emperor?" she said in curiosity. "It's not passed from father to son?"

"Any child of the current emperor is indeed a candidate," Socrato explained, "and such children are near always the favorites to succeed their parent. But it is not necessarily the case. Any venerated citizen, which royal children are by default, can seek and be elected as ruler of the empire."

Pirogoeth's mind swam. "How do the people of this empire keep track of all the rules?"

"Some would argue we don't," Socrato snarked. "I'm not convinced they are wrong."

The shop that Socrato stopped at was located directly on the main street, and was every bit the opposite of Lanka's Clothiers. Well kept and maintained on the outside, and lacking any sense of style on the inside. Racks of the same types of garments were neatly ordered, with little variety in fabric or style.

Then again, half this store probably cost about as much as one outfit from Lanka.

A servant worker almost immediately pounced on them, though becoming immediately deferential once he identified Socrato. The Dominus offered little small talk, instead following Pirogoeth as she grabbed four or five items from each rack to try for fit before she retreated behind a curtained off section at the back of the sales floor.

Socrato began to ask her questions as she tried on the various options that had been selected. "While I wait, I suppose I can get a gauge of what exactly Torma taught you. What did she tell you about the schools of magic?"

"There are two primary schools of thought in the arcane arts," Pirogoeth answered, reciting Torma's own words as best she remembered them. "Material and Ethereal. Material emphasizes the elements and mastery of the body. Ethereal focuses on the mastering the mind and perception."

Socrato's voice was muffled both by the curtain and by the shirt she was pulling over her head. But she was able to hear well enough to know he wanted her to continue.

"Each school has four different manifestations. Material magic is divided into heat, cold, wind, and stone. Ethereal magic is divided into illusion, spirit, mind, and entropy."

Socrato hummed thoughtfully before saying, "Hmmm... Go on."

"Go on?" Pirogoeth asked, having just found the trouser size that at least came closest to fitting her correctly, though still not particularly well. Fortunately if there was one thing Aramathea did not lack, it was belts.

"I sincerely hope that wasn't all Torma taught you," Socrato prodded. "I'd have to be horribly disappointed in her knowledge retention, her teaching method... or the quality of her student."

Pirogoeth momentarily forgot she was trying on belts as her mind raced trying to remember what else she had been taught. She highly doubted that he was looking for practical application, so she moved further into the theory. "Material magic is balanced among itself: cold stills wind, wind weathers stone, stone suffocates heat, and heat thaws cold. Ethereal magic is balanced in a similar way; spirit denies entropy, entropy unravels illusion, illusion deceives mind, and mind dominates spirit."

"Clearly, Torma was simplifying the way of things for you," Socrato concluded. "But what I will say to you now is that the world of the arcane is much more varied and complex than that, as you will learn under my guidance."

Pirogoeth emerged from the curtained area, her expression neutral. She didn't like the idea that Torma taught her incorrectly. She had *liked* Torma.

Socrato caught the displeasure, and correctly identified the source. "Now, still your glare. I didn't say Torma did not teach you well. Sometimes you must ignore the tree in front of you to see the forest behind it." Quickly changing the subject, he asked, "Did you find what size you needed?"

"Yes," she huffed, softening her expression, but not by much. She gathered the rest of her clothes largely in silence, choosing different colors and styles now that she knew what fit, figuring whatever slight differences existed could be managed. Socrato insisted on eight complete outfits, so that the maids could limit the load to once per week, which *was* rather thoughtful of him if she was being honest.

The process took so little time, in fact, that Socrato's timing for the return trip fell way short, and they found themselves emerging onto a crowded street full of people swarming to get to their jobs or finishing their own errands. While the mass parted for them as much as was possible, it was slow going on the return trip to the tower.

"As much as I would like to avoid the rabble of diplomats again, I fear I really cannot shirk my duties as lord of the keep today," Socrato said reluctantly once they crossed under the arch and columns that demarcated the common grounds of the keep from the tower. "So, in the front we go. We will meet after the midday meal in the hall arcana. Taima will guide you. Be sure to be wearing your training clothes."

"Yes, Dominus," Pirogoeth said, allowing Socrato to enter first as the guards stationed at the doorway pushed the doors open. Taima was waiting for her, guiding her back to her room before excusing herself to return to the kitchen.

Pirogoeth entertained herself with setting her clothes into a standing wardrobe that must have been provided for her while she was out that morning, changed into her training clothes, then gleefully studied her tome, becoming more familiar with each page and what they contained. Torma had taught her that the "flow" of each tome, and even each page *within* a tome, was different, and sought different paths through the body. The better she learned its contents, and what ways the magic wanted to flow, the easier and faster she could channel the powers inside.

Pirogoeth found this process surprisingly simple, considering how Torma had regarded such study as a painful chore, though she tempered her pride with the thought that it was probably harder keeping it all straight when you had several tomes much larger than the thin apprentice's manual Pirogoeth was working from.

She was going through her fifth read through when Taima entered with the lunch cart. "The Dominus extends his apologies for not being able to attend to lunch with you, such is life when you are the keeper of the land," She said. "But I am to take you to the hall arcana once you are done eating."

"You are welcome to join me," Pirogoeth offered, "and you can consider that offer an open one from this point forward."

Pirogoeth was rewarded with another pleasant smile, then Taima described what was on the cart. "This is pita bread." She picked one flattened half loaf, then pressed the edges until a pocket formed in the center. "You fill the interior with sliced meats, greens, cheese, and dressing, and eat it much like a sandwich."

Pirogoeth liked this item already. "A sandwich that doesn't have everything fall out when you take a bite? I approve."

"I brought an assortment of meats for you to try," Taima said. "I have beef sausage, lamb, chicken, and veal. My personal favorite is the lamb; I helped Vargat smoke and slice the side this came from this morning."

"Lamb it is, then."

With pitas prepared, lunch began in earnest, and it was Taima who broke the silence. "Tell me about where you came from. Bakkra, was it?"

Pirogoeth shrugged. "Not much to say. It's more a collection of farms than a real city or city-state. Maize is about the only thing that can grow up there reliably, but there are a few potato and wheat farms. Beef is the primary livestock, a lot of grassland for them to graze on."

Taima bit her lower lip nervously before asking, "has your family lived there long?"

"My great grandfather on my father's side was born in the region, so at least seventy years or so."

"What about your mother's side?"

Pirogoeth was becoming wary of the line of questioning. "From the South, in the area of Timin, from what I'm told. Why?"

Taima cringed at the suspicious glare being cast in her direction. "Well... I had heard... from... it was just gossip... *I* didn't believe it... but I thought I'd ask... just in case... it... might be true?"

Pirogoeth rolled her eyes. "Oh, Coders take it. I am *not* some long lost Avalonian princess. While I'm sure there's Avalon blood in my family, I can say with near certainty that it's not royal blood or even noble. And even if it were, it's become so diluted over generations in the Free Provinces that I'd not be recognized by *anyone* there."

Taima placed a comforting hand on Pirogoeth's arm. "I'm sorry, my lady. I should have known better." She cast her eyes down on her half eaten pita sandwich, and said, "Did your parents... How did they react to your decision to come here and learn under the Dominus?"

"They were obviously sad that I was leaving, and that I would likely be gone a very long time." Pirogoeth decided to say. "But they understood it was necessary. Torma, one of Socrato's old apprentices, couldn't teach me everything herself, and I... I needed the time and space that Kartage provides."

"I remember Torma," Taima laughed weakly. "I had just started working here as she was finishing; she was sent off as a journeyman about a year and a half after I arrived. The serving staff used to pick on us both endlessly that our names sounded so similar."

Socrato had told Pirogoeth to avoid this line of conversation... But considering Taima had started it, she couldn't exactly shut the whole conversation down, could she? "Why do you ask?" Pirogoeth queried, hoping to nudge the discussion further without appearing to pry. "Why wouldn't my parents have felt any other way?"

For every bit of brightness Taima's smile offered, her sad eyes and vainly hidden frown stole the light from the room. "My... My parents weren't nearly as supportive."

Pirogoeth was not one for tactile contact. Her father had never particularly been one to physically display emotion, and while her mother was inclined to hug and smooch, Pirogoeth had often found it more imposing than comforting. Pirogoeth gave it her best attempt, bringing an arm around Taima's back. "What happened?"

"My parents... thought I was making a mistake. I tried to tell them that Dominus Socrato wasn't like that, but they didn't believe me. They think all venerated citizens take advantage of lower citizens like me."

Pirogoeth felt certain she was missing some vitally important context. "What do you mean?"

Taima sighed. "Traditionally, a lower citizen offers servitude to a venerable citizen in exchange for learning a craft that they can master and ascend the social ladder. But lately, there have been venerated citizens who have been *charging* those lesser citizens for the opportunity of a better life." Taima frowned as she continued. "Most lower class families and citizens can't afford what the venerated citizen charges up front, so they offer themselves as servants until the debt is paid. I think you can see what happens next."

Pirogoeth shook her head. "What?"

"The venerated citizen has no incentive to truly prepare a lower citizen. They intentionally claim the lower citizen failed to meet their obligations, which they demonstrate by showing how little the lower citizen truly knows, then takes anything and *everything* from the lower citizen and their immediate family. Entire families have been thrown onto the street."

"And no one stops this?" Pirogoeth gasped.

Taima shook her head. "There's little anyone can do. Lower citizens don't stand much chance before a judge when their word is met by that of a venerated citizen. The complaint is often tossed out before the hour has passed."

Pirogoeth had found she had lost her appetite. "I'm sorry, Taima."

"Why? I'm in no danger of such chicanery. I did my research, I knew who could be trusted and who couldn't. It's no accident that a young woman from Grand Aramathea is serving a Dominus in Hermia."

"I'm sorry that this entire messed up system exists. It shouldn't be like this."

Taima smiled wanly. "There are always going to be people who find a way to abuse the system, no matter what that system is. I'm sure there was even someone in Bakkra who gained wealth or prestige unfairly off the backs of others."

Pirogoeth was about to protest that, when she remembered her father grumbling about that "lazy, good-for-nothing mayor who hadn't worked a field in years yet made enough money off of taxes paid to live in a manor three times as large as any other home in the province." Not that the memory helped much.

"That still doesn't make it right!" Pirogoeth protested, somewhat shocked at Taima's lack of fight on this issue. "Just become some people will always be terrible doesn't mean you should give up!"

Taima's face tightened, and her voice grew stern. "*I* don't have to do *anything*. It's not a fight I have the power to win at this point, even if I *wanted* to." Her expression softened, and her lips pulled upward warmly. "But thank you for wanting to."

Pirogoeth understood why Taima felt that way. To be honest, it's not like Pirogoeth had any power in the matter either.

But they both knew someone who did.

"I suppose we're done eating then?" Taima asked, standing and making sure everything was situated on the cart. "It's getting about time to take you to the hall arcana, so I'll just leave this outside and pick it up on my way back. Are you ready?"

Pirogoeth nodded, though her mind was still mulling over the previous conversation.

Taima noticed the apprentice mage's distraction, and said with a chiding yet friendly tone of voice, "You may wish to pay attention to where we are going. I'm not going to be permitted to lead you everywhere for the entirety of your stay."

Pirogoeth snapped her eyes forward, locking with Taima's, a hint of color creeping onto her cheeks. "Right," she said sheepishly. "I will do so."

The hall arcana was five floors up, and Pirogoeth could feel all five of those floors in her legs. That was *not* an easy climb. "It's depressing how tired this poor farmer's girl gets walking around. I promise you I was *not* a pampered princess." She declared as she rubbed her abused calves.

Taima was sympathetic, however. "Oh no. I do not blame you. I was exhausted going more than two flights of steps when I first arrived here. I swear to you that the Dominus intentionally designed these stairs taller than normal. He denies it, but he must have."

Pirogoeth was comforted by that. At least it wasn't just her. "Alright, well, lead on to the hall arcana."

Taima simply pushed open the door. "There."

Pirogoeth understood when she crossed the threshold. The entire floor was one circular room with the enclosed stairway in the center. Unlike what she had seen anywhere else in the tower, the walls of the hall arcana were study gray stone and mortar. She understood why. She could feel the crackle of magical energy lingering in the air, ruffling the hair on her head, telling her that the sort of activity that occurred here was *not* friendly to wood or fabric.

Making sure her gloves were snug, she called out Socrato's name, and got an answer.

"South side, dear girl!" He called out from what seemed like some distance. "Come around!"

Pirogoeth circled around the stairwell, and on the opposite side found Socrato waiting at the far wall. A large part of the floor, roughly fifty feet square, had been cleared, save for an iron cauldron wafting fingers of white smoke.

Socrato said, as he noticed Pirogoeth's quizzical expression, "I was brewing a draught for congestion the last couple of days. Occasionally this area has a summer flu that is carried by mosquitoes, and I like to have this medicine prepared just in case. So don't worry, we won't be working with any potions or anything today. We're just going to be exploring some magic theory. Besides, it's too heavy to move."

Pirogoeth fought back a giggle. She *really* didn't want to encourage him.

"Torma taught you that magic exists in a balance," Socrato began, "but it is but a selective observation, just as flawed as the theories of the previous age. Did you know that, not even a hundred years ago, mages believed that ice and fire were foils? And that the balance came from elemental forces in conflict?"

Pirogoeth shook her head.

"Hmmm... History studies may be of use to you as well, then," Socrato mused thoughtfully. "It is as important to know from where you've come as it is to know where you are going. Oh yes, I hope you were anticipating book learning, and a great deal of it."

"I'm not scared of reading," she replied with a scoff.

Socrato exhaled in relief. "A good many eager minds are. They prefer their plays and operas, as much as I am loathe to use generalities. While it's a perfectly acceptable way to engage minds and thoughts, it's not quite as portable or on demand."

He interrupted his own segue with a cough. "At any rate, all magic, be it material or ethereal, both complements and conflicts among itself. Rather than study finding order within the chaos, we have discovered chaos within what we thought was ordered.

"Wind can feed a fire just as easily as snuff it. It can wear down stone just as easily as build the hills children roll down. Fire can melt stone to lava, and also forge it into the hardest steel. Even fire and ice can work together to make quite the spectacular show."

Pirogoeth's eyes perked.

"Have you ever seen frostfire?" Socrato asked. "I hope not. I really don't want to think that Torma did anything this dangerous around you. But here, with me, I think it will be safe enough."

He pointed to the west. "The apothecary shelves are that way. Third rack facing you, second shelf from the bottom, there should be a reddish-brown colored powder in a ceramic urn. Bring it to me, could you?"

The shelves were arranged along the exterior wall, seven racks with five shelves each, containing powders, liquids, crushed herbs, rock salts, and many compounds she couldn't even hope to identify, like the one she took off the shelf. It was indeed a red-brown, but it was more a mix of red and black powders that created the effect. She figured that Socrato would explain when it was time for her to know.

"Ah, very good!" He cheered as Pirogoeth returned with exactly what he had requested. "Normally, fire requires three things, heat, air, and fuel." He tapped the ceramic container. "However, *this* catalyst allows us to make a fire without air. You'll see why this is important."

Socrato set the container on the floor, and escorted Pirogoeth further back until she bumped into the stairwell. "You'll want to keep your distance, just in case."

He closed his hand into a ball, and within seconds, the container was sealed tight within a block of ice nearly a foot thick. "Now, watch this..."

With the same hand, he snapped his fingers, and a flicker of flame appeared in the ceramic container. Then the powder ignited creating a brilliant white flash, and a violent explosion that startled Pirogoeth into a frightened screech. Shards of ice crashed against a wall of fire Socrato had conjured, melting them before they could do any harm.

"Impressive, no?" Socrato asked. "Granted, this sort of thing has little practical purpose, but as a demonstration that the world has many wrinkles to it that can't be summed up in two sentences, it works splendidly."

With the display ended, Socrato began a lecture about the history of magic and the first mages. While it would have likely kept Pirogoeth's attention under normal circumstances, current events began creeping into her mind and slowly began to mute her master's voice.

And Socrato noticed this. "There is something else weighing on your mind," he noted, though his tone of voice was more curious than annoyed by her lack of attention. "It is distracting you."

Pirogoeth's jaw set, deciding there was no better for it than to face the issue head on. "Are you aware about citizens like you exploiting lower class citizens?"

Socrato's eyes narrowed, though he kept them straight ahead. "I have been aware of some cases in which it happened. It has been more prevalent within Grand Aramathea itself, where an insular community of elites have found kindred spirits in senators to create an environment ripe for such abuses of power."

"And you don't do anything to stop this?" she asked, trying to figure out why *he* would have such a resigned opinion.

"What do you propose I do, young lady?" Socrato answered sternly. "Should *all* venerated citizens be punished for the legally criminal acts of a select few? I understand the Free Provinces have few coded laws, especially between different city-states, but there are procedures and processes that empires require in order to maintain themselves."

Pirogoeth shrugged, "Then change the process."

"And how would one go about that? The venerated acting in this manner have bought influence in the senate which makes new laws. They *are* the judges that conspire amongst themselves to refuse a fair voice to those manipulated. They even have the ear of Emperor Macedon, who enforces the laws of the land."

Pirogoeth went silent for a moment before asking, "Have you tried approaching the Emperor? Surely you'd be able to get his ear too."

In just two days time, Pirogoeth had seen many different emotions play on Socrato's face: amusement, mischievousness, annoyance, regret, and mirth. But this was the first time she had seen anger. The sage's nostrils flared as his upper lip curled up menacingly. His pupils narrowed and his brows dove downward towards his nose. From there, his chest rose sharply, and what followed was one of the most frightening moments in Pirogoeth's fifteen years.

Socrato's bellow nearly deafened her and seemed to shake the floor beneath her feet. "How *dare* you lecture me about things you know *nothing* about, you infantile *brat?* If I wanted a barely cognizant, screeching juvenile in my tower, I would have bought myself a *howler monkey!*"

Pirogoeth winced, covering her face with her arms while she trembled. She was hardly a coward, but this was well beyond what even the staunchest of wills would be willing to face unmoving. "But..."

"Return to your chambers," Socrato snarled as he lowered his voice. "I will summon you again when I am not in the mood to send you back to Bakkra in a barrel."

Pirogoeth tried to stammer an apology, but she couldn't even form one syllable before Socrato interrupted her. "*Leave!*" he ordered, the full force of his lungs returning. "*Now!*"

Pirogoeth hastily fled, her eyes so filled with moisture that she almost flew completely past the floor her room was on. She felt so horribly guilty as she slinked despondently into her chambers, throwing herself face down onto her bed.

She forced herself not to cry. Crying never helped. It only showed weakness that could be exploited in the future. At least, that's what her parents had told her. The advice hadn't helped her back then, but it was a lesson that had ingrained itself nonetheless.

Not that holding back her tears helped hold back her guilt.

How could she have been so cutting? Why would she assume that Socrato would have been complacent in something so wrong? That was hardly fair of her. Why did she always lash out like that at people who didn't deserve it?

She was not feeling much better as evening arrived. She didn't acknowledge the first knock at her door, nor the second. It wasn't until Taima called out, "Apprentice? Are you... Are you there? Please answer me."

Pirogoeth raised her head from her pillow, hastily trying to wipe the moisture from her eyes. "I am sorry, Taima. Please... Enter."

The servant girl again wheeled a food cart in front of her as Pirogoeth sat up. "Oh, my lady, you look horrible! Whatever happened up there? The Dominus was absolutely irate! I don't think I've ever seen him so angry!"

Pirogoeth's face fell. "He must be furious at me."

Taima blinked. "At you? Odd. He didn't mention you at all. Why, what happened?" As Pirogoeth relayed the events in the hall arcana, Taima frowned. She sat down onto the bed next to the apprentice and put both arms around Pirogoeth in a warm hug.

"Oh, you poor dear... It most certainly isn't your fault," the servant girl said reassuringly. "There are few things that upset the Dominus, and you happened to poke one of those scant sore points. That's probably why he was so angry... he lashed out at you and feels horrible about it."

Pirogoeth grasped onto that thin line of hope. "You... think so?"

"This... scandal... is something that has troubled the Dominus for some time. He has argued this case before the Emperor *twice,*" Taima explained. "It's why I tried to keep you out of it."

Offering a weak smile, the servant girl asked, "Now, why don't we have some dinner in the hopes that it will soothe the nerves? I brought a special treat for the occasion. Sweet orange cake with a vanilla glaze. Perhaps, on this occasion, we can have desert first."

Pirogoeth discovered that cake didn't actually make her feel better. But it was part of a pleasant diversion that kept her from thinking about the inevitable next meeting with her master. She could only hope that Taima had the right of it.

Otherwise, Pirogoeth was about to have the shortest apprenticeship in the history of the world.

Day 3: Books All the Way Down

That anxiety led to a fitful sleep. Nightmares of being sent back home in shame, forbidden to use magic, having to deal with the abuse and bullying of her peers. If she had totaled more than two hours of sleep, it was not by much.

When Taima arrived, without a cart, that dread only built. "No breakfast here?" Pirogoeth asked tentatively.

"I fear not," Taima replied, flashing a reassuring smile. "You've been summoned to the Dominus's dining room. It's okay, I saw the menu, and I don't think you're on it."

Pirogoeth dropped her head, and breathed deeply. "Let's get this over with."

Taima shook her head disparagingly, but realized that there was nothing further she could say to ease the apprentice's worries. "Would you like me to lead the way?"

Pirogoeth shook her head. "I'd rather you not get caught in the aftermath. I can go myself."

"Very well, my lady."

Taima took her leave, and Pirogoeth began her personal walk of shame, forcing herself to not make eye contact with anyone she passed in the halls. This was harder than she anticipated, as Socrato's tower was bustling with no small amount of activity, contrary to what she assumed would occur in a mage's tower.

The already unnaturally tall steps felt like climbing a mountain, and her legs heavy as lead. She had to stop at her destination floor to regain her bearings. Circular buildings were terrible on a person's direction sense, especially when one wasn't paying close attention. Once she sorted herself out, she took the proper fork and stopped in front of Socrato's dining room door.

She knocked so slightly that she was worried that it wouldn't be audible. But as she prepared to do so again, she heard the stern order, "Enter."

Pirogoeth nervously pushed open the door, sliding through the moment there was enough of an opening to do so. Socrato was at his usual seat, head down and his chin on his hands.

"You will not interrupt me," he said, his voice measured and controlled. "You will not speak until I am finished, and you will not try to argue with me. Am I understood?"

Pirogoeth nodded swiftly with fearful eyes, forcing her breathing shallow just in case even *that* would be construed as an interruption.

With that, her master said, "As your mentor and teacher, my duty is teach you how to think, how to observe, and how to challenge the world around you. After two days, I have already failed in that task, allowing my own frustrations to suppress the curiosity I should be encouraging. That is unacceptable for a man of my standing, and for that, I humbly offer my apologies."

Pirogoeth's eyes widened, and her lower jaw hung loose.

"This is where you are supposed to say, 'I accept your apology, master', then you sit down, eat, and we can discuss the matters of the day," Socrato said with a bemused half grin.

The apprentice flushed bright red, and bowed, "Yes, master. I accept your apology."

Socrato's apology came in more than words. Once she sat down, she was presented with wheat toast with sweet cream butter, three thick strips of peppered bacon, and a fried egg with an unbroken yolk.

"Taima's idea more than mine, if I'm being wholly honest," the venerated sage said, "but I think it wouldn't hurt occasionally to see fare more to your custom."

Pirogoeth smiled, and graciously responded, "I appreciate the gesture, master. But while the food of the empire is different, I've liked what I've experienced so far."

"The empty half of your plate would suggest otherwise," Socrato replied, noting that Pirogoeth had launched into her breakfast with considerable vigor. "Vargat can make anything delicious. Taima is quickly catching up to him too." Then his tone turned serious. "Small talk aside... I think I know just the thing for you to do."

"Hmm?" Pirogoeth asked, her left cheek bulging with a mouthful of toast.

The sage tapped the table with his fingers. "The citizen's conundrum has *not* been something I've taken lightly. I've tried on more than one occasion to sway the Emperor to act against the practice... but even *if* the venerated didn't closely have his ear, their position is remarkably legally sound, using the balance of power in our system to their advantage."

Pirogoeth swallowed, and asked, "how so?"

"The senate has three levels: local, provincial, and imperial. The two lower branches do not have the authority to pass laws that target venerated citizens without the approval of a seven-tenths majority of venerated citizens within that city or province. Within Grand Aramathea, they have enough of a presence to block any legislation, and the provincial level doesn't have the authority to impose laws on the First Capital."

"So why doesn't the imperial senate do anything?"

Socrato sighed. "For one, the senate and the venerated citizens are closely tied. Most members of the imperial senate got their post through the influence of venerated citizens, and as such are loathe to act against them. In addition, the imperial senate can only enact laws on an imperial scale. Such broad sweeping laws can have disastrous consequences. It would be akin to sending a phalanx of soldiers to handle a rat infestation in a wheat field."

Pirogoeth nodded sadly. "It might work, but they'd probably wind up burning the whole field down."

Socrato frowned. "The judicial system is run by the very venerated that take advantage of the laws, which means there's no help to be found there. As I quickly found out when I argued my case."

"What happened then?"

"I argued before the Emperor that the venerated guilty of this act were fraudulently trading, offering services that they had no intention of honoring. They in turn argued that that the only thing they were *truly* selling was room and board, which they could more than adequately prove they were providing. The 'education' they were offering fell under the Law of Free Information."

Pirogoeth asked, "And what is that?"

"The Imperial Aramathea's Great Library within Grand Aramathea had always charged a small fee to use the information within for the sake of the library's upkeep. But the fees kept steadily increasing as more books became centralized within the library itself." He took a breath, and a bite of his food. "With the development of the press, it looked like the Great Library would lose its monopoly on information, until it claimed that any book that had been copied from the library technically was the library's property, and tried to have those who sold or distributed books arrested or fined.

"It culminated with the Imperial Senate passing the Law of Free Information, that education can be readily available to all, without charge. And as it cannot be charged or paid for..."

Pirogoeth completed the statement. "It's not being traded and therefore no fraud is taking place."

Socrato tipped his head in confirmation as he swallowed.

"The Emperor agreed with them... albeit reluctantly. The Emperor's power here is not absolute. While he has the final say on laws, he cannot make them himself. He could have the power to reign in these venerated citizens specifically... if we could find a way within the current laws to do so." He then stood, leaving his breakfast mostly uneaten. "Which brings us to the task at hand. Finish up, and I will show you what I mean."

The apprentice hastily shoveled her remaining breakfast down, and abandoning proper etiquette wiped her mouth with the sleeve of her shirt. "Should I change into my training clothes, master?"

Socrato smiled. "Not as of yet. Where we are going hopefully will not go up in flames." He then leaned forward, looming over Pirogoeth, and added firmly, "Because if it did, it would take you five lifetimes to repay the damage."

Pirogoeth nodded animatedly, and Socrato led her out towards more new areas of the tower. It was during this latest trek, another six floors up, that she was reminded of her mentor's oddly inexhaustible energy for his age.

He was looking down from at least one floor up through the gaps in the wooden steps. "Are you coming?" he asked brightly and teasingly.

She huffed, forced air into her lungs and her legs to march upward. How could someone well into his sixth decade be more physically capable than her?

The destination, however, was worth it.

Books. A countless number of books awaited her in the room directly ahead on the ninth floor of Socrato's tower. The *entire room*, stacked from floor to ceiling with shelves brimming with books of all different sizes and colors, along with scrolls and even stone chiseled *tablets*, though those were behind glass. No doubt extremely rare and expensive.

Socrato noticed his apprentices awestruck glee, and pleased with that reaction said, "The entire *floor* is but *one* floor of my library, dear girl."

Pirogoeth wasn't sure her eyes could get any wider.

"The eighth, ninth, tenth, *and* eleventh floors of the tower are devoted to my public library, available to any and all who wish to explore. Not as many people do so as I'd like, but more than I expected. I *also* have my *private* library on the fifteenth and sixteenth floors... but those are devoted to the magical arts: tomes and apothecary recipes and such. You will become *very* familiar with those floors by the time your studies are done."

His apprentice was about to go catatonic, which made him decide to get to the point. "But as to why we are here... This particular room, and the next two over, are where I have stored every law and judgment and imperial decision over the last fifty years."

Pirogoeth looked up at Socrato with the a dazed, overwhelmed expression. "That... why?"

"Because this is my challenge to you: find something that my contemporaries and I have missed in our arguments against the class fraud that my despicable peers have been engaging in. You will have your evenings free to do this research, if you wish it. I won't expect it to take up *every* evening... Every mind needs its rest, after all."

"But... if *you* couldn't find a solution, what makes you think *I* can?" she asked, dumbfounded.

Socrato shrugged. "Sometimes a different perspective can find things that others overlook. It's entirely possible that there is something that I have become so used to seeing that I never considered it, a nuance to a law, or an interpretation of a legal precedent that I haven't noticed, but that you would."

Pirogoeth steeled her expression. While she was dubious that she'd have any success, it would hardly look good to not even *attempt* to meet her master's challenge. "I will do my best."

"Very good. *Now,* I would recommend going down and changing to your training clothes. Meet me in the hall arcana in one hour. You are going to start channeling from that tome of yours today, and that isn't always a smooth process."

It would promise to be for Pirogoeth, though, which she quickly demonstrated once she had returned to the hall arcana.

Just like with her personal practice on her first night, she had little problem moving the magic from the tome, through her, and into a "ready" state at the tips of her fingers. Proving it wasn't just a matter of knowing how one particular spell worked, she replicated that ease with other spells on other pages Socrato chose randomly.

"Remarkable," he had finally said, visibly amazed and impressed by her swift mastery of the matter at hand. "I'll be quite honest that the process of properly channeling magic from a tome is often the hardest thing to teach a prospective mage. It really *is* an unnatural thing for most mages to grasp. Having experience only with using the small spark within them, they have a hard time drawing it out from an external source."

Pirogoeth didn't understand that much at all. "Draw it out? I have to fight to keep it *in*."

Socrato's eyes rose, and he requested, "do explain."

She demonstrated instead, sweat beading on her brow as she forced the magic pooling in her hands back towards the tome. "The magic in this tome here *wants* to come out. It *wants* to... explode. I know that the goal is that the tome will feel like an extension of myself, but when I channel... It feels more like *I* am an extension of *it*." Pirogoeth could not gauge Socrato's reaction, as his face had become absolutely unreadable save for a sense of intense scrutiny, like he was searching her face and body language for any hint of mistruth or exaggeration.

Finally, after what felt like an eternity of silence, he said, "That will be enough hands-on practice today."

Surprised by the abrupt end of the lesson, she asked, "Master... Did I do something wrong?"

He gave her a wary smile, and replied, "Oh no, dear girl. Quite the opposite, in fact. You did something far too right, and I need to revise my teaching plan almost entirely because of it." He then took her hands and held her palms up. "What you are doing naturally is normally the result of *years* of training. The tome you have has almost instantly become submissive to you."

"Submissive... to me?"

"Tomes are not normal books, as you well know, but the lengths of their uniqueness extend far beyond even the obvious," Socrato explained, even as she could see that he was choosing his words carefully for reasons she didn't understand. "Tomes have... something akin to a spirit. They aren't 'alive' in the sense that we perceive it, but they all have unique behaviors. Training tomes, like the one I gave you, tend to be more cooperative by nature, but even then, you generally have to prove your worth before it offers its power fully and willingly."

Pirogoeth blinked as her mind swam trying to process what was being told to her.

"The behavior you described is one that normally comes from a tome that has become so in tune with its owner that it seeks nothing but to provide everything demanded of it. It fights your trying to force the magic back because in this purely submissive state, magic wants to nothing but to fulfill the spell that is being channeled." He smiled reassuringly at his apprentice's continued confusion. "I apologize if this seems a bit off. The vast majority of mages never even reach this level of understanding, much less so naturally and readily."

Pirogoeth actually wasn't confused. With it all sorted out in her head, what she had been told made sense... yet was incomplete. It felt like she had a wonderful puzzle in front of her, but was missing several crucial pieces that would allow the image to truly take shape. She told herself those pieces would no doubt come in time, and shook her mind free from that exercise. "I'm sure I'll get it one day," she finally said with as disarming a smile as she could manage.

Socrato accepted that. "I have no doubt you will. Now, if you will follow me, I will bore you to tears with more history of magic and its role in building the The Imperial Aramathea..."

She honestly didn't find it boring. She really didn't. It was merely that there were so many things on her mind that were more engaging that it *seemed* like she was disinterested and distracted. So she really hoped he understood if her eyes drifted and glazed over.

Once Socrato identified that he was losing the battle for his apprentice's attention, he asked, "Would you like to start your evening study a little early today?"

Pirogoeth blushed guiltily, and admitted, "If that would be acceptable."

"Get going. Would you like dinner in the library? Or will you be able to curb your enthusiasm long enough to eat with the rest of us?"

Pirogoeth blinked. "The rest of us?"

"Yes... the evening meal is generally taken in the main banquet hall on the first floor of the tower. All are invited in a buffet style meal."

Pirogoeth's eyebrows raised. "Even the serving staff?"

"Even them. As a result, you are expected to serve yourself. I do suspect that wouldn't be a bother for you though."

Pirogoeth made an uncomfortable connection. "So... you mean... the last two days when I had dinner in my room..."

Socrato sighed, and offered a comforting smile. "Taima was more than willing to forgo the normal way of things to serve you a private meal. She was also quite flattered when you asked her to join you."

Pirogoeth shook her head. "Well, I won't do it again. If the serving staff aren't supposed to serve me in the evening, then they will not. Of course I will attend to dinner as per custom!"

"I'll have Taima show you the way, as I don't believe you've been there yet," Socrato said. "Now up to the library you go. You'll have a few hours to spend before dinner."

Pirogoeth spent those hours more getting a feel for the rooms that Socrato told her would carry the information most relevant to her task than actually reading it. She had expected the documents and books to be sorted by year, but had found that to not be the case. They were initially sorted by theme: land disputes, trade disputes, political treaties, civil rights, among other things. *Then* they were further sorted by year. She found that fairly handy, as it meant that she wouldn't necessarily have to dig through entire rooms to find a related case in a different year.

Deciding it would be best to start with the most recent cases, like the one that Socrato personally argued, she had just about been ready to open that book when the headmaster of the library arrived and showed her something that rendered much of that first hour fairly meaningless.

One floor down, on the eighth floor, was what the librarian called the catalog.

The near entirety of the floor, save for three offices reserved for the librarian and her two servants, was devoted to an index of *every* book in the public library, with relevant information written and bound into volumes then sorted by multiple topics. "In your case, the law and judicial catalog is over to the Northwest on the gray painted shelves," the librarian explained with the practiced patience of a woman who offered this sort of instruction often. "The shelves are sorted not only by topic and year, and by the judges and advocates involved, but also where the case was heard. I suspect you will find it useful."

Pirogoeth nodded dumbly. Having never been used to seeing more than ten books in any one place, this sort of sorting tool would be *invaluable.* But for now... She needed context, which required her to go back to reading.

It was slow going, as it turned out legal arguments and decisions were dry reading. It wasn't exactly high theatre, after all. While Socrato no doubt spoke well and with great passion, that emotion was lost in the transfer to the printed word, and the judge's statement to his final decision was wordy, prolonged tripe.

So, Pirogoeth found it a hint of mercy when Taima arrived to take her to dinner. "Are you ready, my lady?" the servant girl asked.

"Coders, *yes,*" Pirogoeth admitted, nearly jumping to her feet. "And *please* could you *stop* calling me 'my lady'? You're older than I am!"

Taima seemed aghast by the idea. "Oh, I couldn't! At least not until I was of higher standing. You are an honored student of the Dominus, and proper decency demands I address you as such."

Pirogoeth sighed. "And there's absolutely *no* chance you're going to relent on that?"

Taima grinned in apology, and replied, "I fear not... my lady."

In defeat, Pirogoeth took stride behind Taima, and departed for the banquet hall.

The first floor, as well as the two above it, were part of the larger interior keep, and as such had more room to house such spaces like the main banquet hall of Kartage. And unlike any of Socrato's private rooms, it was indeed a spectacular sight.

Firstly, it was massive, larger than most houses in Bakkra. At least fifty feet square, if not more, with enough space to hold four rows of tables along with a center island where food was being set out. The tables and chairs were made of a dark stained mahogany, draped with red velvet and gold trim. The island was similarly decorated, though made of stone to help keep the food on it at a proper temperature.

Lighting came from above, in the form of six crystal chandeliers hanging from the ceiling in a hexagonal pattern, holding the most unusual candles she had ever seen. Twenty such candles were mounted to each chandelier, and looked to Pirogoeth like the flames were being held in a glass bowl... Which made no sense to her. Covered flames died, even magical ones.

Taima noted where the apprentice's eyes were. "Amazing, aren't they? The newest thing in lighting, powered not by fire, but by the river currents."

"How?" Pirogoeth said in amazement. "How can water make fire burn?"

"I'm not entirely certain myself," Taima admitted, "Just that the flow of the river generates energy, and that energy is used to power these lights. I'm told the Dominus wants to have them expanded to the whole of the tower by the end of the year. Anyway, come. If we want some of the best portions, we'll want to move quickly."

Plates were available at the head of the center island, along with utensils, and it gave Pirogoeth a good look at the varied and abundant spread available. Much of it was obvious, slices of lamb and beef, chicken and pork. There were noodles, rice, and sliced bread along with the pita bread and wraps she had seen earlier. There was also *four* different types of rice, which took Pirogoeth by surprise, having only known of one.

"This is brown rice, which you've probably seen before," Taima explained. "Further east they are famous for white rice, which can be prepared many different ways like you see here. It can be fried," she said, pointing to a slightly yellow variety, "steamed," pointing to the pearly white variety, "or boiled in stock with a pasta called pilaf. This particular variety has been boiled in beef stock," she finished, pointing to the light brown mixture with small oval shaped pasta noodles mixed into the rice. Pirogoeth took a slice of the beef and the rice pilaf, thinking that they'd compliment each other.

They then moved further down to a steaming section of the island, where sausage of varying colors from red to brown, and steamed vegetables like maize, carrots, and sweet peas were available. Still further down and separated by a stone partition was the chilled section; leafy greens, tomatoes, and fruits such as oranges and bananas rounding out a hearty and balanced meal.

Taima then blocked Pirogoeth's progress to the next section with a chastising shake of her finger. "No desserts until dinner is done!"

"Yes, ma'am," Pirogoeth acknowledged playfully, taking her laden plate and turning to look for an available seat. She didn't have to look far, because at a table at the head of the banquet hall, her master was beckoning her over with a raised hand.

"You best be going, my lady. When the Dominus beckons, one must answer."

Taima turned to part ways when they heard Socrato bellow, "And where do you think *you're* going, Taima? I do not request your presence so I can be ignored!"

Pirogoeth had to stifle back a chuckle as Taima's face turned so red it showed through her almond complexion. "As I said, when he beckons, one must answer," she said with a trembling voice.

Socrato gestured across the table where he wanted Pirogoeth and Taima to sit, then introduced the apprentice to the fourth member at the table. "Apprentice, I do not believe you've had the opportunity to meet our master chef. Pirogoeth, meet Chef Vargat."

At this point Pirogoeth became aware of the man sitting to Socrato's left. She had never seen such a dark skinned person. Vargat was nearly as black as pitch, definitely an older man, with curly black and silver hair sneaking from under his broad white beret. He stood, took her hand politely with a gentle shake, and said, "greetings, young apprentice. The Dominus speaks highly of you in such a short time." Then he graciously bowed to Taima. "And good evening to you as well. Your broth for the beef was indeed excellent. I should not have questioned you."

Taima colored again, and she returned the bow. "You are the

master; it is your duty to question me."

Socrato laughed heartily. "The evening meal is meant to put aside rank and title, my friends! Could we do so and eat this wonderful food you both can't stop talking about?"

Pirogoeth wasn't sure Taima *could* do that.

But the servant girl could eat, at the very least, and keep her head down, which is what she did the moment she felt it proper to take her seat.

"Coders, Taima. You've been here nearly five years. You'd think you'd stop being frightened of my station at this point," Socrato chided playfully, noting the same behavior Pirogoeth did.

Taima gulped, and nearly choked on what she was swallowing as she learned her strategy of making herself as small as possible had failed. "It's a matter of respect, Dominus. I have much to prove before I can pretend we are equals."

Socrato asked Vargat, "That reminds me, Taima is about to be a citizen of her own merit within the month, if I recall correctly. I trust you've put all those affairs into order?"

Vargat nodded vigorously. "Of course, my friend. The certificate of merit should be in your queue already. She's more than passed by my measure, and will definitely serve the empire as a proper citizen."

Socrato answered, "Well then, I shall have to dig it out of my queue and have it sent to the Registrar at the First Capital first thing tomorrow morning. I will not make you wait a day longer than your twentieth birthday, Taima. You can rest assured of that."

Pirogoeth interjected, asking, "Chef Vargat, are you also a venerated citizen?"

Vargat gently shook his head in denial. "Oh no. I cannot be, as I am not a natural born citizen of Aramathea, and I doubt I'll be winning any wars to gain that exception."

That led into the question she hadn't wanted to ask so bluntly. "May I be so bold as to ask where you are from, then?"

Socrato offered Vargat a look of concern, but the chef shook it off with a tired smile. "It's all right, friend. My lady, I was born far to the south on a continent called Tanzibar, nearly sixty-one years ago to this day. There, within that jungle canopy you could find my home of Canno, the cradle of life, and contrary to what any Aramathean will tell you, where the *true* First Empire and First Capital could be found."

Socrato scoffed, and groused. "No evidence of that outside of your word."

"What was it like?" Pirogoeth asked, her curiosity piqued. It was rare to hear tales from other lands living in Bakkra, much less lands that lied beyond the great oceans.

Vargat seemed to enjoy the memory, smiling blissfully. "Nothing like here, or anywhere on this continent. The trees were so tall, with branches and leaves so broad they could blacken the sun. We built our great ziggurats tall to break the canopy so our priests could pay homage to the coders who we believed lived on the sun.

Our cities were small because of it. The lands were untamed. Your cats are but small bundles of fur. Our cats were *gods*, tall, powerful beasts up to eight feet long, with teeth like daggers, and fur as black as a moonless night. *They* were the true lords of the land, and we understood that. At least, until my ancestors finally crossed the dunes of the great sands, and onto the fertile coasts, where Canno was founded."

Vargat's hands spread to animate his tale, "Our empire stretched from the Western Endless Ocean to the East. Our ports were five times the size of even the docks of Grand Aramathea. They had to be, for we didn't fish for salmon, we fished for *sharks*, great sharks twenty feet long. Their teeth were used in jewelry, their blubber for sealant on our boats, and their meat... oh their meat was succulent. To this day I try and bribe the naval vessels that moor here for supply to try and hunt those deep ocean sharks... to no avail."

"Why not?" Pirogoeth asked, "Are they that dangerous?"

Taima's eyes bulged in shock. "No ships dare brave the waters that far off the coast of the Gibraltar Isles! The Void lies not even a mile past!"

Socrato sternly corrected Taima. "That is *not* true, girl. The Void waters are far out to sea, but it *is* true that vessels dare not sail too far, for the difference between the ocean and the void can be subtle, and once you cross there is no return."

Pirogoeth had heard of the Void. It was a frequent horror story that her father would tell to scare her when she was younger. She somehow doubted the truth was anything like those scary stories. "Is that why you can't return home, Vargat? The Void gets in the way?"

Vargat's lips flattened, and what followed was the voice of a man long resigned to his loss. "My lady, the whole of Tanzibar, Canno and all, fell to the Void forty-eight years ago. I was on one of the last boats that sailed away from the doomed land. I watched the last golden spire sink below the dire water."

Alright, maybe the Void *was* like the horror stories she had been told.

Taima whispered in a nervous tone to Pirogoeth, "Some say it's only a matter of time before the Void starts eating *our* continent."

Socrato again chastised the servant girl. "Do not go trying to scare my apprentice, Taima. There is *no* evidence that the Void is encroaching from *any* direction." He clapped his hands, and said, "Let us move the conversation to more pleasant things, can we?"

It managed to do so as Vargat turned the tables on Pirogoeth, asking her no end of questions about Bakkra, which was no doubt as alien to him as Canno was to her. The four then shared stories until Pirogoeth yawned loudly, startling Socrato as he was in the middle of one of his tales.

"Goodness, I would have never thought any of my alchemical mishaps would be considered *boring,*" Socrato said in tease.

Pirogoeth shook her head. "I... didn't sleep well last night. I think it's catching up with me."

"Then do get your rest, for I will not be *nearly* as easy on you tomorrow as I was today, now that I have a better idea of what you are capable of," Socrato said both in warning and in parting. Taima started to stand as well, but Pirogoeth gently pushed the servant girl back down. "I can find my own way tonight. You aren't going to escape these two *that* easily."

Pirogoeth then made her retreat, glad that she didn't stumble from fatigue until *long* after she was out of sight of the banquet hall. She didn't even change out of her clothes once in her chambers, collapsing onto her bed, asleep almost the instant she hit the mattress.

Day 17: A Lunar Celebration

And those days would not get any easier. True to Socrato's promise, he had put her on what she could only figure was an accelerated training program, thrusting more reading and practice into her hands as soon as she had just finished the previous lessons.

In addition, her research into the lower citizen dilemma consumed near the entirety of her remaining hours, with not much progress to speak of. There was so much she had to learn before she could even *begin* to propose ideas to Socrato, and she could only read so fast.

It's not that those were problems, exactly. Her study was in fact very engaging, and her spirits were buoyed when, one night, her master granted her a genuine tome, rather than the thin training manuals she had had before.

Like Socrato had implied, the full-sized tome wasn't quite as... willing to please... as the training manuals had been. Pirogoeth's touch needed to be more delicate, and the energy didn't flow nearly as cleanly, requiring legitimate channeling to move the way she wanted.

She had been so eager to study it that she stayed up far later than she should have, and as a result was rather dreading this morning, as she knew she wasn't at full speed and it would take some time for the sluggishness to fade.

Blissfully, she got a break when she arrived at breakfast. "Lanka delivered notice that she has completed the rest of the clothes that were ordered. We should attend to that promptly." Pirogoeth's ears perked at the announcement, not so much because she was looking forward to getting more clothes, but that it would give her an hour or so to finish waking up... if not more, considering how particular Lanka could be about clothes.

Socrato grinned teasingly. "That should give you ample time to find your bearings before I start pounding your beleaguered brain full of more half-useless information, right?" Seeing Pirogoeth's guilty reaction, his face softened. "Oh, dear girl... you would hardly be the first one who spent all night playing with a new toy. Coder's curse, I don't think I slept for three days straight when I got my first 'real' tome."

"I honestly can't imagine you as a boy," Pirogoeth admitted.

Socrato huffed in mock insult. "I was a handsome young man,

so you know. Quite the charmer. The girls all adored me."

"Did they?" Pirogoeth goggled in mostly mock disbelief.

"They did," Socrato insisted. "Though, in the spirit of total honesty, I had little interest in them for the most part."

Pirogoeth couldn't help but ask. "Why was that?"

"The general design of ladies that sought my favor were, at the risk of sounding slanderous, not particularly intelligent. Their desires and thoughts were base, and they offered little to engage me beyond the physical. It was not particularly satisfying."

"Surely they weren't *all* like that."

Socrato paused, and it was a rare moment of discomfort that dropped upon his face. "No... but that's a tale for another time. Lanka is waiting."

Pirogoeth wasn't content with another time. Not even fifteen minutes later, once they left the tower on the road to Lanka's Clothiers, she smiled sweetly as she asked, "So, tell me about these others."

Socrato played dumb, and not convincingly. "What others?"

"The other women. The ones that interested you."

The sage huffed, and supplied a half answer. "I have loved, and I have lost. Why do the details interest you?"

Pirogoeth began to get the hint that she was treading in dangerous waters again, and didn't want to risk her master's wrath, especially for what was a trivial curiosity. "I'm sorry. I just wanted to know more about you."

Socrato became apologetic himself. "No, I am sorry. I tend to keep my personal life closely guarded, for a somewhat good reason. I have been... a target... of political games at times, and I like to keep those close to me as detached from that as possible."

Pirogoeth nodded. "That's understandable."

"But in this case, I suppose I shouldn't be so reserved. I haven't had many companions, but those I did have I am still close to. We are going to meet one of them now, in fact."

The apprentice jerked. *"Lanka?"*

Socrato bristled. "And what is wrong with that?"

"She... how old is she?" Pirogoeth always had the impression that the age gulf between the clothier and the sage was significant.

"If you must know, she is only eight years younger than I," Socrato said. "No, she doesn't particularly look her age. Our relationship was not particularly meant to be; neither my master nor our parents approved of it. She was far too clever to keep her tongue still, and that didn't sit well in the more... strict generations of the past."

"I'm sorry."

"It was for the best. We were of two different social strata as well, something that was not encouraged... and in some parts of the empire still isn't. We have remained close over the decades, and I really cannot complain. It was actually through her that I met my since departed wife Mila."

He answered her question before she could ask. "Mila passed away eight years ago. She developed a horrible heart condition that was prevalent in her family. Of all the ways it could have ended, hers was more merciful than most, peacefully in her sleep."

Pirogoeth nodded. "I suppose it would be." One of her neighbors had the patriarch of their family suffer a similar event. It had apparently been very traumatic for everyone involved. "Do you protect your children in the same way?"

Socrato shook his head. "Yes. Mila... couldn't have children. I have two sons through Lanka that Mila and I raised as our own. They are both serving in the Aramathean First Army as officers. While they know, it is not entirely common knowledge, and we all prefer to keep it that way."

"Imperial politics makes my head hurt at times."

"If you ever have to deal with it for six decades, then maybe I'll give your headaches sympathy," Socrato teased, then pointed to his right to the side road heading to Lanka's shop. "Anyway, we are almost there. I'd recommend not talking about this to Lanka, she's even more of a private sort than I am."

"Really? I wouldn't have guessed," Pirogoeth snarked. "About the only thing her shop doesn't have is a 'GO AWAY' sign in the front window."

"It *did* at one time." Socrato chuckled. "She eventually took it down when I was able to convince her that it wouldn't hurt to have a few customers not by appointment."

At least now Pirogoeth had a better idea as to why Lanka had been so warm and welcoming during her first visit when the exterior of her store reflecting anything but. Pirogoeth was also impressed that two people could actually have a relationship break apart and still remain close in spite of it. That was not something she had observed to be terribly common.

Those thoughts fell by the wayside as Lanka revealed the outfits that she had fashioned for Pirogoeth. They were absolutely exquisite, and Pirogoeth had no problem acknowledging they were lovely and beautiful and magnificently crafted. This was no doubt the reason why Lanka could run a business without walk-in customers, because Pirogoeth had no doubt the three outfits that Lanka displayed likely could have been used to purchase half of Bakkra.

"Yes, Dominus, they are more northern and western in design," Lanka said. "I figured they suited your apprentice better. Longer skirts, smoother fabrics, such vibrant colors... Oh, I do enjoy them. Aramathean clothes can be so dreadfully *simple*."

Socrato shook his head dismissively. "I said nothing."

"You were thinking it," Lanka retorted. "Such is the bliss of living here, where cultures merge! Go on, try them on!" she then ordered Pirogoeth, pointing to the curtained-off rear of the store.

"What of her training clothes?" Socrato asked. It was clear what *he* thought was important. "No offense, but you can only wash one set so many times before there's no removing the smell."

Lanka waved off the concern as Pirogoeth slid behind the curtain. "Yes, yes... I have those too, Dominus. Ease your mind."

Pirogoeth actually liked the forest green dress the most, even if it perhaps wasn't the best color for her. Not that the other two were poorly made, by any stretch, but they were similar to the one she already had.

The green one, however... she liked how the skirt wasn't an even length; while it was ankle length on her left side, it was barely below her knee on the right, with a trim that looked like ruby dust. It very well might have been ruby dust, but she really didn't want to think about it. The more she thought about how expensive it was, the less she'd be willing to wear it.

That same trim decorated the shoulders, which, while puffed, weren't *nearly* as exaggerated as she had seen on some of the more elaborate dresses back home, and the wrists, highlighting the full length sleeves that were a slightly darker shade than the rest of the dress.

"I really like the green one," Pirogoeth called out.

"Oh, fabulous!" Lanka replied happily. "I hoped you would. The inspiration really took off on me with that one! Are you finished trying them on?"

"Yes."

"Very good. There *is* one more, but I need you personally to finish the touches on it. I shall be right there."

Pirogoeth was stepping out of the dress as Lanka slipped through the curtain, holding a bundle of gray cloth. "This, I fear, rather has to be of Aramathean design, my girl."

"What is it?" Pirogoeth asked.

Lanka unfolded the bundle and held it up. "Your toga, which is largely required clothes for official functions, which I can promise you will encounter at *some* point. Socrato does host very important dignitaries from time to time, and you will no doubt be expected to attend as well." Lanka began wrapping the cloth around Pirogoeth's frame, explaining how exactly it went on and tied together as she made the subtle alterations necessary.

"Why is this gray? Aren't they supposed to be white?"

"You are foreign born," Lanka explained. "For you, the toga is gray. If you were native born, then it would be white. In addition, as you are a layperson without citizenship, your belt is brown. If you were to become a lower citizen, you would be expected to wear a bronze sash. If you were to ever attain higher citizenship, your sash would be silver, and if somehow you were to be venerated, the sash would be gold."

Pirogoeth thought about this, then noted, "So... Dominus Socrato walks around in his daily business in what is equivalent to a full dress suit?"

Lanka chuckled. "He is a vain one, always strutting around in his finest. I can't entirely blame him though. Unlike those bulky suits that the men of your homeland would wear, Aramathean togas *are* very comfortable."

Pirogoeth couldn't disagree with that, as first impressions of her toga were positive; it wasn't bulky or cumbersome, allowing for plenty of freedom of movement. Her primary concern was not securing it properly and having it all come unraveled in public.

"Well then, I suppose I need you to try on the sets of perfectly boring training clothes I made for you as well. The Dominus insists. Some men just don't understand the important things in life, no?" Lanka added a teasing wink to her words to convey her lack of seriousness, moving to the other side of the enclosed space for the clothes in question.

The trip successfully gave Pirogoeth the time she needed to fully awaken, and allowed the rest of the day to proceed normally. Much of Socrato's tutoring was spent refining the skill of channeling now that she had a tome that wasn't as cooperative. She was getting a sense of the delicate balance needed in order to impose her will on the magics within, steadily gaining the strength to bend it to her whim. It *felt* easier by the end of the lesson... but she could have just been fooling herself.

"The mind is good at that," Socrato said. "Telling us what we want to hear, showing us what we want to see. It's why the art of the illusion and other ethereal magic can be so very effective. It preys on the weaknesses inherent in the human mind."

"And why I'm terrible at it," Pirogoeth said glumly.

"Yours is a practical mind. It prefers knowing what is real, and resists accepting what it sees is not always real," her master said reassuringly. "It takes time to break that programming... and is something that you have only really been studying for the last four days."

"But..."

Socrato held up a warning finger. "You are used to magic coming easily to you. You will not always find that everything is so trivially mastered in life. You should not be discouraged when such times happen."

His advice might have been more easily received if learning ethereal magic was her only source of frustration. The evening task she had agreed upon was bearing even *less* fruit the last few days, only her stubborn refusal to *never* quit on a task forced her forward through long hours of studying just to get the context she would need to even *begin* looking for ways to solve the lower citizens' dilemma.

Pirogoeth began to understand why Torma seemed rather put off by book learning, a trait the apprentice could not have imagined a mage having. She was finding it increasingly hard to crack open a book herself, now that it had become mostly an obligation.

She had one such moment one evening, as the sun began to peek through the window behind her. With a heavy breath, she rolled up the long, meandering scroll that contained a judge's decision that supposedly was the precursor for the Law of Free Information which lay at the heart of this mess. It had not been pleasant to struggle through. How could such educated people be so tedious to read?

Taima's voice drifted to her ears from the stairwell. "My lady?"

Pirogoeth sighed. It just wasn't worth fighting the honorific anymore. "Over here, Taima!"

The servant girl followed the sound of the voice and appeared in the open doorway. "I was told you were likely up here. Are you studying still?"

Pirogoeth didn't really want to tell Taima what was actually going on. It seemed to be a topic the servant girl wasn't keen on discussing. "Of sorts. Socrato has me reading at every opportunity it seems."

Taima had never looked mischievous before. "Is it of vital importance?"

Socrato *had* said he didn't want her spending *every* evening doing this. "No. I suppose it isn't," Pirogoeth answered.

"Then perhaps you can join me in the center square tonight?" Pirogoeth blinked. "What for?"

"There's a lunar eclipse tonight," Taima answered. "I'm sure Socrato mentioned something about it."

"He did," Pirogoeth acknowledged. "And that he was going to study it from the observation deck tonight. Why would we be going to the center square, though? We wouldn't be able to see much from there."

Taima bit her lower lip. "We wouldn't actually be going to watch the eclipse. There is a celebration that occurs among younger folks whenever there are celestial events like this one. There's dancing, games... though you have to bring your own food and drink. It's nothing base or carnal, but revelry is something the older folks tend to frown on nonetheless."

Pirogoeth somehow doubted there wasn't any debauchery present at a young adult gathering. She wasn't *stupid* as to how teenagers and young adults minds worked. But at the same time... she had never been invited to peer gatherings back home. "I trust you have the food and drink covered."

"A basket just outside the door. Filled with sweets and goodies from lemon cake to my attempt at Avalonian Chocolate. I fear I didn't do it quite right. I also have a fine fortified cherry wine that in theory should go very well with the chocolate."

"I suspect you did amazingly as always," Pirogoeth replied. She gave herself the once over, then said, "Can I change into something else first? I was playing with brimstone this morning, and I doubt the smell has completely faded."

Truth being, Pirogoeth just wanted the opportunity to change. She didn't want to head to a celebration still in her training clothes. And it gave her a chance to show off her new green dress.

"Of course!" Taima answered.

The apprentice smiled. "Then let's go."

Taima regaled her on the sort of happenings that occur at these gatherings as they made their way down the steps to the ground floor and then to Pirogoeth's chambers. She seemed particularly interested in the dancing, which apparently used the central square itself as the dancing floor. "It's amazing the routines that people come up with between gatherings and in such short times!" The servant girl said.

"Lunar eclipses aren't *that* common," Pirogoeth replied. She remembered one when she was eight or so, and that was it.

"The eclipse is more an excuse to gather than a reason," Taima admitted. "There have been gatherings for the fall harvest, the first day of spring, an election day, among others."

There were worse reasons to have a party, Pirogoeth figured.

At the door to her chambers, Pirogoeth held Taima back, and wagged a finger. "No. You wait out here while I get changed. I want you to tell me what you think once I've changed."

Getting changed into the dress was easy enough. Deciding which shoes to wear along *with* it was another matter entirely. It wasn't just a matter of color; as she had three different pairs of brown shoes that would have matched the colors of the dress well. She had suede high heeled shoes that made her look taller – a definite plus – but were very unwieldy to walk in. She had a pair of boots with a similarly platformed heel, but were very bulky and not very attractive. Finally, she had more casual rough leather shoes that were more like slippers, comfortable and easy to move in, but didn't offer any height boosting effect and were remarkably plain.

Worried about keeping Taima waiting, Pirogoeth settled on the comfortable shoes, just in case she wound up embarrassing herself dancing. She then returned to Taima and asked, "Well? What do you think?"

Taima's eyes lit up happily. "Oh, Coders be... is that... that *has* to be one of Lanka's dresses! You are *so* lucky!"

Pirogoeth flushed slightly, not expecting quite such an exuberant response. She really didn't want to mention now that she had *four* dresses from Lanka.

"The Dominus must have paid for that. I had wanted to have one tailored for me... but I won't see that amount of coin until I am a higher citizen myself!"

Pirogoeth's curiosity got the better of her. "How much did Lanka try to charge?"

"Thirty-seven Imperial Gold. That would have been twice a year's stipend for me!"

Pirogoeth spun about, the color draining from her face. "I'm going to change into something else." Taima caught her before she could even cross the threshold again, and started insistently pushing Pirogoeth towards the exit of the tower.

The apprentice was a bit surprised that they were heading

towards the main exit and not one of the more conspicuous side exits. "Why are we going out the front? I thought this gathering wasn't approved of."

Taima rolled her eyes playfully. "It's not *illegal*, my lady. Old men stuck in their ways just think it's too loud and we're not respecting proper decorum, then spend much of the night shaking their walking sticks at us."

Dusk had settled upon Kartage by the time the pair had left the tower and entered the city section of the keep, and immediately the pair drew every set of eyes... or more accurately, the foreign apprentice of the Dominus did.

Pirogoeth was far too used to being a social outcast, and becoming the center of attention so quickly by a score of people she didn't know was disconcerting... which quickly turned to a mild annoyance when unsolicited questions suddenly reminded of the gossip she had been isolated from for the last two weeks.

"Is it true you're from Avalon?"
"No."
"Did you know your father was a king?"
"That would be news to him, I'm sure."
"Do you remember anything about the court?"
"Can't remember somewhere I've never been."
"Is life in Aramathea anything like life in Avalon?"
"Wouldn't know."
"Is it true the Dominus is protecting you from assassins?"
"They'd be the dumbest assassins in history."
"Come now, people!" Taima interjected futilely. "We're here to have fun!"

Groupthink had conjured an entire narrative out of nothing, as far as Pirogoeth could tell. She was the lost Princess of Avalon, after a revolution that had deposed the royal family twenty years ago. All of that family had been confirmed executed save the youngest daughter. Socrato was teaching and protecting her so that one day she could reclaim her throne and restore the monarchy.

While the entire backstory of the Avalonian Revolution was true, Pirogoeth's supposed role in the story fell apart by applying simple logic. This "lost princess" was a young girl at the time of the revolution, yes... but she was *alive*. Pirogoeth hadn't been born until nearly five years later.

And while it was true that her father's side of the family came from Avalon, that was five generations and more than seven decades ago, and they came from the northern part of Avalon that was just as frequently Daynish lands, depending on where the ever fluctuating border was.

Through the barrage of questions, a firm and powerful voice cut through. "Now, kind men and women, I highly doubt that even if the apprentice here *were* a member of the Avalon royal family that she would be interested in holding court here and now! Scatter and give her space!"

The man's authority of voice did the trick, as men and women quickly found somewhere else to be, and this allowed her to get a good look at her rescuer.

Pirogoeth recognized him, though he did look a bit different in civilian clothes, a brown leather tunic and trousers held together with a black belt, than he did in Aramathean Phalanx armor. "Thank you..." she began, coming to an embarrassed halt when she discovered she didn't remember his name.

"Daneid, my lady," he answered, not showing any sign of insult. "Don't worry yourself; we have met all of twice, I believe, and both times I was in uniform. I'm told I look rather different then in it."

"Well, thank you again, Captain," Taima interjected. "I'm a bit surprised to see you here."

"Someone has to keep the peace and appease the seniors of the keep that nothing inappropriate is going on," Daneid answered. "I'm just glad it isn't me tonight."

That drew a laugh from both girls, then Taima lifted her basket and offered, "I have prepared some desserts for the celebration, Captain. Would you like to join us?"

"I would be glad to, my ladies. I think I can appropriate a good spot for us as well. Come with me."

The phalanx captain did as promised, even if he probably had to use his authority inappropriately in convincing a group in front of the font in the square to find a different spot. Pirogoeth found the misused authority to be barely above the bullying she was all too familiar with, but at the same time didn't want to make a scene and ruin Taima's night.

It helped that lemon cake had an uncanny ability to soothe tempers. Especially lemon cake crafted by Taima's expert hands. A perfect blend of sweet and tart, which would have been a dangerous combination had Pirogoeth been alone... because she would have probably eaten the whole cake herself.

Night had completely fallen, and the lamp on top of font behind them lit, like it did every night. This, coupled with long torches mounted into standing steel frames, served to give enough light for the party to continue.

Then Taima revealed the wine she had brought. "Be careful with this, my lady," she said in warning to Pirogoeth as she filled the apprentice's glass a quarter full. "This is probably a little bit stronger than anything you've had before."

"What about the chocolate?" Pirogoeth asked.

"That will be for later," Taima replied.

Daneid nodded in agreement. "Too much sugar doesn't always mix well with stronger alcohol. It's a bit of an initiation trick in the phalanx. Superstition goes that if you vomit, you won't have what it takes to survive army life. It's a stupid superstition; plenty of men have had perfectly respectable careers and not been able to handle that stomach curdling mess."

"Like you?" Pirogoeth asked.

"Oh, Coders no! I handled it just fine."

Both girls giggled at the comically defensive response, and used that as an adequate break in the conversation to drink.

Taima hadn't been joking. The burn of the wine was very evident and overpowering, to the point that Pirogoeth could barely taste the fruit, and it caused her to sputter. This was far more like the potency that she had sampled before, back home. Up until now, that small sip from her father's mug had been plenty enough for her.

Taima immediately showed concern. "My lady? Are you well?"

The apprentice coughed twice, and waved off concern. "I'm fine. Just took me by surprise." Not wanting to make Taima feel bad, Pirogoeth resumed drinking, forcing herself to ignore the burn. It got easier the further into the glass she got, but even by the end she still wouldn't have called it pleasant.

As Pirogoeth finished her glass, Taima clapped her hands and squealed in delight. "The dancing has started! My lady, come with me!"

The apprentice shook her head. "I think I'll decline... for now. Give my stomach a chance to settle."

"I'll keep the lady company," Daneid encouraged, shooing Taima towards the cleared section that had been reserved for the dance floor. "Have fun. I'm sure we'll all get our chance to strut by the time the night has concluded."

Taima was initially torn between staying with Pirogoeth and dancing, but the encouragement from both convinced her to take the latter option, gleefully dashing to the rapidly filling dance floor.

Aramathean dance was far different than what little she had seen of dancing back home. People didn't "pair off" here, instead forming into groups or even solo, with fluid improvised movements rather than the carefully scripted patterns that girls and boys had to learn. Pirogoeth was astonished that in the wild swarm no one seemed to collide with another.

"To be fair, I don't like dancing because normally when I'm in close quarters with someone, it's either sparring or fighting," Daneid admitted. "My reflexes as a result have made me unwelcome on the dance floor."

Pirogoeth laughed.

Daneid picked up Taima's bottle of wine, and asked, "wWould you like some more?"

Pirogoeth visibly cringed at the idea, as an unfamiliar voice cut into the conversation much like fingernails across a chalkboard.

"Oi! Cap'n! Shouldn't you be playing with someone more your age?"

The sound came from above, Pirogoeth craning her neck back to identify the source. Along what was normally the upper pooling lip for water in the font was a woman, perched in a crouch upon the edge.

To call the woman rough looking would have been an understatement. Her clothes were faded, tattered and frayed at every end, her blue denim shorts held to her waist by a hemp rope. A red shirt, visibly strained by the woman's chest, looked like it would split in two with a particularly deep breath. A yellow, flower print bandana wrapped around the top of her head and battered, unpolished leather boots completed the haggard ensemble.

Yet it was more than her clothes that seemed off. As the woman grinned menacingly, her canine teeth commanded her mouth, more like fangs than teeth, really. Her gaze seemed almost predatory despite the smile, and she looked like she was about to pounce.

Daneid appeared to know the woman; he jumped to his feet, and accused angrily, "You pirate scoundrel! When did you get here?"

The woman hopped down to ground with a huff, and straightened as she dismissively replied. "Pirate? You can't prove nothin'. I come and go as I please, and I don't answer to you."

From the different angle, Pirogoeth finally figured out what was so off about the ragged visitor; evidence in the form of a bushy fox tail, protruding from where part of the shorts' backside had been sliced off with what appeared to be a knife. The new line of sight also allowed Pirogoeth to clearly see a pair of fox ears twitching aggressively at the top of the woman's head.

She had heard of such people, "chimeras" Torma had called them; cursed with a partial animal form through either magic or influence of spirits of nature. They were so rare that in most parts of the world, like Bakkra, they were considered a myth, but Torma had insisted chimeras were very real indeed.

Pirogoeth wasn't going to doubt Torma's stories again.

"When did you get here?" Daneid demanded.

"When you weren't at your post," the woman replied. "Whatcha gonna do about it? I haven't broken none of your laws. Don't plan to either. Though you could make me change my mind."

"Is that so?"

The woman leaned on her toes to meet Daneid's eyes. "Yeah. If you're willing to explain to your men tomorrow morning how you got all scratched up, I'll fight ya right here and now. No skin off my teeth. I'd be back out roaming free by this time tomorrow."

Daneid's silence was his only response.

"Otherwise, why don't you go back home and leave this little girl alone?" the woman then offered.

"One of these days, wretch, I'll see you in a dungeon, and I'll laugh," Daneid growled, but apparently decided retreat was the better part of valor. "My lady, be careful with this one," he said in parting to Pirogoeth, and disappeared into the night.

"Feh!" the woman spat, keeping her eyes on the soldier as he walked away. "You gotta be careful with the likes of him! Aramathean men have some very loose definitions of consenting age, let me tell ya."

Pirogoeth really didn't get that sense from Daneid; while perhaps trying too hard to be friendly, there hadn't been a particularly sexual vibe. There was certainly some history there between the chimera and the captain, though. Before Pirogoeth could formulate a question, the chimera had grabbed Taima's wine, and chugged half of it straight from the bottle.

The woman frowned in distaste. "Feh! Aramatheans can't make a good brew to save their lives. No bite at all." She then set the bottle back down and still without even giving Pirogoeth a sideways glance said, "See ya girl. Watch out for the men around here."

The chimera then also vanished into the night, several minutes before Taima returned to the scene, understandably confused to see Pirogoeth alone. "Where did Captain Daneid go?"

How could Pirogoeth answer that question truthfully in a way that didn't sound insane? "He... apparently some business came up unexpectedly. He had to leave."

Taima frowned. "Well, that's a shame. Phalanx have such difficult jobs and little free time. Oh well, we can't let that ruin *our* fun! Come on!"

And Taima wasn't about to let Pirogoeth go without sampling *all* the fun the party had to offer. The apprentice learned that she was as unwelcome on the dance floor as Daneid, for similar yet different reasons. After inadvertently striking a fourth person, Taima quickly decided to find somewhere else Pirogoeth should be.

Not that Pirogoeth fared much better at the games. Testing her strength had been depressing. She fared little better in the sprints. And no matter *how* much Taima begged, Pirogoeth steadfastly refused to step into the wrestling circle.

She *did* win a silver piece at a "guess your age" game... though it was little consolation considering the game master offered a guess of twelve. Pirogoeth was half of mind to shove the coin straight down his throat for the indignity. Attempting to write it off as just some crazy, blind, old man also failed when he correctly guessed the next seven contestants within a year.

"You're not *that* short," Taima offered helpfully after Pirogoeth declared she was done having fun, and was going to return to her chambers. The apprentice had been on a slow burn the entire walk to the tower, to the point where she didn't even acknowledge the soldiers at the front gate through her surly self-loathing.

"Yes I am," Pirogoeth grunted, refusing to be mollified. "I look like a child. I've got no chest, my hips are non-existent, I'm tiny, slight, with no curves or anything to make me look taller than a twelve-year old girl."

"It's because the men who run such games have trained for years to spot the telltale signs of Aramatheans as they age. For someone outside of the empire from an entirely different stock, their accuracy plummets drastically. It'd be like asking a horse tender to tell me details of a breed they had never seen before."

Both Taima and Pirogoeth looked upward with a start, surprised to see Socrato looking down at them from just inside the gate. While he didn't look displeased, he didn't look exactly *happy*, either. Despite Taima's assurances that they were doing nothing wrong, Pirogoeth dropped her head guiltily.

"And what are you so shameful about?" Socrato asked. "The

only thing you did wrong was not bringing your tome with you."

Pirogoeth's eyes jolted wide. She had been in such a hurry to show off her dress to Taima that she had completely forgotten it on her bed.

"A mage without a tome is asking for trouble," Socrato reminded her. "I expect you to be much more careful in the future. Good night, girls."

Pirogoeth held back, waving Taima farewell. Once the servant girl had left earshot, Pirogoeth spoke up. "Master, I saw something unusual tonight."

"I presume you aren't talking about the eclipse." Socrato said warily.

Pirogoeth nodded. "I saw a chimera in the town square. A fox-girl, in fact."

That rose Socrato's eyebrows. "Did you? Chimeras generally draw attention, especially when they don't want it. Odd that I heard nothing about one arriving in Kartage."

"Captain Daneid claimed she was a pirate," Pirogoeth continued.

Socrato confirmed, "That is quite possible. Chimeras often wind up pushed into that lifestyle by civilizations that find their presence offensive, and even worthy of extinction. Quite sad, really."

Pirogoeth couldn't quite understand the casual dismissal. "But if she's a pirate, why didn't Captain Daneid do anything? He seemed almost scared of her."

"Was the chimera wearing a yellow bandana or scarf?"

Pirogoeth eyes bulged at the random question. "How did you know that?"

Socrato took a deep breath. "There are two types of pirate in this world. The first are the ones that you hear about in stories and rumor. Vicious, bloodthirsty scourges of the seas; thieves and murderers. They are more nuisance than anything, for their numbers are few and there is very little organization. They prey on vessels that take unnecessary risks, and put themselves out of naval protection.

Then there is a second group, who call themselves 'pirates', but there's no evidence of any actual piracy on their part. They are most noted for having a yellow article, usually a scarf or bandana, that marks them of this group. These pirates are very organized, as much as any naval force in the world, in fact. They stay outside imperial waters, and generally avoid conflict. At this point, we understand to leave them alone, and they will leave us alone.

They've established very powerful friends in all three major empires. I've had magisters of the emperor himself *order* me to release any gold pirate, as they are called, within twenty-four hours of their detainment. Not that I've ever had reason to do so. The scant few times one of their number has appeared in Kartage, they've done nothing to warrant arrest."

Pirogoeth blinked as her mind wrapped around the information. "So if they aren't criminals, and aren't really pirates... what *do* they do?"

Socrato reluctantly answered, "I don't know. And that's what troubling to me. They're an enigma. And I really don't like mysteries." He waved off further questions or concerns. "But there is little we can do about it, especially now. Sleep well, dear girl. You have studies in the morning."

Curiosity didn't want her to leave it there, but a long day coupled with a lack of sleep from the night before quickly caught up to her in the form of a heavy yawn. At that point, her bed became much more appealing than trying to learn more about pirates.

At least she was going to sleep a lot better tonight, if for no reason than she was amazed she was able to keep her eyes open long enough to plop lifelessly onto her bed.

Day 61: Further Up and Further In

Pirogoeth became increasingly certain she would never quite "get" ethereal magic.

It's not that she didn't know *how* to channel such techniques. The process was actually the exact same as any other type of magic. It wasn't that she couldn't make the spells do what she wanted. She had the technical details solidly down. It wasn't a tactical issue, either. She knew precisely when and where ethereal magic could be put to its greatest effect.

It wasn't even a matter of breaking down what she had learned. She perfectly accepted that the theory Torma taught her was nigh wholly incorrect, that ethereal magic didn't have forms in the sense that material magic did. It was a hodgepodge of spells that refused to be classified in any conventional sense, and behaved in ways that could not be easily predicted.

But there was something she was missing that really brought the best out of that particular school of magic.

"Ethereal magic doesn't have the raw power of material magic," Socrato reiterated with the patience that she had come to expect when he was actively teaching. "You can't sear an opponent to cinders with an illusion. The power isn't in the spells themselves."

Pirogoeth had heard this, many times, and it didn't make sense.

"The best way that I can explain the trick behind this school of magic is that it is as much observation as it is misdirection. You need to know how your opponent perceives reality, identify his tendencies, his patterns, and shape a reality that conforms to that perception yet bends ever so slightly in the direction *you* desire."

In the time it took her to figure out all *that*, she could have razed her opponent to cinders, taken what she wanted, and ripped apart half of whatever building he was found in.

"Ethereal magic is in many ways, an art of subtlety, and it's not best suited for every personality. You know *how* to do it. That really is the important thing. The rest will come to you in time, I am sure. Would you like to move on to something else, perhaps?"

"Could we?" the apprentice pleaded hopefully.

Socrato agreed with a nod. "These next lessons may even indirectly help you understand ethereal magic better, come to think of it. Because now the lessons get a little more advanced, we'll discover how material and ethereal magic can be used in unison. But I do believe that will require a new tome for you..."

His voice drifted off, then he looked up towards the ceiling. "How do you feel about another climb? I think it's time you got the chance to access my personal library."

On one hand, Pirogoeth *loved* the idea of getting a first-hand look at the veritable *mountain* of mystical items and books that her master was said to possess. On the other... she was *not* looking forward to the twelve floor climb to where said library was.

"Well... I suppose we can use one of my shortcuts," Socrato said, noticing Pirogoeth's apprehension, and the relief that followed his suggestion. He snapped his fingers, which appeared to be the trigger, as the entry to the stairwell turned the telltale black that Pirogoeth remembered from her arrival in the tower.

"Ladies first," he said, motioning for Pirogoeth to take the lead.

Pirogoeth found this fairly unusual, but didn't argue, stepping through the veil of darkness and popping into an open floor filled with wonder and magic, quite literally.

Unlike the public library several floors down, Socrato's private library was not nearly as ordered. It wasn't cluttered or messy by any stretch – that would have been exceedingly dangerous – but tomes were shelved next to artifacts, scrolls tucked underneath tables that had larger trinkets resting on the top. Pirogoeth had no doubt there was an order to the seeming madness, but it was likely an order only Socrato understood.

She stepped forward, her body tingling as her mystic sense could literally *feel* the mystical energies radiating from the chamber. It was both intoxicating and frightening... that such power was right in front of her, but she didn't dare actually try to interact with any of it.

One very large object caught her eye, a solid table made of obsidian. The volcanic glass was extremely rare, extremely sharp, and extremely brittle, and as such Pirogoeth had never seen it used to make a table. She had seen old Daynish weapons made of the stuff, and they were supposedly frighteningly damaging if unreliable... but never a piece of furniture.

As she got closer, she realized that what she thought was the base was actually a hollow compartment with a ceramic interior, with sliding panels that locked together to seal the top closed. Sensing that didn't have any magical properties in and of itself, she toyed with said top repeatedly, opening and closing it to try and figure out exactly the mechanism that caused such a tight seal. She wasn't sure what to make of it... what could such a thing possibly be used for?

Socrato finally made his presence known, startling Pirogoeth. "That is a supposed alchemical table, an item that I purchased when I was far younger and far more foolish. I don't regret it... I think it was good for me to finally abolish the idea of practical alchemy once and for all."

Pirogoeth had heard of alchemy, had heard of some claims of people who had transmuted metals like lead and iron into gold, but had never heard of any concrete evidence that it had truly been accomplished. "Practical alchemy? You mean it's *possible*?"

Socrato shrugged. "In a sense. Through immense amounts of experimentation, tremendous amounts of energy, and at great personal risk, I discovered that it is indeed possible to alter the fundamental properties of heavier metals. But doing so creates something that you would be wise to never touch or try to handle. I was ill for a good many days, and it took the healing of many of my peers to pull me from death."

He then shook his head. "But to make gold from iron? That, I suspect, will remain a flight of fancy for many, many years. The amount of power needed to do so, and also make it fit to be used in *anything*, is beyond anything short of the Coders themselves."

He turned away from Pirogoeth and the table, the memories tugging at him. She figured that must have been a scary time, and let it go without any further comment. Although the more she learned about the earlier life of the venerable sage, the more she found herself intrigued by his adventures, and thus found it difficult to bite her tongue.

"But that's not why we're here, so let's not dwell on it, shall we?" he declared. "I need to find a particular tome, and that may take some time. Try not to touch too many things, if you would be so kind."

Socrato's concern was warranted. Pirogoeth knew just enough about magical artifacts and trinkets to be dangerous to herself and others. She also knew this, and that very real danger was enough to keep her curiosity from getting the better of her.

Her master begin running his fingers along the shelves, muttering with increasing annoyance as he did so. He abruptly yelped in triumph, pulling out a book, only for his expression to turn into a snarl as he grunted, "Wrong version. I want the sixth edition *I* made, damn it."

Socrato crossed the room, passing in front of Pirogoeth,

grumbling, "Did I move it over here?" He continued with another round of rummaging through bookshelves, rapidly growing irritated by his lack of results. Finally he stopped and tapped his foot rapidly as he drummed his index finger of his right hand on his chin.

Then with a snap of his fingers, Socrato's face brightened. "How silly of me! I put it on my desk last night because I knew I would need it today." He then crossed in front of Pirogoeth with a tired sigh. "You'd think I was getting old with the way my memory is falling apart." Socrato stepped behind Pirogoeth to a distressingly cluttered pine wood desk. Somewhere within that mess, the sage emerged triumphant with a blue leather bound book, entirely plain on the cover, as per Socrato's tendency.

"Here we go. I prefer this version as it is one that I personally transcribed with proper corrections that make it more effective than the edition that preceded it," Socrato said, handing the tome over to his apprentice. "This is the Book of Life and Death, and it is every bit as dangerous at its name implies. It possesses many of the spells that define the magic arts of restoration and decay."

"These are *not* techniques to take lightly," Socrato warned. "They are extremely advanced, and most mages aren't fit to even *try* to use them."

Pirogoeth understood that much. Torma had noted that while she had a book of restoration spells, she was loathe to use them. "Torma had said that healing spells scared her more than decay spells, which still seems odd to me," Pirogoeth admitted. "I don't understand why."

"Decay is the natural order of things," Socrato explained. "Restoration is a rejection of that natural order, and mages can feel it in their bones when they try. Unless you have absolute domination of the tome you are channeling from, healing has a tendency to steal your own life essence to help fuel the spell. It is as unpleasant as it sounds. I am eternally grateful for the mages that came to my aid from every corner of the world to restore my health, for they no doubt paid for it with a bit of themselves."

Making someone else's arm rot didn't sound so bad after all.

"Restoration and decay are examples of spells that have material *and* ethereal elements. They are techniques that draw their energy from beyond nature, like ethereal magic, but they very clearly have effects that are physical in ways that ethereal magic isn't." Socrato had his apprentice's full attention. "Now do you see how the lines blur? Magic is not something that is, or ever will be, neatly defined."

Pirogoeth nodded. "I suppose so, though I suspect that I'll have an entirely different opinion once I start trying to actually use these skills."

"Perhaps. For now, get acclimated with this tome as always. But I would strongly advise against attempting to channel any of them like you have in all the other tomes I've given you." Pirogoeth flushed guiltily at the words, but Socrato waved off her worry. "Oh do not be like that. I know you are exceptionally gifted with such self-exploration, and you would probably be perfectly fine doing the same here. But as the techniques get more complicated, the more it would ease my mind for you to start playing around with them with my supervision."

Pirogoeth nodded again. "Yes, master."

Socrato shooed her away, then called out to her as she started to leave. "Oh! One last thing. Be sure to have your toga cleaned and ready by the day after tomorrow."

"Why is that, master?"

"I received word that a very important visitor should be arriving by evening the day after tomorrow, one of considerable prominence that demands formal and traditional attire. As a result, the usual dinner buffet will also be a more traditional meal. I suspect our guest would not care on either count, but it's a matter of appearances and proper respect for a man of his station."

Pirogoeth couldn't help but note that Socrato hadn't mentioned exactly *who* was coming. "Who is coming, master?"

"I'm not really at liberty to say. You see, he is *supposed* to be on orders to go straight back to the First Capital, and he is somewhat bending those orders to stop here to resupply. I'd rather not implicate him just yet. Now off with you. Clean up and be ready for dinner in an hour."

Pirogoeth couldn't gossip about the news at the meal with Taima, and thus had to wait until the pair were excused to their evening business. She hurried Taima towards her chambers, pulling to a stop just short of the door.

"Hold on, one second. I want to try and change the color of the room," the apprentice said, realizing an opportunity to test her skills of illusion. She focused on the room inside, changing its color. "Okay, *now* you can go in."

Taima did so and squealed in delight. "Oh! You changed the color! I *love* red!"

Pirogoeth sighed in defeat. "It was *supposed* to be green..." She had forgotten that she needed to influence Taima's mind first, lead the servant girl's vision in the direction Pirogoeth wanted. Lacking that, Taima latched onto a different color, either from personal taste or from some other unexpected outside influence.

"Oh! Now I see it!" Taima yelped. "How very clever!"

"Not clever enough yet," Pirogoeth grumped sourly, finally stepping into the room and dropping the illusion so that Socrato's initial blue once again commanded the room.

Taima patted Pirogoeth on the shoulder warmly, "You'll get there!" She then turned conspiratorial, and closed the door. "But something tells me that what you wanted to talk about so eagerly during dinner wasn't your attempts at decoration."

"I trust you know that you'll be working the day after tomorrow instead of the buffet dinner."

Taima shrugged. "That happens from time to time. I'm sure that means someone important is coming."

"He's done this before?"

Taima nodded. "Though he's never been secretive about who or what the matter of business is. I can only imagine who it might be. I wouldn't worry about it terribly much. In less than two days, the secret will be out."

Pirogoeth acknowledged this. Besides, she had too much on her plate to worry about some secret event happening in forty-eight hours. Some of which she should get to. "Well, I suppose it's back to study for me then," the apprentice said.

"Back to the library?" Taima surmised. "Studying more history, are you?"

Pirogoeth shook her head. "More current events now. I'm thinking Socrato just wants someone he can debate with."

"I should return to help with cleanup anyway. Vargat says I don't have to, but I'll have to get used to always being at work once I have my own restaurant. Might as well get used to it now, yes?"

The girls parted ways, each to their tasks, even as Pirogoeth's treasonous mind continued to mull over the coming mystery in two days' time.

It was going to be a *long* two days...

Day 63: Important Guests

Pirogoeth blamed her complete logjam of thoughts on the upcoming important dinner. It was easier than concluding she was completely and hopelessly stumped.

Socrato had given her the day off from her magical studies, citing administrative business that he needed to get done so that he'd be able to devote the evening to entertaining their still secret visitor. Pirogoeth decided to occupy her time with another attempt to solve the conundrum created by the venerated citizens abusing their power.

It seemed better than letting her curiosity run wild... though the frustration she was currently facing was probably a wash. She felt reasonably caught up with all the twists and turns in the case, or at least as much as she could hope to be without devoting *years* to studying Aramathean law, and she could see now just why it frustrated Socrato so.

It was clearly and blatantly evident that the venerated citizens charged were abusing their power and ruining the lives of others in order to gain material wealth. While it was true that lower citizens should have gotten the hint these venerated were bad news and to stay away, that didn't excuse the fact that these venerated citizens were destroying entire families in their lust for property and money.

And yet, despite this wrongdoing – one of the citizens charged actually went on record bragging about being untouchable – they were using the law and bureaucracy as a shield in a way that was never intended.

Every idea she came up with, Socrato already had, and had run into the same roadblock: that the schooling was not what was being traded, and so long as the venerated citizens offered something tangible in exchange, it was entirely legal. The quality of schooling, or lack thereof, was "free", and thus not something tradeable, and thus not something that could be contested as fraud.

She dropped her head into her hands and groaned. Why did she agree to do this? Why was she still even *trying*?

"My lady!" Taima squealed in excitement; Pirogoeth was able to hear the servant girl charging up the staircase and into the library. The noise startled both her and the librarian, who angrily hissed at Taima to quiet down.

Taima did settle herself, at least vocally. When she appeared in the room Pirogoeth languished in, the servant girl was still shaking visibly, like a tightly pulled harp string.

"Have you been chewing Socrato's coffee beans again?" Pirogoeth asked sharply.

Taima's grin broadened until Pirogoeth swore she was half teeth. The servant girl raised her arms and brandished two things: a bronze sash, and a large envelope. "They finally came! The Registrar in Grand Aramathea finally accepted the Craftsman's Writ, and I am officially a lower citizen! I can wear this to dinner as a true citizen of the empire!"

Pirogoeth jumped to her feet, and threw her arms around Taima. "Congratulations! One step closer to your dream!"

"I try not to think about it as being ten years away," Taima said. "It's rather amusing that the only thing that is changing is my official title. I'm now a chef, and not a chef's assistant, but I've been doing that work and had those responsibilities for the last two years anyway. But still... it matters to me!"

"And it should!" Pirogoeth insisted. Then curiosity got the better of her and pointed to the envelope. "And what is that, exactly?"

Taima replied, "Oh, that's the Writ itself. I don't particularly need it, as I will be staying here working under Chef Vargat, but if I wanted to get employment elsewhere I'd need it to prove that I am actually certified to do what I claim I can. Another copy is with the Registrar in Grand Aramathea that I can appeal to if this one is ever lost or stolen."

Pirogoeth blinked. "So you need *that* as proof of your education?"

"Of course. Did you think that people of the empire as a rule took a citizen's word for it and just hired them?"

"I... I'm not sure what I was thinking," Pirogoeth admitted, her mind churning as a thought bubbled in her head. She quickly dashed back to where she was seating, rifling through one source after another quickly to see if this most serendipitous idea was one that had been argued.

She squealed in triumph. It had not.

"My lady?" Taima asked with curiosity. "What...?"

Pirogoeth dashed back to Taima, and gave her a thankful hug. "No time. I want to try and catch Socrato before I have to get all dressed up for dinner. I'll see you later tonight."

Taima certainly wanted to know more, but Pirogoeth didn't give her the opportunity, leaving in a rush, and the servant girl had her own business to attend to that prevented her from giving chase. Which was probably a good thing... Pirogoeth didn't want to have to explain herself until she got Socrato's opinion.

Not finding him in his public office on the first floor, she dashed madly through the halls asking anyone she ran into if they had any idea where Socrato could have been. The search proved to be unnecessary, as Socrato was doing the exact same thing looking for her.

"Where have you been?" Socrato demanded angrily. "I have been looking for you for the last half hour!"

"Master, I think I've found a solution..." Pirogoeth began excitedly.

The sage cut her off. "Later! Right now, you must get changed and meet me in the banquet hall as soon as possible."

"But... the evening meal isn't for another hour at least." Then she added tentatively, "Right?"

"The schedule has changed. We're getting another 'guest' and as much as I'd rather not, proper decorum would be to entertain and dine him after such a distance traveled."

This new arrival was clearly announced with very little warning, as Socrato rarely showed such visible annoyance otherwise. While a very adaptive and pragmatic personality, that did not mean he liked deviations from previously made plans.

"This doesn't have to do with the secret guest you were planning to host, does it?"

Socrato's expression grew dark. "No, it does not," he grumbled. "And I suspect he will want to see you, specifically."

Pirogoeth was confused. "Me? Why me?"

Socrato sighed. "I'll let you guess. Our visitor is an ambassador from Avalon."

Pirogoeth snapped her eyes shut, her face twisted in anticipation of the coming headache. "Are you serious?"

"Yes," Her master said tiredly. "Now get changed. The sooner we get this ambassador in and out of my keep, the better the chances he leaves with our dignity still intact. Quickly now."

Pirogoeth dashed as rapidly as safety would allow to her chambers, where she immediately discovered one fairly significant problem: she had forgotten Lanka's instructions on how to put the damned toga on.

She experimented with different methods of wrapping the long, singular length of cloth around her body, but it either didn't look right or would fall open in very inappropriate ways, if not fall off completely.

A knock on her door made her squeak frightfully before Taima's voice from the other side calmed her. "My lady? The Dominus sent me. He thought you could use my help? But I don't know why?"

With a heavy release of breath, Pirogoeth covered her chest with her right arm as she cracked the door open with her left. "Oh Coders thank you, I can't figure out how to put this accursed garment on."

Taima smiled broadly. "Just like an Avalonian princess."

"I will burn that toga clean off your body in the middle of you serving dinner if you make another comment like that," Pirogoeth warned with a hiss.

Taima, of course, had slung her pristine while toga across her frame, proudly sporting her new bronze sash. "I understand, my lady. Now please allow me inside and I shall properly instruct you on traditional Aramathean dress."

Pirogoeth complied, and Taima began her assistance. "Firstly, let's get you properly wrapped up. Sometimes, even when properly put on, the toga can slip. I don't even have that confidence, and I've been putting these things on for years."

Taima rummaged around for some linen that could service as a top. "The trick is to have a wrap the same color as your toga, so that no one can tell the difference unless they are looking *very* closely. I don't think anyone will hold it against *you*, though, so this should suit." The servant girl held up a roll of white gauze, intended for first aid purposes, after tightly wrapping it around Pirogoeth's chest, and securing it in the back with a pin, Taima moved on to the toga itself.

"Now, watch carefully." Taima started by folding the large rectangle of cloth in half. "It really helps to have a second person working with you to put these on *anyway*." She explained as she draped the section of material over Pirogoeth's right shoulder. "Even with experience, an extra set of hands makes this easier."

She then adjusted the front side of the cloth until it was the longer of the two, then took it around Pirogoeth's chest, under her right arm, then over the left shoulder, that part hanging to form the front side of the "skirt", then shifted the shorter side so that it formed the back half.

"The sash helps keep it together, somewhat," Taima finished, tying the brown belt around Pirogoeth's waist, "but it really is more for show than anything. And all done! Now, I must get back to the kitchen promptly. The time for dinner has been pushed forward, and Vargat needs my hands."

"Then go!" Pirogoeth yelped, pointing animatedly at the door. "And thank you again for your help."

Taima nodded, and made haste leaving, moving so quickly that Pirogoeth could hear the servant girl's footsteps in the hall. It reminded Pirogoeth that *she* had somewhere to be quickly as well, and within seconds, she was charging right down Taima's same path towards the banquet hall.

Socrato gestured to her as she appeared, silently motioning for her to sit next to him at the main table. "Still no word on our Avalonian guest's arrival," Socrato said. "Captain Daneid is supposed to be sending word once the envoy is spotted. I hope he doesn't run too late. Message via hawk from Helenus is that our *desired* guest should be arriving on schedule."

"Would it be *that* much of a problem if they both arrived at the same time?" Pirogoeth asked.

"Our wanted guest is one that should not share hospitality. He also would not be pleased to see foreign entities imposing themselves onto Aramathean territory on what he would consider trivial affairs... and he has not exactly refined his diplomatic tongue."

"You're worried about one or both of our guests making a scene if in the same room," Pirogoeth concluded.

"Quite." Socrato gestured to a servant standing at the side of the door that led to the kitchens. "Send in the appetizers once they are ready. We may be here a while."

Small talk with her master was a very unnerving thing, Pirogoeth discovered. Not because she wasn't used to such banter from a teaching figure... but that the sort of things that Socrato deemed small talk was quite frightening.

Like, "Did you know that human skin melts at a little over one hundred and sixty degrees? I didn't until yesterday."

Or, "Did you know it's possible to lower air pressure enough for your blood to boil at room temperature?"

He finished with, "And close your mouth, girl. It is most undignified to chew with your mouth open."

Any reply Pirogoeth could have made was interrupted by the tower herald appearing at the main entrance. "Dominus, our guest from Avalon has arrived."

Socrato animatedly gestured at the herald to get on with it. "Yes, yes. Very good. Send him in."

The herald nodded and disappeared momentarily. When he returned, it was with proper pomp and circumstance, declaring with a hearty voice, "Dominus, I present to you Cavalier Norman of West Snake River."

A tall yet thin man appeared behind the herald, dressed in a royal blue vest with silver lapels dotted with golden pins and red ribbons, and a white full length dress shirt underneath, complete with ruffles in the chest and sleeves that flared at the forearms before hugging tight at the wristband. His trousers were the same color as the vest with a silver stripe down the exterior of the legs and ended with dutifully polished black leather boots.

He was an older man, judging from his full head of gray hair, though not so old that his face showed any significant wrinkles or a heavily receding hairline. He moved confidently, more *through* the herald than *around* him, an arrogance that came from a lifetime of authority.

"Cavalier, is it?" Socrato said. "Odd to see such a title from a man representing the Republican Provinces of Avalon."

"Not all noblemen supported the crown during the revolution," Norman answered crossly. His voice was graveled, and laced with irritation. He didn't want to be here, that much was evident.

This was a good thing, Pirogoeth figured. Socrato didn't particularly want the Cavalier here either. Perhaps it meant Norman would take one look at Pirogoeth, shake his head, and leave without further theatrics.

There would be no such luck. "Rumor has reached Caravel that you are harboring a fugitive member of the deposed royal family here," Norman said with annoyance. "I would sincerely hope that is not the case."

"And if it were?" Socrato asked.

"The royal family, any who may live, are criminals in the eyes of the Republic. Our response would be the same with any other high criminal fugitive being harbored in a foreign land."

Socrato seemed more than willing to poke the Avalonian. "Oh, so you mean bluster impotently for months, if not years, until the harboring entity finally tires of your whining? In case you have forgotten where you are, Cavalier, this is *my* keep. I will do as *I* please, whether Avalon likes it or not."

Norman didn't respond verbally, though his slowly clenching fists spoke volumes as to how he truly felt.

"But you can return to Caravel, and inform your paranoid

parliament that I am harboring no one outside of a young girl from the Free Provinces who I can assure you is no princess of any land," Socrato finished dismissively.

Norman, not surprisingly, wasn't the least bit assured by Socrato's say so. "I will be the judge of that, Dominus..." Then hastily adding with what was the closest tone to polite he had offered so far, "if I may."

Socrato gestured with an upturned palm to Pirogoeth, and said, "Apprentice, do present yourself to our guest."

Pirogoeth made a sour face as she stood. She bristled at the distasteful staredown Norman offered her, even though she should have found it a good thing, really. The less this nonsense continued the better... but it still wasn't nice to receive such a baleful eye.

"This girl looks *nothing* like Princess Viola," Norman scoffed. "If you are going to present a pretender to the throne, I think you should try harder."

"Good! Because I'm not trying to!" Pirogoeth finally snapped with all the venom she could lace into her tongue. Implying her master was a liar did not set well with her. "I'm sorry you came all this way for nothing chasing some ghost that isn't, and never has, settled here."

Norman's jaw set angrily. "Now see here, child. I have it on good ears that a woman matching the rumored princess was seen here, taken from the Free Provinces. So pardon me when your patron tries to pawn off an obvious misdirection on me."

Socrato's temper started to boil, "Then your good ears aren't nearly as good as you think."

"I'm not going to give you too many chances, Dominus. I will not accept much stonewalling on this issue. Present to me this woman that my sources have seen, and we can end this charade. If you think to destabilize Avalon *again* with this nonsensical rumor of a lost princess, we will..."

"Will *what*?"

All three heads whipped in the direction of the main entry and the source of the voice. It was powerful and authoritative, and the man it belonged to matched that voice admirably. He was not very old, Pirogoeth guessed, maybe his early thirties, with rich coal black hair and an equally lush if trimmed beard. Heavily muscled and imposing, he was easily a foot and a half over her, and every inch of his frame was packed with more muscle than it should rightfully be able to carry.

He was dressed similarly to the Phalanx soldiers that guarded the keep, though his armor was much more elaborate, with etched patterns across the bronzed steel chestplate. The spear and shield on his back were also decorated elaborately, notably the large ruby colored stone embedded into the spearhead. His helmet, tucked under his left arm, carried a plume of red with gold stripes, unlike the solid red of the soldiers she had seen previously.

This man was a member of the army. And even though Pirogoeth had little knowledge of the indicators of rank, even she could tell it was very high ranking member at that.

"Cavalier Norman, allow me to introduce you to General Argaeus." Socrato said, his ire dissolved into nervousness. This was clearly the intended guest, and judging from the very deliberate and loud footsteps from the general, Pirogoeth sensed that his worry was justified. Sparks were about to fly.

"You seem to forget your place, Cavalier," Argaeus growled, menacingly. Every hint of his body language seethed aggression. "This is *not* Avalon." The next three words were delivered with clear enunciation to emphasize them. "This. Is. Aramathea. This is *my* land. This is *my* home. It is under *my* protection, and you are currently violating that boundary. You are in no position to be issuing demands or making threats. I, on the other hand... am."

The short sword dangling at the general's hip moved with a flash, the hiltless blade's tip coming to a stop less than an inch under Norman's head and in front of his throat. "For a self-admitted pointless search of fantasy, you and your fellow Avalonians seem to put an undue amount of time and effort into dispelling it."

For once, the Cavalier was content to be silent, though Pirogoeth doubted there were too many men of enough courage to even attempt to muster a voice in his situation.

The general's voice lowered, but every bit of menacing power remained. "I care little about what stones you overturn in Avalon. I also don't care what city-states you turn inside out in the Free Provinces. But your mad crusade stops at the borders of Aramathea from this point forward. If the Dominus tells you no one by that description resides in Kartage, that means no one by that description resides in Kartage."

The blade danced subtly upward until it tapped Norman on the chin. "Unless you wish to declare the Dominus, a venerated citizen of the First Empire, a liar. At which point, I am terribly afraid I would have to take offense. And rest assured, that would end very badly for you."

Argaeus lowered the sword, returning it to its sheath, his growl steadily increasing in volume until he was at full bellow. "Now, return to your hole in your swamp. Tell your Parliament that if your lost princess resides here, she is beyond your reach. And impress upon them that this will be the end of it. For if it is *not*, if Avalonian boots tread upon *my* land again searching for *anyone*, princess or pauper, without the expressed permission of the Emperor... that the response will be *my* steel, and *my* army, burning your filthy growth of a kingdom down until all that is left is the peat moss!"

Pirogoeth recoiled. She didn't dare air her thoughts, but if she had, it would have been to remark on the nature of disproportionate responses. Then she wondered if General Argaeus even *had* the authority to do such a thing. A look in her master's direction, and the color drained from his face in horror, told her that he even if Argaeus didn't, the general had an authority close enough to it to make very little difference in the end.

But it seemed to work on Norman, at the very least. Even if the Cavalier thought it was just bluster, there was no way he was going to test that theory. "Very well," he said slowly. "I will deliver your words to the Parliament. Though I doubt they will be intimidated into compliance."

"If they value their existence, they will," Argaeus replied, turning aside to allow the Cavalier to leave, which mercifully Norman did, taking step behind the herald who would lead him out of the inner keep."

Once alone, Argaeus's demeanor changed. He was much more reserved, even friendly. "I apologize for that. This is not the first time agents of Avalon have crossed into the First Empire. I have grown tired of their incursions, both official and clandestine."

He then looked over the direction of Pirogoeth's right shoulder. Taima was hovering in the doorway between the hall and the kitchen, holding a tray of roasted duck, her poor knees visibly trembling from fright. Argaeus waved his arm animatedly to beckon her forward. "Oh come now, dear lady. I only bite mangy dogs of Avalon. Your Dominus and his apprentice are no doubt hungry!"

Socrato had regained his composure by that point. "Only if you would join us, General."

"Delighted to, my friend," Argaeus answered amiably, pulling forward a seat across from them before sitting as Taima and the kitchen staff began serving the main courses.

"I was supposed to receive notice of your arrival," Socrato said, though it really was more of a question than a statement.

"I ordered Captain Daneid to *not* report to you when I saw Avalon's standard in the keep," Argaeus explained. "I knew that you would try to hide him from me if you knew of my arrival."

Socrato sighed in defeat. "You know me too well at this point."

Pirogoeth stepped in, her curiosity getting the better of her. "Why would they secretly poke around Aramathea? Surely there are official channels they can work with."

Argaeus regarded her. "You must be the new apprentice, Pirogoeth. I apologize for the lack of proper introduction, but sometimes pleasantries can't always be properly exchanged. Anyways, they don't bother trying to beseech our aid because they know they will be rebuffed. Aramathea does not consider being born into the wrong family a crime."

"Even if the youngest daughter of Avalon's royal family *was* here, we would not aid them in her apprehension," Socrato added, "and they know it. Not that it matters. They could tear this entire continent apart, and still come up empty."

"Why is that?" Pirogoeth asked.

"Because the Princess Viola is most assuredly dead with the rest of her family. She would have been barely old enough to walk during the Revolution," Socrato said. "Where could she have gone? The only reason that the myth has any legs is because supposedly no one was able to find the royal bunker that she and her nursemaid would have been hiding in. There's no other evidence, no signs that *anyone* from the royal family survived that midnight raid."

"Personally, my suspicion is that there is a rebel somewhere who knows exactly where the child is. Her body at any rate," Argaeus said between bites. "I certainly wouldn't want to admit to killing a babe. That silence gives the rumor legs."

"Besides, if there were a refugee princess out there, the first place she would go is Domina Morgana's keep, who has given asylum to *any* nobleman who has come to her gates," Socrato said with finality. "Even now, the Parliament dares not impose their will on her lands, for they know it would be folly. She has seen no one from the royal family."

Argaeus coughed loudly. "Enough gossip on foreign lands. So, if you have a new apprentice, I trust you have heard from... what was her name... your last one?" He looked up at Taima who had abruptly appeared to refill wine glasses with a nod of approval.

Socrato's eyes narrowed suspiciously. "Torma. And don't

84

pretend you didn't know that. She is still a journeyman, traveling through the Free Provinces. She was actually the one who discovered Pirogoeth here."

"Did she?" Argaeus said, giving Pirogoeth a warm smile. "Well, if you pass muster with both her and the Dominus, you must truly be a formidable mage in training, my dear." Then to Socrato, he asked, "Is there any timetable on her return?"

"I suspect you will know better than I, General," Socrato said darkly. "As I suspect she will appear on your doorstep upon her return to the empire long before mine. Oh yes... I know exactly how familiar," he coughed conspicuously after that word, "the two of you got over her time as my apprentice. Though I admit that I am surprised you are still pursuing news of her."

Argaeus grinned smugly. "Then you don't know quite as much as you think, my friend. I asked for her hand upon her departure from the empire."

That got Socrato's eyebrows to raise. "And your father approves of this?"

"Not his decision to make," the general answered with a shrug. "Though, yes, he does approve for the record. Torma is hardly of mongrel stock or of low status, for what little it should matter."

Socrato nodded. "I suppose that's true enough."

Pirogoeth couldn't help but slip in a dangerous tease, "I think my master is so used to treating any apprentice like a worm that he forgets their station in life."

It got the desired effect; Socrato glowered in insult while Argaeus belted out a burst of laughter. "I only laugh because I know that's not true," Argaeus said when Socrato's silent ire turned on him.

"And I only say it because it's not true," Pirogoeth added with a smile.

Two could play at that game, Socrato demonstrated; "Far too late to prevent you getting mop duty in the hall arcana tomorrow." Pirogoeth cringed, even though she got the joke for what it was. She was hardly upset with cleaning work, and had always taken those tasks without any complaint.

Taima appeared again, bearing a tray of sweet rolls, and a refill of their wine. Remembering Taima's warning at the party about sugar and alcohol, Pirogoeth asked, "General, out of curiosity, I was told that there was a tradition within the army about eating lots of sweets and strong wine..."

"Oh yes, *that* stupid thing," Argaeus replied with a roll of his eyes. "Many institutions have strange rituals that make very little sense beyond building camaraderie. That is one of ours."

Socrato grinned mischievously. "Yes... do tell her your experience."

Argaeus laughed. "It is a bit of an encouragement to those who fail, and a great many do. I dare say I vomited three times during that little trial. I don't think it stunted my career growth any. My skill with my spear and tactics weighed far more heavily than my stomach."

And then Argaeus's tone and expression turned grave. "There *is* a reason I came here, Socrato. I think it is best we deal with that business shortly."

Socrato nodded. "Pirogoeth, could you inform Chef Vargat to have dessert prepared outside my lower study? I will get to it once I am able."

Pirogoeth agreed, and went to the kitchen as Socrato and Argaeus took the opposite path to the exit. After the apprentice relayed Socrato's orders, Taima approached her, still in a daze. *"That* was Socrato's secret guest?"

"Who is he?" Pirogoeth asked. "I mean, outside of a general? Because I sense there's more to him."

Taima nodded slowly. "Much more! General Argaeus is the son of Emperor Macedon, and the Emperor's likely successor!"

That would explain Socrato's panic at Argaeus's implied threat of war. And that reminded her of her findings before all the drama at dinner occurred. It was a perfect chance! "Could... you tell Vargat to have dessert ready outside my chambers too? I just realized something I have to do." Taima nodded as Pirogoeth dashed away, hoping to catch the two men before they reached Socrato's study and began their private business.

It wasn't a long trip, just across the inner keep, and she cut through the court hall to save time. Nonetheless, she was just a shade too late, the door to Socrato's study closing with a click five strides too soon.

She decided to wait, as this was an opportunity she simply couldn't miss. The pair inside started talking in hushed tones, though she could almost make out what was being said despite the door and their attempt at quiet. Curiosity got the better of her, and she quietly approached, pressing her ear against the door. If only they would talk just a little bit louder...

"And you're sure of this?" she abruptly heard Socrato say, as if he had complied to her wishes.

Argaeus did as well. "The company mages definitely sensed the ley lines in the islands weakening. One of our scouting vessels... was nearly lost to the Void. It's definitely closer than it's ever been." Pirogoeth's eyes bulged.

"Of all the times I had wished my observations were wrong." Socrato said bitterly. "So... South Gibraltar."

Pirogoeth had heard of the islands in the South Forever Sea. They were sparsely populated at best... there had been a surge of interest in potential precious metals being found deep in the caves from the dormant volcanoes that formed the islands, as well as trolls, thought long extinct after the fall of the southern continents.

But once that interest had faded, it returned to the mostly uninhabitable land it had been before. While she doubted many would miss it, that it was in danger at all was the troubling part. It meant that the Void was indeed approaching. Her heart dropped into her stomach as the harsh truth hit her hard.

The Void was coming. No place was safe.

"How long do we have?" Argaeus asked.

Socrato answered, "The Void moves slowly. It could be another four months before it reaches land, from what you're telling me on these maps. That does *not* mean we can delay, though. The void expands through regions rapidly once the energies from the Code vanish completely."

"I will inform my father of your findings the moment I return to the First Capital. It won't even be a month before we will have the island cleared."

"Do so," Socrato agreed. Then asked, "Were the gold pirates *also* there?"

"I was going to bring that up myself. Because they were. In force, in fact. At least five ships, as they were anchored near the islands, and perhaps more in open water. They weren't particularly cooperative or conversational. The best my men could gather was that they had business on the island, and were not inclined to share what that business was."

Socrato hummed thoughtfully.

"You don't think they have something to do with the coming collapse, do you?" Argaeus wondered. "Because I'm not entirely certain anymore."

"Explain."

"One of the gold pirates vessels saved one of mine from falling into the Void, drawing it away from dire water. Secondly, It would seem that if the gold pirates had that sort of power, to collapse entire regions, that they would have no doubt used it before this."

"And yet every time there is movement of the Void over the last sixty years, the gold pirates are seen in force," Socrato countered. "That is *not* coincidence. At the very least, they have information that we do not, and I do not like it in the slightest."

Argaeus then nervously broached the obvious topic. "Dominus, once the South Gibraltar Islands collapse, there won't be any way to hide the truth. My father is going to want to know when we should inform the public, preferably before it actually happens."

"As soon as he is comfortable with our findings," Socrato said, sounding intensely defeated. "I agree it needs to be before the islands actually fall. The people will need to trust us in the coming years, and that will be impossible if they think we have been lying to them."

"You still think there's a solution?"

Socrato didn't sound nearly as confident as his words suggested. "There has to be. The Coders didn't grant some of us the ability to manipulate the Code of the World if they didn't want us to..."

His voice died off, as if he just realized how loudly he had been talking. "Speaking of which... hold a moment, Argaeus," he said warily, then grabbed the door and yanked it open as Pirogoeth staggered backward in a panic.

Socrato made no attempts to hide his displeasure. "Apprentice, *what* are you doing?"

She didn't know if Socrato had some sort of arcane trick to detect falsehood, or if experience simply gave him insight on how and why people lie. So in a surprising bit of cleverness, Pirogoeth told a carefully edited part of the truth. "I... I was waiting for your meeting with the general to conclude. I... I had something I wanted to ask him."

Her master's eyes narrowed, but before he could say anything, Argaeus stepped in. "Well, I am here, and I think the general thrust of my business is concluded. Details can be worked out shortly, my friend. Come in, apprentice."

She nervously shuffled forward, still worried about being punished for eavesdropping. She jerked when Socrato closed the door behind her, and took his seat behind his desk. Argaeus was leaning against the wall to her right just in front of the cabinet where Socrato was known to keep a small mountain of paperwork.

"What do wish to ask of me, my lady?" Argaeus queried, his voice pleasant and disarming.

Pirogoeth gulped back her nerves, took a breath, and said, "Is it true that you are the emperor's son?"

Argaeus nodded, though he seemed put off by the question. "One of five children. Yes. I'm the second youngest, for what it is worth."

"And the only one of the five to actually accomplish anything of note in his or her life," Socrato sternly added. "You are indeed looking at the next Emperor when Macedon passes away or retires."

"Maybe," Argaeus countered.

Socrato turned to Pirogoeth and asserted, "He will. Don't let his attempt at humility fool you."

"Then you know about the venerated citizens who are fraudulently offering opportunities of higher citizenship?" Pirogoeth asked.

Argaeus nodded. "I am not familiar with *all* the details, as my duties often take me away from the First Capital, but I do know of the problem. It has bothered my father considerably, especially over this last year. As I understand, as long as the fiends offer something tangible, they can claim the education is free, and there's little else that can be done."

Pirogoeth smiled. "But what if I told you they *are* trading something tangible other than room and board?"

Socrato's eyes narrowed. "Like what?"

Pirogoeth turned to him and chirped sweetly, "The Craftsman's Writ and the Writ of Mastery. Both of those are very physical things that prospective citizens need to prove their worth or claim employment."

Socrato's eyes flared open in astonishment. "Of *course!* That's *brilliant!*"

Argaeus wasn't nearly as convinced. "I think that would be stretching the definition of tradable goods a little thin."

Socrato, on the other hand, was already sold. He cheered, "Hah! Considering how long those fiends have been able to defend their illicit doings with careful word play and twisting definitions beyond their original intent, it would be poetic justice for such tricks to be their undoing!"

"But how would that help matters? The problem from what I can tell isn't that the venerated aren't issuing these writs; it's that the prospective citizens are ill prepared and unable to pass muster," The general wondered.

Socrato countered. "But if the writs were declared tradable goods, they would fall under imperial trade oversight! The venerated would have to demonstrate they are properly preparing their prospects, and that would completely undermine their entire scheme!"

"Or just mean another level of bureaucracy they'd have to bribe," Argaeus said sourly.

"There are established ways *that* can be countered," Socrato said, undeterred. "But this... this is the argument I needed!" He jumped to his feet with speed betraying his age and lifted Pirogoeth off the ground in an enthusiastic hug. "Brilliant girl! You're lucky you are so clever, for I'll forgive your attempts at eavesdropping!"

He hastily set her down, and shooed her off with a smile. "Now, best be off. The general and I do have to finish our business. Off you go!"

Pirogoeth was elated, and rightfully so, as she skipped back to her chambers... at least part of the way. Then as the euphoria of her master's approval wore off, the rest of the news she wasn't supposed to hear sank in. And much like the source of that news, it sank her enthusiasm and her mood, leaving behind an empty, lifeless pit in her stomach.

By the time she flopped onto her bed, staring up at the ceiling for what would prove to be a restless night, there was nothing left but that gnawing pit of despair.

The Void was coming, and no place was safe.

Day 66: A Healing Touch

One of the most underrated tendencies of the human mind was the ability to block out uncomfortable or unmanageable truths, and bury them deep into the back of the mind where they can't interfere with more benign worries.

Pirogoeth discovered she had that ability, burying herself in her studies so well that she didn't even stop to think about the news she had overheard in Socrato's study. Socrato also didn't press her on the matter, not even bringing up that eavesdropping the morning following. Or the day after. Nor did he address it this morning, either.

Instead, he had something else to discuss.

"I will be leaving for the First Capital today," Socrato declared over breakfast. "I should be gone no more than two weeks."

"Oh?" Pirogoeth said. Usually, her master declared even the most minute of details long ahead of time. To make such a spontaneous announcement of that scale was unprecedented. "Whatever for?"

"I will be presenting your findings and my proposal to the Emperor," he replied. "No time like the present to repair the damage that has been done."

"I haven't packed..." Pirogoeth noted.

Socrato shook his head. "No reason to. You wouldn't want to come along anyway. Boring, stuffy legal arguments. I wouldn't subject you to that. My lectures are enough. Consider it a break, dear girl. A vacation, if you will."

She thought about a vacation. Two weeks wasn't nearly enough time to...

Socrato seemed to sense where his apprentice's thoughts were going. "Considering all the drama surrounding you and lost Avalonian princesses, it probably wouldn't be a prudent decision to leave Aramathea, or Kartage specifically. I'm sure you miss home terribly, and you'll have your chance to go back... but only when I can ensure your safety during the trip."

Pirogoeth nodded, accepting her master's verdict on the matter. Meanwhile, her mind was racing off in a different, and more guilty, direction. She hadn't really thought about home or her family since her first couple of days at Socrato's tower, and only thought about it now when the prospect of a vacation had arisen. Contrary to Socrato's claim, she *didn't* miss it all that much.

Did that make her a bad person?

It was a question she posed to Taima when they decided to spend that morning window shopping in the bazaar after Socrato had officially departed for Grand Aramathea. It was an otherwise wonderful day, an unusually strong breeze coming off the sea cooling what would have been an otherwise sweltering summer as it approached noon.

Taima's reaction cooled the environment further. "I can't say I've given much thought of home or my parents over the last five years."

Pirogoeth winced. She really *should* have given thought to Taima's strain with her family before bringing up the issue. "Life in Bakkra wasn't exactly easy for me, either. My parents weren't cads, true... but the rest of the town wasn't exactly friendly to me."

"Well, I know those backwa..." Taima stopped herself from saying 'backwater', "places tend to have some perverse opinions about mages. I can understand why you wouldn't miss it."

Pirogoeth shook her head, "No one had any idea about my magical talents, not even me, until I was fourteen. I was bullied by my peers for whatever reason they could think of. I've always been small... never had much of a figure... never was strong or fast... never good at talking to people... and all those things were excuses to treat me like a mangy dog."

Pirogoeth continued her tale as Taima leaned in with concern. "When I was younger, I would get abused on the playgrounds at school. I'd be picked on during games, knocked down, tackled, kicked, punched, bitten. I had my face buried in mud, spit on... one boy a year older had his friends hold me down while he... urinated on me."

Taima's eyes bulged. "That's not just terrible, that's disgusting and unsanitary!"

"I was told it would get better when we were older, and that the abuse of my peers was just part of growing up. That it would make me stronger in the end. But it never really did. And it stayed that way until..."

"Until?"

Pirogoeth shook her head. "During a lunch recess last year... some of the girls in a higher grade attacked me. One of them picked up a rock, and was going to throw it at me when..." the apprentice choked up before finishing, "I... conjured fire, burning her face and hair. Not badly... but it was enough to scare my schoolmates, and the whole town at that.

"I was put in the stockade for a week while the mayor and the town elders decided what to do with me. For once, I was lucky that our leaders took forever to make a decision, because that gave time for the news to spread to nearby city-states, and more specifically to Socrato's previous apprentice, Torma. She was able to convince the mayor and the elders that she could teach me how to control my power and that no one had to be burned at the stake."

Taima put an arm around Pirogoeth's waist warmly. "Well, then I can understand why you wouldn't miss that mud hole. Let them live in their barbaric ways."

Pirogoeth sobbed, "But... I feel like I *should*, and in way I *do*. Why should the *good* parts of my home be cast aside and forgotten because of the bad? What sort of selfish little monster doesn't even give a second though to..."

Taima silenced Pirogoeth with a more forceful hug that muffled any further words into the servant girl's chest. "You are *not* a monster, though I have no doubt you heard that said about you far too many times. And you *are* giving second thoughts to those good things, if you've been paying attention."

She held Pirogoeth out at arm's length, and said, "The Dominus has had you studying morning, noon, and night for over two months! What time would you have had to think of *anything* else?" She then looked across the cobblestone street, and said, "I know what will make you feel better. Semi makes some wonderful almond bread at the bakery across the way. Not as good as *mine,* of course, but if I know you, you'll like it. Come on!"

They were halfway across the street when a loud commotion interrupted them from the north. A single cart, drawn by two horses, had rushed past the guards, who were now giving chase. A familiarity struck Pirogoeth, like she should know who the horses belonged to... until she saw the humongous man leading them. She couldn't place the name, but she definitely remembered the large merchant that she had run into the first day she arrived in Kartage.

She broke free of Taima's hold, and sprinted to the cart as it was forced to stop just short of the town square by the masses of people. She arrived just as the Phalanx did, the soldiers angrily demanding the merchant surrender.

"I need help!" the large man shouted frantically. "My brother is hurt! Please!"

Captain Daneid intercepted Pirogoeth, but she would have none of it.

"My lady, stand back..."

"Get out of my way!" she shrieked. "He's frightened, and I'm going to find out why!"

"He could be dangerous, and Dominus Socrato would flay the skin off my bones if you were harmed."

"He's a *merchant,*" Pirogoeth growled, tapping into the training tome looped into her belt for a surge of visible energy that she ignited into a flame that was harmless, though Daneid didn't need to know that. "Now, if you do not step aside this instant, I am going to try and confirm my master's claim that skin melts at one hundred and sixty degrees."

The Phalanx captain reluctantly complied, deciding that the danger of melted skin *now* was greater than the danger of flayed skin *later.* He stood down, allowing Pirogoeth to pass, and ordered the soldiers trying to force the merchant off of the cart to stand down.

The large merchant saw her, and also recognized her. "You... are the Dominus's apprentice."

"Yes. I'm Pirogoeth. I'm sorry I don't remember your name."

"Pierre," he said, his eyes repeatedly dashing towards the back of the cart, which had been covered by a white sheet. "Is the Dominus available? We need his help immediately. We were attacked by bandits on the road, and Julian was wounded."

Pirogoeth rushed to the rear of the cart, ordering two of the soldiers to pull back the sheet. Indeed, Pierre's brother was lying on a bed of sheets on his side, his skin a deathly pallor, the side facing up sporting a vicious puncture wound, with a shard of steel still sticking through, blood soaked dressing wrapped tightly around it.

It was remarkably good first aid, Pirogoeth noted, and no doubt the only reason Julian was still alive. But he needed more complete attention, and quickly. "Captain! Escort these men to the loading gate for the inner keep. I need to get the proper tome, and I'll meet them there."

Pierre was wary of those orders. "Why can't the Dominus aid us?"

"Dominus Socrato is away," Pirogoeth replied, fighting back insult. "I'm going to be the best you can get." Then she snapped to Daneid, "Now, Captain!" She took off again into a sprint towards the tower, Taima catching up in the process.

"What is going on?" The servant girl asked.

"We're about to find out just how well I've learned healing magic." Pirogoeth intentionally left out the "in five days" part as she took to the steps in a full sprint, and only barely slowed down through the interior halls of the tower.

"I'm going to need to get myself a shoulder bag," she grumbled once she reached her chambers, flinging the door open and crossing the distance to her desk in three strides. "I need to start carrying all my tomes on me, that's all there is to it."

Pirogoeth grabbed the necessary tome off her desk, and turned to Taima, who had been waiting in the doorway. "Damn it... Taima, do you know of a liquid called Norine Lavender? It would be in a red clay pot with a brown stripe on the third row of shelves of the hall arcana, smells like... well... like lavender. Can you get it for me?"

Taima snapped her fingers with a smile. "Can do you better my lady. Chef Vargat has some that he uses when the keep gets food from foreign lands. How much will you need?"

Pirogoeth shrugged. "Enough to test a piece of steel. Not sure how long the piece is though."

"I'll grab a washbasin then. That should be enough."

"Then go. Meet me outside the loading gate as quickly as you can," Pirogoeth ordered as she grabbed a roll of linen gauze from a lower drawer of her desk.

The girls quickly parted ways, and Pirogoeth took as direct of a path as she could to the gate used for large deliveries on the east side of the inner keep. Unlike the front entrance, the loading gate was just a single-door entry into the dry stock chamber, so small that Pirogoeth would have been more than able to push it open herself even if the Phalanx hadn't already been there and opened it for her.

Pirogoeth was rifling through the pages of her tome, trying to commit to memory all the spells she might need. Mending for deep tissue, assuredly, but toxin and disease purging spells as well. She just sincerely hoped she didn't need to use all of them, as she suspected just the mending spell would tax her horribly.

Daneid had done as requested, and Pierre had nimbly backed the rear of the cart to face the gate not even ten feet away, allowing her to hop right in to tend to the wounded man without having to break stride.

She was now able to give the patient a closer look as Pierre hopped into the back of the cart, clearly sick with worry. The metal stuck roughly three inches out of Julian's side, was polished very well, and had etching that she couldn't quite decipher from what little was visible. That didn't set well with her. It could be runes that carried any number of malicious intentions.

"He's fortunate, as I don't think the blade hit anything vital. I'm going to need to pull the metal out in order to heal it, but I don't want to do that until I get the lavender I need," she declared.

"What for?" Pierre asked.

"Because if this blade is poisoned or cursed, just healing the wound won't do any good," Pirogoeth replied grumpily.

"I think it's a bit of stretch that it would be."

"You can *think* all you want. I'd rather *know*."

Pierre bit his tongue, and she sensed he knew more than he was letting on. But she had little time to press as Taima's voice drifted to her ears from the dry stock room. She emerged seconds later in a brisk walk holding a basin that hopefully held the Norine Lavender Pirogoeth needed.

"My lady! I have the lavender!" The servant girl shouted.

"I need pliers!" Pirogoeth barked, holding out her hand behind her. "Now!"

She wasn't sure who pressed the tool into her hand, and really didn't care. She was too busy moving on with her instructions. She shoved the roll of gauze into Pierre's hands, and said, "I'll need you to hold him down while I pull out the shard. Because it's going to hurt, I'm sure. After that, you're going to need to unroll that, and apply as much pressure on the wound as you can until I'm ready."

Pierre nodded silently, unwrapping a long length of gauze around his right hand and forearm, then put both hands on Julian's shoulder and ribs.

Pirogoeth took that as her cue. She clamped onto the exposed steel with the pliers as tight as she could, then pulled. As she expected, Julian jerked and howled in pain as Pirogoeth pulled out a five-inch long narrow piece of very well maintained steel that tapered more to a point than an edge. It wasn't like any weapon she had seen before, but she was reasonably sure it wasn't any bandit blade.

She couldn't give it much more thought, as time was of the essence, and without that imposing piece, the bleeding would increase significantly until healed.

"Taima! Come here quickly!" She ordered. The servant girl complied, bringing the basin over to where Pirogoeth could drop the shard of steel into the liquid it held. "Tell me if it changes color. It should only take a few seconds."

Pirogoeth then took a deep breath, and prepared herself for something she was not going to find pleasant. She focused on her tome, opening the path through her body, readying herself until she knew exactly what she would need to channel.

"No change, my lady." Taima informed her.

Now she knew what to do. "Okay, step aside, Pierre," Pirogoeth ordered. She took position, placing her hands over the wound, and added, "Captain, Pierre, I may need you to catch me."

"My lady?" Daneid asked in concern.

"What I'm about to do might drain me badly. It's possible I will black out once I'm done. Just... try and make sure I don't crack my head open falling out of this cart."

She didn't wait for them to argue further, focusing on herself and channeling the spell she needed. As she expected, it did not flow easily, merely a trickle that wouldn't have been able to mend a paper cut. She demanded obedience, and the flow of energy increased reluctantly... still not enough to heal the wound, but enough that it was showing a tangible effect. Crackles of energy sparked off her hand, and it did seem like the bleeding was starting to slow.

Pirogoeth's vision blurred abruptly, and she shook her head to clear it. She set her jaw, closed her eyes, and again imposed her will on the resisting tome. She wasn't going to fail this man's life just because of some uncooperative *book*.

Her sense of hearing started to fail next, whatever Pierre was trying to say to her reaching her ears a garbled, slurred mess of sound. Pirogoeth was reduced more to working on instinct than what she could see in front of her... which was fortunate because she couldn't see much.

The last thing that she really remembered was being forcibly pulled away from her patient, despite her slurred protests, before her vision completely collapsed upon itself. Within that internal blackness, time held no meaning. So it was hard for her to tell just how long between that moment and when she started to hear voices from the outside again.

I do believe she is who we are looking for.

Do you now? From what I have gathered, what you have is a meager talent unable to maintain consciousness for a simple mending spell.

That she learned to channel less than a week ago. Tell me, Morgana, how well you fared the first time you tried such a skill on a real person.

Your pupil may be a swift learner, Socrato, but how can you be so certain she has the type of talent we've been searching for?

I've seen signs of her power to dominate, Augustus. I plan on making a better observation in a more controlled environment, obviously, but I do believe she will meet my expectations.

Or we can continue our search and not put all our hopes in this waif of a girl. I could have another prospect easily enough...

Your last apprentice tried to kill you and take control of your tower. I think we've seen enough of your ability to judge character.

Augustus, Morgana, enough. We do not have time for more searching. We do not have time to keep scouring the continent. The Void approaches the South Gibraltar Isles as we speak. Time is no longer our friend. The both of you need to focus solely on your experiments and observations. I will test my apprentice, and prepare her to my fullest for the trials ahead.

I hope you are right about this, Socrato.

As am I, my friends. As am I.

Whatever she had overheard had already started to fade from her memory by the time her eyes started to flutter open. She desperately tried to remember it, but the voices slipped through her fingers like water, then dashed entirely when a cold wet towel was pressed against her forehead.

Her eyes flashed open, and Socrato's voice instantly said soothingly, "At ease, dear girl. You are well. No doubt extremely tired, but well."

Socrato? Here? "How... how long have I been out? Has it... has it been *weeks*?"

Her master laughed lightly. "Not even half the day. Captain Daneid sent word to chase me down after you collapsed. Poor man was at a loss with what to do; thought you had killed yourself to save some damn fool merchant who had gotten on the wrong side of some bandits."

Her attempt to heal Julian's puncture wound slowly came into focus again. "Did I... did it work?"

"Yes. Yes it did." Socrato said in assurance. "He is recovering, as are you. The only thing I would suggest in the future is that with a wound that deep, you cast a cleansing for disease even if nothing has tainted the blade. In this case, there was no harm, but it's a simple enough spell to cast that can prevent some nasty ailments down the road."

Pirogoeth nodded slowly. "I should have. I should have thought about that. I also shouldn't have moved him so much once it was determined what was wrong. And... Pierre was right that I wasted time testing the blade... what were the chances that bandits would curse their weapons, or even have the *ability*..."

Socrato shushed her. "You were presented with a problem. You provided a solution."

"But... it was a *bad* one. I could have done better."

"There is no such thing as a bad solution. There may be *better* solutions, but any solution that solves the problem cannot be a bad one. One of our greatest failings as humans is that we waste time and let problems fester waiting for the perfect solution. You did not, you solved the problem to the best of your ability, and there is one life saved for it."

He smiled. "I am very, very proud of how you stood up to the challenge, and took the lead when I could not. If it eases your mind so you can rest, I promise I will berate you for hours in the future about your horrible missteps in this venture. But for now, rest. In the morning, we will have a long talk with our merchant friends."

That reminded her of another detail she had almost forgotten. "I don't think they were..."

He silenced her again. "I don't think they were attacked by bandits either. But that is an interrogation we can get into when both you and the peddler are *able* to field such questions and answers. Now. Sleep. I shall see you in the morning."

Day 67: Interrogations and Old Legends

"My lady?"

Taima's voice started softly, but with each appeal grew louder. "My lady?"

It turned out that the servant girl wasn't getting louder, but that Pirogoeth's alertness was sharpening. The apprentice's eyes opened, and the morning light caused her head to throb painfully, making her wince and groan in protest.

"My lady!" This time Taima was most certainly louder. "Coders' thanks, you are awake!"

Pirogoeth's head rung with each excited word. "Unfortunately." She tried to move her arms to rub the sleep out of her eyes, only to find they were made of lead. Her legs were equally uncooperative.

Taima noticed this, and yelped, "Oh! I was supposed to give you this when you awoke!" Her hand slid under Pirogoeth's head, tilting it up, and a steaming mug appeared under the apprentice's chin. "Drink this. It's a fortified tea to help restore the energy you lost. The Dominus feared you might still be drained when you awoke."

"Thoughtful," Pirogoeth muttered, opening her mouth and weakly grabbing the mug as Taima assisted Pirogoeth in taking a pair of tentative sips. Despite the steam, the beverage was not terribly hot, and Pirogoeth could feel her vitality returning. A tingle began in her fingers and toes, and the warming sensation quickly spread through the rest of her body.

Breakfast followed in the form of a bowl of porridge topped with bananas. "Easier on the stomach, my lady," Taima explained. "The Dominus was really worried that you had overdone it. I am glad that you are recovering."

Pirogoeth didn't realize just how hungry she was until she took that first bite. At which point, anything Taima might have said never reached her ears for the next three minutes. When the bowl was empty, she looked up quizzically at Taima and asked, "What time is it?"

"About an hour to noon, I would guess," the servant girl replied. "I was supposed to inform the Dominus when you felt up to questioning the men you aided yesterday. Would you like me to do so now?"

Pirogoeth nodded in silent confirmation as she went back to

her tea. Even as she struggled with consciousness last night, the inconsistencies between what she had seen and what Pierre had claimed nagged at her. There was something slightly off about it all, and she certainly desired sorting it out. She was actually surprised that Socrato had been waiting for her to start.

Taima came back ten minutes later, the normally almond color to her skin paled. She shuddered and said, "The Dominus says he will meet you in the penitentiary. I don't know why the merchants are *there,* but that is where the Dominus wants you to go. If you do not know the way, I am supposed to lead you."

With a nervous bite of her lower lip, and pleading eyes, Taima added, "Please tell me you know the way."

Pirogoeth didn't, but she wasn't going to ask Taima to take her somewhere that the servant girl was obviously uncomfortable going. "I suspect I can have one of the Phalanx show me the way. Besides, I'm sure Chef Vargat will have no end of things for you to do."

The apprentice shooed Taima off with a hand as she finished the mug of tea, and tested her recovering constitution by sliding out of bed. The world swam for an instant, but righted itself quickly. Confident that she could at least walk, she left her chambers, and headed to the main exit where she could no doubt find a soldier to lead her to the dungeon.

The only things she really knew about Kartage's dungeon was that the entrance was actually *outside* the keep proper, and that the facility itself was *underneath* the sea floor nearly a half mile past the shore. It made for a prison not easily escaped from, and even if you did, your only way out put you in open terrain at arrow range of the keep walls.

Pirogoeth found an escort, who helpfully offered her an oil lantern, and he took her west towards the river delta, and what at first glance would have looked like a sealed storm drain with a latch, until the soldier pulled up the grate and the stonework steps became visible.

She could understand why Taima was unnerved by the place once inside and the grate closed behind her. Even with the lantern, it was a dark, dank, gloomy tunnel that bored ever deeper into the earth, and out towards the sea.

Pirogoeth was expecting to see signs of the ocean above, like dripping or pools of water, but even once the tunnel expanded into the dungeon proper, no such indicators occurred. She supposed *that* should have been the expectation, as Socrato kept everything else in Kartage in near pristine condition.

The large hall she found herself in was a massive domed structure a hundred yards to a side, with teams of Phalanx along the perimeter, and especially flanking four of the five other exits to the dome, which she figured were where the prison cells were located, and the fifth was for prison staff.

She was momentarily stopped by a line of Phalanx just inside the main prison, but it didn't take much to confirm her identity and for the warden to personally take responsibility. "Dominus Socrato is waiting for you in Section Beta. I will take you there."

Section Beta was one of the four distinct "blocks" in the dungeon, each with fifty individual cells for various people found guilty of crimes in Kartage. "Though not even a third of them are being used," the warden noted as they passed Section Alpha. "Crime in Kartage is well below the imperial average. There are many reasons for that, I'm sure... but that sort of theory is a bit beyond me and my pay grade."

Pirogoeth could think of a handful of reasons off the top of her head. She suspected life in Kartage was well above the average standard of living in Aramathea. And while populated, Kartage was hardly crammed tight with people, keeping tensions down. And there was the entire "venerated citizen who could probably incinerate any disturbance with a stray thought" as well.

That last reason was probably the most effective one.

Pirogoeth crossed into Section Beta, and where the spacious dome turned into a cramped hall flanked by black iron gates on both sides. A wrinkled hand slowly reached through the bars of one gate, only to be slapped back by her escort.

"Touch her and lose the hand that does, worm," the warden growled. He explained when he noticed Pirogoeth's sympathetic look back, "That man murdered his wife and child after the wife found him with another woman. He then fled here where we apprehended him and are holding him until his execution. I wouldn't feel sorry for him if I were you."

They met Socrato at the far end of the section, and the warden made his leave. Socrato put his hands on Pirogoeth's shoulders and said, "Good to see you up and about. You look well enough, I suppose. Though probably still a bit drained, I'd wager."

Pirogoeth didn't try to lie, nodding in reply. The walk here had taken a bit out of her.

"You'll feel a bit under the weather for a while, I fear," Socrato said with sympathy. "Even when you have considerable experience under your belt, healing magics will tax you more than any other. But you will recover, I assure you."

"I was never one for walking anyway. That probably has more to do with it than any lingering fatigue from spellcasting," Pirogoeth said with a tired shrug.

"Then you feel you can properly question these men?"

Pirogoeth's eyes flew open. "Me?"

"Yes you. You're the one who was there. You have a much better idea of the situation than I do. You're the one that treated them. Why not you?"

She took a deep breath, and said, "Very well. If you think that is best."

Socrato then pulled her aside, and back five strides towards the exit. "We've been keeping them separate, but I suspect they had plenty of time to put together a collaborating story. Nonetheless, there *are* some details you probably don't know that I need to get you up to speed on."

Pirogoeth nodded in silent confirmation.

"First, the shard of metal you extracted was a piece of an Avalonian rapier. Those weapons are most commonly found in the hands of Cavaliers. Which rather fits the time line established by the wound Julian took."

"They encountered the Cavalier who visited us," Pirogoeth surmised.

Socrato nodded. "In addition, the merchants' cart had a false bottom. Inside it was a cache of Reahtan weapons. I suspected that these two dabbled in the weapon trade for some time, so that isn't particularly much of a surprise to me."

"Cavalier Norman was someone who *supported* the Revolution," Pirogoeth said. "Julian and Pierre attacked *him!*" She quickly put together the rest of her theory, "Julian and Pierre were running weapons for the royalists and they saw an opportunity to take out someone the royal supporters would consider a traitor!"

Socrato nodded, though he didn't seem convinced. "That... was a thought I had as well as I put together the evidence. However... I fear there is more to it. Unless they were completely lying about their origins, they would have very little love for the royal family."

Pirogoeth remembered Pierre's miner stance and the tics that came with that trade. While it could have all been an elaborately planned cover, she doubted it very much. "Are you *sure* you want me to question them?"

"I am. I would recommend working on Julian first. As much as he makes himself out to be the leader of the pair, Pierre is a far more formidable mind than he makes himself out to be."

Pirogoeth nodded again in affirmation, then took a breath to steel herself. "Which cell?"

Socrato pointed towards the farthest cell on the right, and that prompted the Phalanx stationed in front to open the gate for Pirogoeth to enter. Julian was stretched out with his hands behind his head across a threadbare cot that really wasn't much more than a stretch of canvas over a metal frame.

"Comfortable?" Pirogoeth asked darkly.

Julian shrugged, but didn't move otherwise. "I've slept on worse, though I must say I heard much better things about Kartage hospitality."

"Maybe if you hadn't lied to me about how you were injured, we would have been more accommodating."

"Oh? And how did you reach *that* conclusion?"

"You were injured by a rapier. A weapon common among Avalon nobles. Which interestingly enough, there was one visiting just a few days before your arrival."

Julian dismissed the accusation. "Rapiers aren't wholly uncommon, and bandits aren't picky where they get their blades."

"Which is another issue. I come from the Free Provinces. Bandits are a very common threat up there. Bandits don't leave people alive. Much less when wounded. You know who *does* leave wounded? People who have been attacked and trying to flee. Like an Avalon Cavalier you and your brother attacked."

Julian scoffed. "On what grounds would we want to attack a heavily protected Cavalier?"

"Perhaps it has something to do with the Reahtan weapons in a false compartment in your cart? And why you claimed you wouldn't be back in this region until fall? Give you plenty of time to supply the royalist supporters and step back into your normal schedule before someone gets curious."

"The Parliament pays good money to get Reahtan steel," Julian replied. "As do the royalists. Aramathea has never had a problem with me and my brother moving those weapons as long as it doesn't happen on Aramathean soil... and it hasn't."

Pirogoeth's eyebrows raised. "So you play both sides."

Julian again shrugged. "I have little love for the royal family. They took me, Pierre, and my sister from our family, forced Pierre to mine coal and iron, and my sister and me to work in the palace as slaves. The king frequently raped my sister while there. So yeah, I wasn't exactly crying twenty years ago when the gate ripped open and every single one of that family was lined up and stabbed to death."

The merchant finally sat up. "But guess what, girl. The Parliament wouldn't be any better to us. The only thing that has happened is that Avalon has traded one oppressive hand for another. They're still charging heavy taxes to fund their war of expansion into Daynish lands. They still offer cartloads of tribute to that witch Morgana."

He finally showed an emotion, a disgusted scowl. "So yes. Pierre and I like to make sure that the royalists have good equipment... and happily take the 'long road' to Reaht to get weapons for Parliament at the same time. Each day on the road is one less day Pierre is working mines and one less day I'm cleaning chamber pots."

Pirogoeth closed her eyes as her lips curled in a frown. While enlightening, it was an Avalonian matter, and had nothing to do with her or why she was here. She wanted to know about their attack on the Avalonian Cavalier, and wasn't going to tolerate too much more evasion. "So then why did you attack Cavalier Norman?" She cut off Julian's attempt at a denial with a scornful hiss, "And do *not* tell me you didn't! I will *not* be lied to again. You *will* tell me this instant."

Julian jerked stiff like a board in fright, and his eyes dilated. "We didn't want him to report what he had learned. That the Princess Viola wasn't in Kartage."

Pirogoeth's mind quickly skipped back to that first meeting... and how the murmurs of the lost princess had started *after* her meeting with those two merchants. "You!" she shouted accusingly. "The two of you started that gossip!"

"It wasn't hard," Julian admitted. "The gentry in Aramathea wouldn't know what the princess looked like, and the rumor that she had fled into the Free Provinces wasn't new. It was easy to start the talk, and let it spread to Avalon."

"*Why?*" she demanded. "Tell me!"

From the next cell over, she heard Pierre say, "Your apprentice has considerable power of persuasion, Dominus."

Pirogoeth whipped back to the cell exit, where Socrato had been watching her quite intently. "Yes... that she does."

"My brother knows little beyond the superficial," Pierre added. "I on the other hand could tell you more, but I'd rather have some privacy in which to do it. I'd rather not shatter his view of me too much."

"A little late for that, I fear," Pirogoeth snapped, considering said brother was right in front of her.

"Oh, I suspect Julian is aware of little else than your browbeating," Socrato said, still very deep in thought. "In fact, I think I shall take you up on your offer, merchant. Your brother no doubt needs some rest."

Pirogoeth turned back to Julian, and had to admit he did look oddly pale, although she tripped on the implication that she had something to do with it. "What... what happened to him? What did I do?"

"He's dazed: a combination of your interrogation and recovering from his wounds," Socrato said. "Lay him back down, and follow me. The warden's office should be private enough."

Pirogoeth found that harder than she expected. It wasn't so much that he was resisting, but that every muscle in his body was stiff, like a puppet with all its strings pulled taut. "Just lay down, peddler!" she snarled in frustration.

That got him to comply, along with a tired, "Yes... I think I need to lie down. I need rest."

"Yes... that you do..." Pirogoeth said, confounded by the merchant's behavior and by Socrato's feeble explanation for it. She couldn't give it too much thought, however, as she heard the door to Pierre's cell open, reminding her that she was supposed to follow her master.

She had to jog to catch up, the protest in her legs reminding her that she wasn't exactly at peak condition herself. But she was able to fall in step behind Pierre and Socrato as they left the cell block then made a right towards the unguarded doorway in the domed central chamber.

The warden's office didn't look particularly impressive, a desk, some bare pine wood chairs, a cabinet for paperwork, and not much else. But once the heavy iron door was closed behind the three, it was certainly very, very private.

"Alright," Socrato demanded coldly, "Talk. What is this nonsense tying *my* apprentice into some damned Avalonian *myth?*"

Pierre looked far more at ease than he rightfully should. "The more Parliament is spooked about a member of the royal family surviving the revolution, the more resources they spend trying to ferret out any rumors. That means fewer resources being spent crushing the last of the royalist supporters *not* hiding in Tortuga."

"That is Domina Morgana's keep," Socrato explained to Pirogoeth. "She was beholden to the royal family, but did not support them during the revolution. She has deemed her lands neutral territory, and has on more than one occasion tossed a noble to the Parliament's mercies for plotting against the current leadership."

"And the two of you decided I'd be an excellent breeding ground for another rumor to keep your Parliament busy," Pirogoeth growled angrily.

Pierre nodded. "You were, and are, wholly safe in the matter. Even if they thought you *were* Princess Viola, they would not *dare* anger The Imperial Aramathea by invading. It's a war they know they wouldn't win. Avalon's military might is too spread out, too small, and reliant on cavalry. The Aramathean Phalanx would rip them to shreds, and both sides know it."

"Then why attack Cavalier Norman? And how would you think it would succeed?" Socrato questioned.

Pierre sighed forlornly. "That, I will admit, was more a confluence of fortune than anything planned ahead of time. I learned of the Cavalier's approach from behind us, and Julian and I set a trap to break the axle of the lead wagon in his procession. *That* part worked. The delay even lured the Cavalier out of his wagon. *That* part worked better than expected."

Socrato was transcribing Pierre's account with what Pirogoeth had identified as his shorthand writing. "And what didn't?"

"The cavalier was faster than I gave him credit for," Pierre said regretfully. "He avoided my attack, and had his rapier ready quicker than I though he could manage. Julian... took the attack for me. It was fortunate that they thought we were smarter than we were."

"Why is that?"

"The cavalier couldn't conceive that it was a suicidal plan by just two people. He guessed our charge had to be part of a larger ambush. As I fled with Julian, Cavalier Norman was rushing all his people to retreat as fast as they could go."

Pierre then turned to Pirogoeth, and said, "For what it's worth, that will be the end of the matter for you. He'll report you are not Viola, and Parliamentary interest in you will end."

Socrato set down his pen, and said sharply, "*I* will decide when this matter ends, peddler. You attacked a diplomatic envoy on Aramathean lands, and most notably lands under the auspices of Kartage. I would suggest getting comfortable in my dungeon until I can inform Avalon of your crimes."

Pierre shrugged out of his vest as he said, "No, I don't think I will." He then rolled up the sleeve of his shirt to his shoulder, revealing a yellow armband. "In fact, I suspect within two hours if I am not released, you will have someone appear with notice from the Aramathean Senate demanding it. I suspect I'd be able to get such arrangements for my brother as well."

Socrato's eyes flared, and his face turned red with rage. "You... you are one of *them!*"

"The Gold Pirates have interests on more than the seas. We also have agents on the continent itself, beholden to no particular allegiance other than the good of the world." He ignored Socrato's breathless huffing as he added, "My brother is not one of us, though I strongly suspect he will be granted my protections. I ask you not think too harshly of him. He thinks he is protecting me."

Pirogoeth interjected, "When it's really the other way around, isn't it?"

Pierre offered her a wan smile. "When he recovers... ask him about why the lost princess story means so much to him. I think you'd find that an interesting tale."

"Well, you'll have two hours at least," Socrato said, his seething anger still at boiling. "I think I'll just wait until your claimed notice of release arrives. Until then, back to your cell."

Pierre shrugged. "As you wish. You can even have your soldiers drag me back in shackles if it will make you feel better."

"Don't tempt me."

"We aren't your enemy, Dominus. I wish you would accept that."

"Secrets are the enemy of knowledge, and your entire piracy ring is steeped in secrets."

Pierre flashed a glance in Pirogoeth's direction. "Secrets can also be a necessary evil until your audience is ready to receive them. You should know that better than most, right Dominus?"

"Phalanx!" Socrato barked. "Take this man back to his cell this instant!"

The door swung open, and Pierre didn't offer any fight, falling in line with the soldiers as they disappeared from view. Socrato settled back into the warden's chair, brooding and making no attempt to hide it.

"Master?" she asked.

"There is much you need to know, dear girl," Socrato said with a measured voice. "And one day, you will know them."

"Master, you're nothing like those pirates."

"Aren't I?" he asked rhetorically. "Because I *am* keeping many things from you. Many things that I don't think you're ready to know. Not yet."

"And I'm sure we'll get back to it once you return from your trip," Pirogoeth said, "unless you've forgotten you have a case to argue in Grand Aramathea."

"I have not," Socrato said, "but... your training also needs to continue. I cannot abandon that."

"This is important, master. Far more important than just me."

Socrato looked up at her, and for a brief moment, Pirogoeth could see the internal struggle in his eyes. "If only that were true, dear girl. You have become far more important than you realize." He paused to think on his options, then said, "Perhaps... yes... perhaps you *are* ready for that lesson. That's something that could be done on the road..."

Pirogoeth suspected she knew what Socrato was pondering, but asked anyway. "Master? What are you getting at?"

"When we return to your chambers, pack for a two week journey. You will join me on my trip to the First Capital," Socrato declared, rubbing his chin thoughtfully. "I'll have Taima pack up as well. Poor girl hasn't been home for five years... and it'll give you something to do while I argue for hours with a bunch of old men in front of the Emperor.

"At any rate, while I intend to sit here for the next two hours, there's no reason for you to," Socrato finished, shooing her off. "Go and pack for your journey. If you see Taima, pass the word on to her."

Pirogoeth bowed in acceptance of those orders, but wasn't quite ready to leave the dungeon quite yet. She returned to Section Beta, passing by Pierre, and stopping in front of Julian's cell. "How is he?" she asked the guard.

"Well enough," Julian answered coldly. "Stiff as a board, but well."

Not responding to Julian, she instead asked the guard, "May I speak with him again?"

The Phalanx nodded, and unlocked the door for her. Julian clearly didn't like this development. "As I understand, my brother told you everything you needed to know. You have no evidence any wrongdoing occurred on Aramathean land, and you're not going to get any. Why don't you just leave me be?"

"I'm actually here because your brother wanted me to ask you something else," Pirogoeth replied, keeping her voice as nonconfrontational as possible.

"Did he now?" Julian drawled darkly. "How considerate of him."

"He said the lost princess story meant a lot to you, and to ask you why that was."

Julian shouted towards the wall separating him and his brother, "Sometimes that lout doesn't know when to keep his mouth shut!" He then said to Pirogoeth, "I don't know why he didn't tell you himself if he's so eager for you to know. She's his sister as much as mine."

Pirogoeth remembered Julian talk about a sister. "What is it about her?"

"Part of the reason why the whole damn lost princess legend has lingered as long as it did." Julian said. "The story goes like this: there was *one* person who managed to flee the palace in Caravel before the Revolution rose up on them. A woman. My sister. Who I warned to escape before we all turned on the royal family."

"But why would your sister be targeted? You aren't noble, are you?" Pirogoeth asked.

Julian shook his head. "My sister wouldn't be the target. Her daughter on the other hand..." He paused and abruptly changed topics. "Tell me, what do you know about chimeras?"

Pirogoeth blinked, and answered honestly. "Not much... just that they are people with animal traits that are usually the result of some curse or spiritual influence."

"They're a bit more common in Avalon than other places of the world, because it's a popular curse for rich nobility to have cast on less than faithful spouses. Illegitimate children of such wayward nobles are born chimeras. The last king was probably the worst philanderer I have ever personally seen. One of the girls he had his way with was my sister."

Pirogoeth knew that from the first questioning. She could see where this was going.

Julian's tale wrapped up with, "That's what several witnesses saw that cold winter night before the people rose up against the king. A woman who was a maid to the royal family, running away with a child bundled up on her back, a child about Princess Viola's age."

"A bastard child of the king," Pirogoeth said.

"It interests me because no one ever found where my sister went. She didn't go north to Tortuga. She went south, towards Lourdis, where our family once lived. I tried to pick up their trail whenever I was in the area, but never had any luck. You wouldn't think it would be so hard to find a red-haired woman with a fox-girl child..." Julian's voice drifted off with a defeated shrug.

Pirogoeth jolted. A memory of the lunar eclipse gathering, and a fox chimera with red hair. But what were the chances of that? It was a silly coincidence to consider, and certainly not something she was going to offer to Julian, even if she felt it had any merit. It would be her personal revenge for those two peddlers dragging her into this drama in the first place.

"I'd recommend not setting up any ambushes for Avalonian Cavaliers in the future," Pirogoeth said flatly, keeping her expression neutral as she straightened out her skirt. "You'd probably have much more to worry about than being in a dungeon cell."

She made her leave of the dungeon, sincerely hoping that Pierre's promise that her involvement in the entire lost princess legend was done with. It made for a halfway interesting tale, but had nothing to do with her. She had far more important things to worry about.

Day 68: A World Worth Protecting

Pirogoeth only had one question once the trio took the road leading to Grand Aramathea: "Why didn't we do this when you led me here from Bakkra?"

The apprentice was referring to the grand wagon that she, Socrato, and Taima were sitting in, easily the size of the bedroom she had in her home town. She had been a lucky child, as many homes in Bakkra weren't large enough to have such a convenience as a bedroom.

And this cabin was luxuriously supplied. The seats were brown leather with red velvet covers. A broad pine table stained deep brown stood in the center where food and drink could be provided during meals when the procession stopped. It even had its own bookshelf, albeit small.

It had *windows*, with red satin *curtains*, for Coders' sake.

"When traveling outside imperial boundaries, especially into the Free Provinces, it's prudent to be unassuming," Socrato replied. "In these lands, however, we can travel with a bit more comfort. Besides, hearing you grumble about walking amused me."

The playful Socrato had returned. Pirogoeth didn't like it.

Unfortunately, Taima wasn't providing much of a distraction, staring out the window to her left glumly. The servant girl had been lukewarm at the prospect of going home, and had only complied reluctantly at Socrato's insistence.

Pirogoeth put a hand on her shoulder, still as unsure what to say now as she had been the entire morning. The contact, however, was enough to draw Taima's attention and a wan smile. "Perhaps I need to do this, my lady. I'll... be all right. I'm sure. Besides, the Dominus is trying to get your attention."

Socrato was indeed drumming his fingers on the table in front of him as Pirogoeth turned her head back in his direction. "I trust you didn't think this would be a pleasant trip through the Aramathean countryside, dear girl. You've got lessons to attend to, and we might as well get started on them promptly." Pirogoeth wondered what sort of magic they could safely study in such close quarters.

Socrato expected that confusion. "What we will be studying here is nothing like any magic you have ever experienced before. It is a much more internal art, one only recently discovered, at least in terms of human civilization. Today, you are going to learn how to scry."

He turned in his seat to reach for a book on the shelf behind him, which Pirogoeth recognized as similar to her training manual. "This will be a good one to start with. Late edition with little power. We won't be able to delve so deep that you drown." Pirogoeth was fairly certain she heard a very quiet, "I hope..." escape her master's lips as he set the sliver of a tome onto the table.

His voice returned to full breath as he said, "I'm sure Torma talked to you about the Code of the World."

She affirmed, "Yes. It was the rules governing magic as created by the Coders themselves. But you've already demonstrated those rules aren't as rigid as most mages are made to believe."

Socrato replied, "As is the Code of the World more complex. It means so much more than just magic. Everything that makes this world, makes people, makes *us*, is governed by the Code. The ley lines are the vessel, the magic the language, that fuels this world and keeps it alive."

Socrato's voice was laced with pride. "Tomes tap into that underlying current, that is what makes the magic we use possible, and when I was a younger man, I discovered that mages can ride that path in reverse, allowing them to behold the Code of the World that the tomes access. That is the art of scrying, and it has allowed mages no end of insights since."

"There are two major factors as to how well an attempt at scrying will be," he explained further. "The power of the tome is one of them; the stronger the tome, the 'deeper' into the Code it reaches, and the more information there is to be found. Secondly is proximity to a ley line, the closer you are, the clearer that information is."

Socrato then pointed at the tome in front of them. "This is a particularly poorly made tome, so it's attunement with the Code is not great, and we are steadily leaving Kartage, which sits right on a powerful ley line, so I don't think it would be particularly dangerous for you to attempt some beginning scrying."

"What are the dangers?" Pirogoeth asked.

"Mages can delve too 'deep' into the Code. Without proper discipline and mental resolve, you can literally lose your mind and soul in the Code."

"So... death," Pirogoeth summarized.

Socrato's tone turned grave. "If only it were that simple. Your body would still live, it is simply your mind that would be erased. You would become a revenant, a walking dead. It is not a pleasant thing for those close to you to witness." He choked up from a long buried memory. "I... I lost one apprentice that way. Even if there was no soul left in his eyes, it was not easy to kill him."

"And you want *me*, an apprentice under your tutelage for barely two months, to try this," Pirogoeth said warily. Taima's attention was fully ensnared at this point, and she offered a comforting arm to her friend, while her eyes bulged in fright like Socrato had just revealed he was a creature from her nightmares.

Socrato said reassuringly, "As I said, there is very little danger in these circumstances. This would be equivalent to wading out into waist deep water. Yes, you could drown if everything went wrong, but if we held ourselves out of anything that *might* do us harm, there would be no advancement in the world." He tilted his head, his voice understanding. "If I did not think you were capable of this, I would not ask it of you. I made a terrible mistake with the apprentice I lost all those years ago, letting him go farther than I should have let him, and it is not a mistake I have any intention of repeating."

Taima *never* questioned Socrato's decisions, so the fact that she was airing her reservations spoke volumes to her concerns. "My lady... I... I don't like this. I don't want you to get hurt."

"I'll do it," Pirogoeth said with more bravery than she actually felt. She sensed a desperation in her master's actions, that not even he was entirely certain he was doing the right thing. But he wasn't wrong either. She wasn't going to improve as a mage by taking the safest path. And he obviously needed her to improve.

Socrato clapped his hands once. "Excellent! A word of warning, however, scrying can be very difficult and very exhausting. You are literally fighting the flow of energy to its source, and that is not easy. It requires a tremendous amount of will..."

At that point, he drew a ritualistic knife from his pocket, not even three inches long at the narrow blade with a pin point tip and a black handle. "And a little bit of blood helps." Socrato finished, carefully gauging his apprentice's reaction.

Pirogoeth had heard and read about blood rituals, and that they were *not* considered acceptable practice for mages in the current day. Mostly because they involved using someone *else's* blood. And since other people generally liked *keeping* their blood, the most common way to *get* that blood was through extraordinary violence and some macabre sacrificial rites. "Unless you're expecting me to cut Taima or yourself, I don't have a problem with it," Pirogoeth finally answered.

"It's hardly anything grotesque," Socrato assured, handing the knife to Pirogoeth. "Nothing more than a slight prick of the index finger of your dominant hand. Magical energy tends to flow easily through blood, and is a remarkable catalyst for magical energy. That's why ancient mages sought blood for their spell casting. For this, your blood will amplify your inherent powers for your scrying. In addition, the pain I've found helps keep me aware of my own body. You might not even need it in this case, but no sense risking it here, right?"

She readied the knife, and asked, "What else do I need to do?"

"First, you must channel the tome normally. As the energy begins to flow, you use *your* energy to move your spirit upstream. If it works, you will see into the Code of the World itself."

Pirogoeth inhaled, closed her eyes, mentally preparing herself for the task. It also helped her to draw blood from her finger, as she might have been more hesitant to do so had she been looking. She chided herself for being silly about a little bit of blood, even if it *did* sting, then opened her eyes and focused on the tome.

The tome, like the training manual she possessed, fell into complete obedience without even the slightest bit of pressure. And yet, even with the tome's cooperation, trying to move "upstream" was indeed every bit as hard as Socrato claimed. She felt like she had barely moved along the path and sweat was already building on her brow.

Her breathing began to labor, and she still wasn't sure she was making any significant progress. Then the tome jumped, as if an unseen hand picked it up a fraction of inch and then dropped it. At that point, Pirogoeth hit a mental wall of force that broke her concentration and stole her energy.

Pirogoeth was vaguely aware of Taima's distressed appeals to her, forcing her body and lips to move enough to pat the servant girl on the arm reassuringly and slur tiredly, "I'm okay... just a little worn out..."

"Give her some water, Taima," Socrato said. "She might be a little thirsty."

Pirogoeth was thirsty, in fact, likely due to sweating like a roasting pig. Taima pushed a cup into her hand, and helped her bring it to her lips, though that last part was a bit unnecessary. The water helped cool her, but didn't do anything about the exhaustion.

"So... did you see anything?" Socrato asked as Pirogoeth's breath rate returned to something approximating normal.

Pirogoeth shook her head weakly. "I... hit something. It felt like... I ran into a wall at full sprint."

Socrato nodded, his expression amazed. "Impressive that you

clawed that far on your very first scrying attempt. You reached the ley line barrier. It's really not so much a wall or a barrier as it is the point where the mystical energies become so dense that it *feels* like something solid to those foraying into those depths."

"And I'm supposed to be able to punch through that?" she grunted.

"As you build your own mental strength, yes," Socrato confirmed. "It takes time and repeated effort. But I am now certain you are more up to the task. In fact, I would bet that you'll crack that barrier before we even reach the First Capital."

Pirogoeth said, "I'm glad you have confidence in me."

"Dear girl, it took two *months* of experimentation for me to reach the ley line barrier," Socrato replied. "My confidence is born of experience." He glanced out the window, then pulled on a string behind him just to the left of the bookcase. A tinny bell chimed, and a small panel of the wall above the bookcase slid open to reveal the back of the driver's head.

"Yes, Dominus?"

"Could we make a stop here? I think my apprentice could use a dash of air and an opportunity to stretch her legs."

The driver complied, and the trio inside the cabin could feel the wagon slow and eventually jerk to a stop. Socrato stood first, able to extend to his full height thanks to the cabin's high ceiling, then helped Pirogoeth to her feet while Taima steadied her.

"I know you think this is a bad idea," Socrato said, "but it honestly will help to move around a bit. It won't be any long hike, I promise."

Pirogoeth knew for a fact that her master's definition of a "short walk" was more than a bit different than hers, but in this case, the distance was not far, and she had to admit that the sea air revitalized her a little. While they were still on the coast of the Southern Forever Sea, the air here was drier and cooler, and as they approached the edge, Pirogoeth discovered why. They had been steadily ascending, and what had been a delta and flood plain around Kartage had become a tall cliff face.

"This is called the Sapphire Cliff," Socrato said, taking a deep breath himself. "You can't see it from here, but it's due to the cobalt salts that have been exposed from ages of erosion, those salts as they wash out to sea also tint the waters."

Pirogoeth was not entirely fond of heights, but gathered the courage to look down. As Socrato had described, the ocean was a deeper blue than she had ever seen water reflect. Such an odd and simple thing, but so entrancing nonetheless.

"This is the first such colored cliff that we will see on the road to the First Capital," Socrato continued. "These cliffs rise steadily, and the further we go, different salts stain the waters, red, green, yellow, silver, and even gold. And at the top, where quartz and diamond sparkle upon the cliff, you will find Grand Aramathea, the First Capital. We'll try to take the boardwalk into the city so that you can see it for yourself."

Taima chirped with glee. "That would be amazing!"

Socrato turned his eyes down towards Pirogoeth, who was still peering over the edge. He coughed to get her attention, then flashed her a warm smile when she looked up. But his eyes were grave and dark despite the turn of his lips as he said brightly, "It's a beautiful world, and worth preserving in any and every way we can. Do you not agree?"

Pirogoeth instantly knew what he was talking about. He hadn't discussed her eavesdropping during General Argaeus' visit, and Pirogoeth had fooled herself into thinking that he didn't know exactly what she had overheard.

There was no fooling herself anymore. He knew *she* knew about the encroaching Void.

"Anyway, I was already delayed leaving Kartage, so we can't dally," Socrato declared, turning full about abruptly, and gesturing for the two girls to follow him back to the wagon. "Let us press on."

Pirogoeth fell into step, her mind churning. Was that why Socrato was pushing her so hard? Did he think there was something *she* could do to stop the coming Void?

If so, she wasn't about to disappoint him. If he wanted her to scry that tome by the end of their trip to Grand Aramathea, then by the Coders, that was *exactly* what she was going to do.

Day 74: Family Matters in the First Capital

As the days passed she was feeling a lot less sure about that determination.

While she was able to reach the ley line barrier more easily, and wasn't requiring hours to recover between attempts, she still hadn't made any headway actually pushing through the barrier and it didn't seem like she was getting any more successful at it with each attempt. She would hit that point and would immediately be jolted out of her scrying trance.

"It is immensely frustrating, I know," Socrato said with sympathy. "There's no real sense of progress when it comes to this step. One day, you'll be trying to push through with all your might with no feeling you're getting anywhere... the next you're through and you're immersed in the Code of the World."

Pirogoeth nodded with a tightly set jaw. She could either choose to take him for his word and keep trying, or disregard her master and give up. The latter didn't seem like an option that would accomplish anything.

The wagon steadily slowed, and Socrato picked up the training tome they had been working with and returned it to the shelf. "I do believe you have earned a day's rest, dear girl, for I suspect we are nearing our destination."

Once the cart stopped, Socrato stood. "I will be needed to confirm our arrival and plans with the Phalanx guards. I should not be long."

He didn't even bother closing the side door behind him, confirmation of his intentions. The reality seemed a little different, as it was at least five minutes before he returned to the wagon, grinning and quite pleased with himself.

"Sorry, ladies," the venerable sage said happily. "It took longer than I expected to get boardwalk access."

Taima's eyes brightened. "We can take the boardwalk?"

Socrato nodded. "It will take us closer to where I need to go as well, as I need to get to the Imperial Quarter as soon as I can. I am told the Emperor has been awaiting my arrival." He then slid over, and tapped on the left side of his seat. "Pirogoeth, you will want to sit here. It will give you the best view."

She complied, sitting down as the wagon lurched forward and

took a hard turn to the right. The feel of the movement also changed as they moved from the cobblestone of the road to the wood planks of the boardwalk.

"Because Grand Aramathea is situated on a high cliff face, shipping from the sea can be difficult," Socrato explained. "Thus the boardwalk was created. From the docks at sea level, it is a gradual incline with broad turns to allow for large shipments to come through. That's why getting access can be difficult, depending on what boats are loading or unloading. You should be able to start seeing it right about now."

Pirogoeth pushed open the curtains, and took sight of what was before her.

The first thing she noticed was the cliff face, shimmering and glimmering like Socrato had claimed, the quartz and salts making what looked like tiny flashes of rainbow color across the cliff. The second thing she noticed was the several wooden ramps extending above and below, two separate boardwalks, in fact, the one they were on for unloading goods into the city, and the other for loading goods for shipping to other places.

Which led to her final observation, being the city itself. As they were already on the top level of the boardwalk, with only a very slight incline, the whole of the city slid into the profile of her vision. Buildings of alabaster stucco, likely made from the same white material of the cliff, dominated the edge of the city and the face, topped with white ceramic shingles stacked like scales. People crossed in front of those buildings and houses in a bustling street with a fortunate rope mesh to prevent accidents.

Something just out of the line of sight prompted her to recklessly stick her head out the window and nearly get brained by a supporting post of the boardwalk. A second attempt, not quite as far out, allowed her a safe, better view of what she was trying to see.

It was certainly a grand palace, with six towers of white stone taller even than Socrato's in Kartage, and a dome in the center, in front of a pearl and gold arch that Pirogoeth suspected was their destination. Two statues, at least fifty feet tall, of Aramathean Phalanx Soldiers flanked the arch, their shields held in front of them with spears raised, as if they themselves were defenders of the gate into the city.

"Welcome to the First Capital, dear girl," Socrato whispered into her ear. "Grand Aramathea, the largest city left in the world, the hub of the continent's trade, and the pot where cultures from around the world, even places long since gone, meet and mingle."

"Over half a million people call this city home," Taima said as Pirogoeth stuck her head back into the wagon. "Not all of it is this pretty."

Socrato nodded in acknowledgment. "It is true. The Lower Quarter is not nearly as affluent, and the Foreign Quarter is hit and miss when it comes to fabulous display. But the Higher Quarter and Imperial Quarter tend to be what visitors remember most."

"But this part *is* breathtaking, I will give it that," Taima said. "I never had the opportunity to come out onto the boardwalk for the fifteen years I lived here. It's unfortunate that it's for official business only."

They came up to the arch, and Socrato stood again. "Official identification is never done," He said. "I shall return."

Pirogoeth moved back to her original seat in the wagon, and gave Taima a gentle shake. "Are you going to be all right?"

The servant girl shrugged. "My last memories of this city were filled with angry yelling and being told I wasn't welcome any longer. I haven't been back for five years. How *could* I be 'all right'?"

"Are you sure you want to do this?"

"I'm going to have to at some point. As much as I love Kartage, there won't be many opportunities for me as a chef there, and I'd *never* dare compete with Chef Vargat. My best career choices as a higher citizen would be here or in the nearby city-states. I can't ignore my family forever. And this way... I have support, right?"

Pirogoeth nodded emphatically. "Right!"

Socrato reappeared, closing the door and settling into his seat. "And there we go. Next stop, the Heart of the Empire: the imperial palace of Grand Aramathea, and the Senatorial Amphitheater."

The palace and the amphitheater were part of the same building, the dome they had seen earlier actually only half of one, with an open air end on the north side. The towers were part of the palace, and the palace itself was underground.

"It was designed that way centuries ago," Socrato finished his lecture as the wagon finally pulled to a stop at the roundabout in front of the main doors of the palace. "After the Aramathean army stalled the Daynes in their great conquest nine hundred years ago. It is meant as the last bastion for the empire. No matter what, the Emperor will not abandon Grand Aramathea."

Straightening the shoulder of his toga, Socrato prepared to depart yet again. "This is my stop, ladies. Feel free to enjoy the sights and sounds of the largest city in the world. I only ask that you return by sundown. I do not envision needing more than this evening to present my case, and would like to depart back for Kartage by first light tomorrow."

Pirogoeth was surprised by that, due to her crash course in Aramathean politics. "Doesn't it usually take weeks for the wheels of bureaucracy to turn?"

"As this is solely an executive matter, the only thing I need to do is convince Emperor Macedon to declare an edict. That is a much quicker path to action, and one that I do not anticipate needing too much time to sway him on." He hopped out of the wagon, gave final instructions for the driver, and dutifully made for the palace entrance.

Said driver, dressed in his finery of a foreign born layman, appeared at the doorway, and asked, "Where specifically would you like to go, my ladies?"

Pirogoeth nodded in deference to Taima, and the servant girl took a nervous breath before declaring, "Lower District, housing number 4550 on Vestige Street."

The driver bit his lower lip. "Going to need to get directions for that, I think."

Taima stood, hopped out of the wagon, and moved to the front, gesturing for the driver to follow. "And I'll give them to you. Let us proceed."

Pirogoeth shrugged as the driver looked at her. No doubt that was a very unusual request for him to handle. He took it in stride however. "Very well, my lady. You lead, I shall follow."

"No one's ever called me that," Taima said with a giggle. "I'm not sure I approve."

"Now you know how I feel!" Pirogoeth shouted out, jumping out of the wagon, and briskly catching up to the others. "No sense me being the only one back there," she said when she dropped down next to Taima.

It was a much different perspective from the front of the cart, with a much wider field of vision. Pirogoeth could see just how large of a city Grand Aramathea was. She had thought Kartage was big, but this made Socrato's keep look like Bakkra. Houses extended to the horizon, the streets filled from edge to edge with people and carts and wagons, though helpfully delineated so that the traffic flowed smooth...er.

"Midday is always a busy time, *anywhere* in the First Capital." Taima said. "Though there never really is a point where the activity is what you or I would consider slow, either. And it's another two miles to get where we want to go. Still sure you want to stay up here?"

"This bench isn't uncomfortable," Pirogoeth replied.

"No, it's not," the driver added. "Dominus Socrato knows how to treat his staff, I'll give him that. Most wagons like this gave me nothing but bare wood to sit on. *Maybe* a leather cover, if the master was being *nice*."

There was a major roadway that separated the Imperial Quarter from the Lower Quarter, and there was a stark difference upon crossing that street. The white stucco vanished, replaced by neutral wood. Thatch and tar shingles replaced the stonework on the roofs. Some houses were painted different colors, but they were a distinct minority.

It's not that the homes and businesses were shanties or wrecks, they were still of higher quality than most of the houses in Bakkra, but there was a definite drop in quality upon the changing the quarter, and that somehow managed to tweak Pirogoeth's sensibilities more than the level of squalor that was common back at her home.

It was one thing that everyone lived in a certain degree of discomfort. But she couldn't imagine being able to live in a city where she could see how much better others lived simply by looking across a single street.

"Turn right here," Taima ordered, pointing to the intersection she was looking for.

Now fully into the Lower Quarter, Pirogoeth could see some signs of very poorly constructed or neglected buildings, but they were mercifully few in number, and two of them were even being restored as the wagon passed by.

She also became aware that they were drawing more and more attention, though understandably. Surely a good many people were wondering why such a fine wagon would be touring through their part of town. She began to worry that Taima's parents would think she was showing off.

"Stop here at the guard post. Tell them who you are and that you will leave by sundown," Taima instructed. "The lady and I will go the rest of the way on foot."

Concern diffused.

"Please tell me it's not a long walk," Pirogoeth pleaded.

Taima laughed, "Not even two blocks. You'll be okay."

Pirogoeth was not nearly as amused. "Good."

It wasn't very long at all, especially as on foot they were able to use narrower walking paths rather than the wider roads for carts and wagons. Their trip ended at a simple house painted white with tar shingles. Certainly not a hovel, and well above the mean for the area they lived in. Taima hesitated at the edge of the street across from her old home, until Pirogoeth bumped her with her shoulder. "We need to be back by sundown, remember?"

Taima nodded, steeling herself, and took heavy deliberate steps as if doing so would keep her legs from scampering the other way. Pirogoeth fell in step a stride behind her, close enough for Taima to know she was there, but no so close to be crowding.

By the time Taima reached the door, there was no more trepidation, and she rapped sharply on the door three times. There was silence at first, and Taima cringed. "There might not be anyone home at this hour."

Instead the door whipped open, to reveal a caramel skinned woman with chestnut hair flecked with gray. There was a long, pregnant moment as Taima and the woman both stared at each other, then finally Taima said weakly, "Hello... mother."

That broke the tension, and Taima's mother threw herself onto her daughter with a smothering embrace. "My baby... my baby girl! It's been... it's been ages! Oh, Coders' blessings! My baby... my baby..."

Taima was stunned catatonic by the response. She was no doubt expecting something much colder. The servant girl nervously returned the hug until the dam of emotions burst, and both women were weeping openly. "Oh, mother, I am so sorry it's been so long... I didn't know how I would be received..."

She was shoved to arms length, the older woman's jaw set, even as her cheeks glistened with tears. "No matter what you do, no matter where you go, you will *always* be my daughter, and you will *always* be welcome. How could you *ever* doubt that?"

The embrace resumed as Taima choked out, "I don't know."

Pirogoeth smiled happily and took a step back, trying as hard as she could to not impose. Ironically that movement only drew attention to herself. Taima's mother straightened to ask, "And who is this exquisite young lady?"

Taima's response was one that showed she had forgotten about her friend's existence. "Oh! This is Pirogoeth, Dominus Socrato's mage apprentice. I am accompanying her and the Dominus on business with the Emperor."

The older woman's eyes widened in amazement as Pirogoeth said, "Your daughter has been the best friend I've ever had, madam," and offered a respectful bow. "It's a pleasure to meet you."

Taima's mother skipped in front of Pirogoeth, then bowed so low that Pirogoeth was afraid the woman would fall over. "Please, my lady, I am Demetra. I am honored by your presence."

She then snapped back and hissed to Taima fearfully, "I have *nothing* clean or ready to entertain such a guest! Your brother has been ill and I've been away from work to tend to him!"

Pirogoeth interjected, "Madam Demetra, I come from the armpit of the Free Provinces. Rest assured I am not some prim and proper noblewoman. I have slept on straw and bathed in muddy water. If anything, your accommodations are likely an improvement from most of my life."

Demetra still looked a bit fearful. "But..."

"You said your son was ill?" Pirogoeth added. "Do you know what is wrong? I might be able to help."

Demetra smiled. "Nothing but the sniffles that pass among children. I wouldn't trouble any mage for something so trifling, but it is sweet of you to offer." She took a defeated breath. "Well... if you are certain that I can provide suitable hospitality, come inside. Best not to keep making a scene. Your father should be home within two hours."

The interior of Taima's childhood home was comfortably furnished. Nothing elaborate, but enough for everyone to have a place on sturdy oak chairs, and a bright red rug across the pinewood floor. The house even had a separate kitchen and dining room, a second floor, and an interior bathroom *with* a tub for bathing.

It made her wonder what Aramathean higher citizens expected from people they visited if *this* wouldn't be enough.

A bench padded with pillows at the north of the living area seemed a good enough seat for Pirogoeth. Taima settled down next to her while Demetra took one of the many chairs. "Since you are associating with mages, I take it your schooling has gone well?" Demetra asked.

Taima bit her lip and nodded. "I think so, yes."

Pirogoeth refused to let Taima shy away from any potential praise. "She completed her tasks for lower citizenship last month, and did so with honors, as I am told. She amazes everyone with her work at every meal."

"And you're being cared for?"

Taima sighed. "Yes, mother. Dominus Socrato is *not* one of the fiends that have been terrorizing laymen for money and land. I have been cared for, I have been trained well, and I *will* achieve what I set out to do."

"I understand your worry, Madam Demetra," Pirogoeth added, "but if the Dominus has treated *me*, a foreigner with nothing but respect and care, I think you can expect the same for people of your empire."

Tears again began to form on the older woman's eyes. A breath later, a sound emerged from the stairs from the floor above, and a young boy's voice called out. "Mother? Who are you talking to?" The boy that slowly shuffled down the steps had all the features of a proper Aramathean, lean and trim, but it seemed natural for his frame.

Taima choked up again at the sight, jumped to her feet and dashed to her brother as he made it to the ground floor. "Suqa!" she squealed happily. "You were barely up to my waist when I left! Now look at you!"

The boy looked up at the woman who had hugged him, and the recognition seemed to send a jolt of energy into him. "Taima? Taima! You're back! You're back! Are you staying? Are you staying for good?"

Taima shook her head, visibly saddened as her brother's face fell. "Just for the day, I am afraid. Dominus Socrato is a busy man, and he can't dally here very long."

"Who's she?" the boy asked, pointing at Pirogoeth.

"The *lady*," Taima put emphasis on the title, "is an apprentice mage under the study of the Venerated Socrato. I would suggest showing her the respect you never showed me."

Suqa did exactly that, bowing as Pirogoeth stood. "Greetings, my lady. I've never met a mage, so I don't know how to properly treat one."

"Oh, like any other per..." she said warmly as Suqa straightened. Damn it, he was taller than she was by half a head. "How... how old *are* you, if I may ask?"

"Ten. My father says I'm tall for my age."

Pirogoeth turned her head so that Suqa didn't see her bitter glower. Ten-year-olds were taller than she was.

Demetra had taken the opportunity afford by Suqa's entrance to gather some appetizers, water and crackers with cheese. "I apologize for the meager fare, but I am not a cook by trade, and I still have to get dinner started."

Pirogoeth grinned deviously, a fact that was not missed on Taima. "But we know someone who *is*..."

Taima shook her head violently, aghast at the very implication. "I wouldn't *dare* impose on my mother's kitchen."

Demetra groaned. "Daughter, *please* impose. I *beg* you." A light of inspiration crossed the woman's face, and she smiled deviously. "In fact... who wants to make a big surprise for your father?"

Suqa and Taima didn't need to be sold. Whatever their mother was planning, they were all for it. "Suqa, you get back to bed. I know you're almost well, but I still want you resting one more day." When the boy tried to protest, Demetra added with a warning finger, "besides, if you're down here and not resting when your father gets home, he'll know something is afoot. So up to bed you go. Now, daughter, you and the lady come with me. Show me what you have been learning in Kartage."

Pirogoeth was not much of a cook. She wasn't *terrible*, having helped her mother for several years back home, but to see Taima at work was remarkable. The servant girl had no fewer than six things going on at the same time, yet still knew exactly what her two helpers were doing and how far along they were. Taima was a flurry of activity, always on the move, juggling all the tasks with grace.

Pork that had been smoking since the morning turned to stuffed cabbage rolls and roasted chops with a light gravy made from its juices. A vegetable medley with seasoned oil... perfectly browned bread rolls... and the eggs Pirogoeth beat became part of a dessert called 'tiramisu', though Taima was wary of it.

"Traditionally, this dessert only uses the yolks. The egg whites might affect the flavor, but there wasn't much for it," Taima explained. There hadn't been enough eggs to use the yolks alone, a fact Taima only realized once she had already finished the biscuit dough.

"*Somehow*," Pirogoeth retorted sarcastically, "I think we'll all be able to choke it down."

Demetra looked out the kitchen window, and giggled childishly. "Your father is coming. Both of you, in the corner!"

Pirogoeth and Taima tucked themselves into the southeast corner of the kitchen, where they'd be out of sight unless Taima's father, Dophici, were to actually walk into the kitchen. The front door opened, and they heard a hearty call, "Dearest! Oh my... something smells remarkable!"

Demetra stepped out of the kitchen, putting on her best face for the show. "I'm just about done with dinner. I think it's gone very well."

"How is Suqa?"

"Resting. He's well over the worst of it. I think he'll be ready for his schooling tomorrow. Did you stop by Metricles?"

"I did. He says to take as long as you need nursing our son back to health. Business tends to be slow this time of year, apparently."

"It is. Everyone has bought their summer shoes, and won't be needing much else until they start to buy their winter clothes. All the work is mending, and I'm not much help for that."

Dophici laughed at that. "More use than you think, love. He'll be glad to see you back, don't doubt that. Anyway, I'll rouse the boy and let you finish dinner."

He took the steps to the upper floor as Demetra returned, giggling with their successful conspiracy. "Splendid so far. Now... be ready for when I call you, daughter."

Taima nodded, grinning from ear to ear.

Demetra starting bringing out the trays Taima had prepared and had gotten to the main courses as Dophici and Suqa came back down the stairs. Taima's father exclaimed, "That looks spectacular, love!"

Suqa stifled a giggle as Demetra said, "I'm glad you like it."

At that point, Dophici noticed the settings. "Why do you have so many chairs out?"

"Oh! I had been cleaning during the midday, and put them there to get them out of the way. I must have forgotten to put them back in the living room."

Taima's father chuckled. "Even your forgetfulness is charming."

"Ewwwwww!" Suqa moaned, presumably because his parents shared a moment of affection.

The scratch of chairs moving across the pine floor told the girls in the kitchen that the family had taken their seats to eat. Almost immediately, Dophici exclaimed, "Love, this is amazing! Did the hands of the Coders come to you this afternoon?"

"You could say that," Demetra said, "Perhaps you should see for yourself."

That was Taima's queue, and she crossed the kitchen, into the door, and took one step into the dining room. "Hello... father."

The next sound Pirogoeth heard was Taima's grunt as her father nearly swallowed her in his embrace. "My girl! My sweet girl!" His voice broke from the sobbing he was trying to hold back. "You've returned! Look at you! You've grown so much. Like a spitting vision of your mother when she was your age!"

Taima tried to talk, but likely was still out of breath from what had been a suffocating bear hug.

Her father took that silence as to continue. "You look well. You look healthy. That is the best news I have seen in years," Dophici said, his voice dropping from his earlier astonishment. "Oh, my dear girl... not a day went by that I hated myself for our last words. Your grandfather would have been so ashamed of me that day. He had told me that he only wanted two things from me: that I be happy, and choose my path through life without regret. I should have given you that same advice. Please, forgive this failure of a man who does not deserve to be your father."

"Only if you forgive me for being stubborn just as long."

"Dears, the food is getting cold," Demetra said with playful chiding, "I don't think you want Taima's hard work to go to waste. I think Taima's friend should come out now too."

Pirogoeth's introduction to Dophici went almost exactly like her introduction to Demetra: a moment of insecurity, worry, and eventually acceptance as Pirogoeth assured him she wasn't anybody that would be insulted by such middle-class surroundings.

And while Taima would deny it to her deathbed, the tiramisu was divine.

The evening went by far too quickly for Taima's taste, as was apparent as the sun crept into the window. "We promised the Dominus that we would be back at the Emperor's Palace by sundown," she said regretfully. "I wish I could stay longer."

"We are all at the whims of those higher than us," Dophici said sadly. "And you still have much to learn and farther to go. These last ten years will fly, I promise you, and then you will return to this city, with silver at your waist, having attained heights your mother and I could only dream of."

"And even if by some disaster you don't, our home and our hearts will always be open," Demetra added.

Taima hugged them both fondly, the tears flowing again. She spared an embrace for Suqa as well. "In five years, maybe you'll join me in Kartage, and I'll show you around!"

Her brother nodded animatedly. "I'm gonna be a dressmaker!"

Pirogoeth had to fight back a laugh, not because of Suqa's declared intent, but because she found herself picturing him as Lanka's new apprentice on Socrato's suggestion. Would that be a blessing or a punishment... and for who... she wondered.

Taima forced further partings to be short. The last thing she wanted to do was disappoint the Dominus by being late. They left the house, their steps becoming longer as the distance increased.

Taima wiped tears from her eyes, and said, "I heard that little laugh of yours, and I know what you were thinking. Why would you want to see my brother suffer as Lanka's layman?" They both laughed now knowing that their minds went to the same horrible place. Taima regained her composure first, and smiled warmly at her friend. "Thank you, my... Pirogoeth. For being there."

Pirogoeth slipped an arm around Taima's waist. "Whenever you need my help, I'll do anything I can, Taima." They stayed like that until they returned to the guard post.

The driver looked up from the book he had been reading. "Ready to return?"

"Have you been waiting here this whole time?" Taima said, distressed by the idea that she would have compelled the driver to sit in that spot for hours while she entertained herself.

The driver shook his head. "Oh no, I figured you'd be no few hours, so I amused myself with some of the shops across the street there. Found a splendid little trinket for my little girl back home. Never out of sight of the cart, of course, so I could see if you were returning. Such is the life of a wagon master."

"Well, we will hold you no longer. We must return to the palace, and try to make as good of time as possible."

At least the traffic in the late evening was slower, though there were still an astonishing number of people out and about. "Grand Aramathea is a city that never sleeps," said Taima. "The evening and night hours often are the only opportunity shop keepers get to tidy up their stores and stock up for the next day."

"Ships sail into port at all hours too," their driver added. "The oceans are fickle, and all it takes is an uncooperative wind to slow your arrival until well past sunset."

Fortunately, there were no winds to slow Socrato's wagon, and they arrived back at the palace with time to spare. So much time that they actually had to wait for Socrato's meeting with the Emperor to conclude before they were allowed into the palace.

Dusk was upon them by the time Socrato emerged. The fruits of labor were quite clearly successful by the triumphant look on his face. "You young folks may not understand how exhausting talking for hours can be," he said, "but the rewards are worth it. The Emperor has agreed to the wisdom of our apprentice, and will submit the edict tomorrow at midday."

Pirogoeth grinned broadly, and Taima threw her arms around her in excitement.

"We even worked out a good many details as to how the new Governor of Education Trade will operate. Several promising names, policies, time well spent. We are both pleased. Anyway, we have lodging waiting for us in the Diplomatic Suite. Let us be on our way, so we can get some rest and make the return trip by first light."

The Imperial Palace was much what she expected... had much of it not been underground. The style and design was similar to what she knew from Kartage, save for a lack of windows. Pirogoeth shivered from a surprising chill, which was in contrast to the normally hot summer air that she had become accustomed to.

"An interesting side effect of the construction of the palace," Socrato said, noticing his apprentice's reaction. "Being underground keeps the interior remarkably cool, even during the hot months of the year. It's rather refreshing."

The place they would be staying was not far from the entrance, just a single left turn off of the main hall, and once inside, Pirogoeth learned why Taima's parents had been so worried about insulting her with their accommodations.

She had thought her quarters in Kartage were luxurious. She had been mistaken. The suite was a mansion in its own right. Blue marbled floors accented brilliant white stucco walls and a map of the continent painted onto the ceiling of the central room. It even had a damned *fountain*, made from granite and sculpted in the form of an impressively built male holding a plate where the water bubbled and flowed down to the basin.

A *naked* male. And impressively built in... many ways. Pirogoeth turned bright red, and Socrato chided her. "We really need to dash those western sensibilities you got living in the Free Provinces," he said disparagingly, correctly guessing the source of her discomfort. "That is a genuine Viviendo sculpture, and they are works of art. Try to be respectful."

"Oh, I think she respects it just fine," Taima said with a teasing bump of her elbow to the apprentice's side.

Pirogoeth forced down the color of her cheeks as Socrato rolled his eyes. "Hormonal young women. I'd chide you more fiercely if I didn't think I was just as bad when I was your age."

Pirogoeth circled around the fountain, trying very hard to ignore that the man in the sculpture had some very well constructed buttocks as well. A semicircular table made of the same stone flanked the fountain, and four large bowls rested on it, overflowing with grapes, oranges, pomegranates, apples, bananas, lemons, limes, and figs. That table sat in front of a comfortably padded bench covered in bleached leather, with backing long enough for all three of them to be able to lay their full lengths on with room to spare.

Socrato in fact did just that, lounging with only his feet dangling over the end, groaning in relief as he grabbed a handful of grapes and began snacking. "Finally off my feet." He said between bites. "The two of you feel free to pick a room, and I will take what's left."

There were in fact four rooms, two on the north side, and two on the east side. All were lavishly furnished with canopy beds with silk covers that were every bit as comfortable as they looked. Each room even had a desk, carved from white marble, which at this point Pirogoeth had decided was just unnecessary extravagance.

Taima pulled open one of the drawers underneath the desk table, and chirped in triumph. "Hah! Perfect!"

Pirogoeth blinked. "What?"

Taima pointed at the chair to the desk, mercifully made of stained mahogany wood rather than marble, and ordered, "You. Sit."

The apprentice complied, and Taima pulled out a sheet of wood pulp paper, an ink quill, and a long white pen. "You helped me approach my parents, and now it's my turn to help you. *You* are going to write your parents a letter, and in the morning, I'm sure Socrato will be happy to take a detour to have it posted."

A letter to Bakkra would *not* be cheap. She began to protest. "But..."

Taima silenced her. "Hush. You write. Now."

"Very well." Pirogoeth surrendered, dipping the pen point into the ink well. She looked up at Taima. "And thank you." She brought the pen to the paper, and found she didn't need to think much about what she had to say:

Dearest Mother and Father,

I apologize profusely for taking so long to write this. My life has become very busy since Dominus Socrato has taken me under his wing. If I have worried you, I am so very sorry. But I am safe and I am well.

Life in Kartage has been the most amazing thing to happen to me. Every day, my knowledge grows, and my confidence in myself grows with it. I've already learned so much in just two months, and I'm only beginning to scrape the surface of what there is to know.

This world around us is amazing, and I'm glad I've had the chance to see it. I've met so many amazing people, and done so many amazing things. Coders, I am sitting at a desk in the palace of the Emperor of Aramathea as I write this. I helped change a law today, Mom and Dad. I've made lives better, and it's a wonderful feeling.

I've even made friends here. Don't laugh, dad, because I know you are. Taima's become my best friend here. She wants to be a chef, and has been working in Kartage for the last five years to make that dream come true. She's helped me in so many ways, and I wish I knew how to thank her properly. I wish you both could meet her.

I thank you so much for making

this possible, for letting me spread my wings and leave the nest you worked so hard to give me. You may not have thought it was as much as I deserved, but it was everything I could have asked for. I miss you both, and I hope you are well. I hope to come home again, but I can't promise when that will be. Until then, stay safe and I'll see you again.

        With love from your daughter,

                Pirogoeth

Day 78: A Glimpse Past the Wall

The road back to Kartage meant that Pirogoeth's training resumed, and it was as frustrating as the first leg of the journey. She slammed her left fist down in frustration while sucking on the index finger of her right, staring balefully at the irritatingly helpful tome that graciously let her slam her head on the ley line barrier time after time after time.

"Think of it this way," Socrato offered. "You're not very tired."

This was true. She was more angry than tired. But what good was getting stronger if it wasn't accomplishing anything? She kept repeated the mantra that this was normal, like Socrato insisted through the entire process, but it was getting increasingly harder to keep that close to heart with each failure.

"Pirogoeth." Socrato barked sharply, grabbing his apprentices attention. "Keep your focus and still your anger. A level state of mind is the most important factor if you are going to scry successfully."

That was easier said than done. Her jaw was so tense that her teeth might have been fused together at that point. She wasn't used to going nowhere, despite her master's claims she was making progress. She could feel Taima's hand on her shoulder, but the words her friend was saying didn't register in her mind.

Pirogoeth reasserted control, forcing back her boiling anger. Even if Socrato was wrong, succumbing to rage wasn't going to accomplish anything. If she was going to succeed, and she *was* going to succeed, she needed to settle her emotions. She took long, steady breaths, holding them a second before exhaling, as if doing so would gather the anger and push it out of her body. The angry red in her face dulled to pink, then vanished altogether. Her hands eased and her jaw loosened. She opened her eyes slowly, her eyebrows unfurling.

The meditative relaxation technique didn't work completely, but it was good enough for her to be able to tersely say, "Again."

Socrato's eyebrows raised. "So soon?"

Pirogoeth shrugged. "Might as well. I don't feel drained, and I might as well give it another go before my finger heals up entirely."

He extended one hand in acceptance towards the tome. "Then by all means."

"Are you sure about this, Dominus?" Taima asked nervously.

Socrato nodded. "She doesn't look strained. No harm in letting her try again. If you wish, you can keep an eye on her for any signs of distress like I am."

Pirogoeth pricked open the scab on her finger again, closing her eyes and focusing once more on the helpfully troublesome tome. She brushed off the surge of energy, steadily and slowly working backwards until she was more within the book than her own body. The only sensations were the sounds of her own breathing, and the slight pain in her right index finger. The rest of her world became black, instinct and the feel of the magic energies pushing against her all the only evidence of where she needed to go... up to this point, everything had been just as it had been every other time.

She hit the wall, exactly where she expected to. Here, the pressure was like a hurricane gale, and it was far harder to keep her focus and position. The sound of her breathing was gone, the prick of her finger fading. She probed the wall, trying to find something, a portion of the flowing power that was a little weaker or slower, a "crack" in the wall that she could exploit.

And this time, she found it.

The difference wasn't much, a momentary lag in the power that rushed in front of her. But it was all she needed to finally, after days of frustration, to push through... and see the Code of the World.

It was magnificent yet also simple, a network of power that ripped right through her and spread throughout the world. She couldn't see very far, the edge of her senses barely reaching the compressed power underneath Kartage, but that alone was nigh overwhelming. She could feel a butterfly landing alight onto a flower to the north. Hear the clop of horseshoes on the road leading to the keep. Taste the grass being chewed by sheep west of Grand Aramathea. It was a tidal wave of sensation from every living thing within her range.

She forced those those things out, simply for the sake of her sanity, remembering her master's words. She could lose herself within the Code.

It was surprisingly easy to reassert her own ego, considering the power rushing through her... perhaps Socrato was right that getting in was the hard part. From her restored perspective, she could sense exactly where the amalgamation of energies were flowing. To the very edges of her scrying vision, everything was strong. Had she not known that far to the south, on the southernmost islands of the Gibraltar Archipelago, the ley lines were steadily weakening, she would never imagined anything was wrong.

This portion of the scrying was not nearly as interesting as the one before. There were no vibrant colors, no rich smells, or anything else that tickled her senses. It was easy to leave this behind, and return to her body where Taima and Socrato were almost hovering over her with concern faces that turned to relief and excitement when the realized she was alert.

"What?" she said crossly.

Socrato laughed, and clapped twice. "Spectacular! After two hours, I figured you had done it!"

Pirogoeth blinked, and turned to the window to her right, where the light definitely was more consistent with late evening than the late morning when she had begun her attempt. "How... how long was I scrying?" she asked in shock.

"Goodness, about seven hours!" Taima whimpered, her eyes welling with tears. "You had me worried sick!"

Pirogoeth hugged Taima reassuringly as Socrato sighed. "I tried to explain to her you were fine, and that time flows differently for those who are scrying, but she would hear nothing of it. Coders, I one time wound up scrying and didn't return to myself for three days. Mila had initially called the undertaker, thinking I had died in my sleep until the poor man noticed I was still breathing."

Pirogoeth grumbled, "Of course you wouldn't *mention that before,*" closing her eyes shut as she imagined tying the old sage to the top of the wagon for the rest of the trip. But in doing so, she found something else... an image, like the after glow on her retinas after accidentally looking directly into a bright light. But instead of a shapeless blob... this was a distinct image, it was definitely not natural, a mess of squares and lines that could not have been formed by chance. She jolted, her eyes snapping open in surprise, then quickly closing them again to try and commit what she had seen to memory, but by then, the ghostly image was gone. "Master! I... saw something! Just now! In my eyes..."

Socrato nodded, reaching inside the shoulder of his toga, and withdrawing a small slip of folded paper. "I know. You saw this..."

On the paper, when folded open and set on the table, revealed a carefully inked series of squares, just like the one Pirogoeth had just seen.

"What... is that?" Pirogoeth asked.

"I call it the Scryer's Mark," he answered. "Anyone who has successfully scryed has seen this image burned into their eyes for a short time afterward. But as to what it is, I do not know. I don't even know what it *could* be. It matches no rune from ancient times, and is far to precise too have been from any mortal hand of that time, either. It is the Coders' work, to be sure... but that is all I can say for certain."

Pirogoeth couldn't be *entirely* certain, but as she scrutinized the mark Socrato had presented, the more she was convinced it wasn't *exactly* the same one that had been etched into the back of her vision. "This one is slightly different than what I saw. Not by much... but it was different."

Socrato nodded. "That is likely. Marks from my peers also had subtle alterations, whether that is because our memories were not wholly keen, corruptions created by our power, or actual differences in the mark is of some considerable debate."

He pushed aside any more questions with a happy declaration. "But now is not the time for such musings! We'll have plenty of opportunity as you delve even further into this art, as we get into more powerful tomes closer to places of power."

Pirogoeth groaned. One victory simply met an entirely new struggle.

Day 97: A Much Needed Respite

And those struggles were really starting to weigh on her.

It wasn't so much that Pirogoeth was having trouble learning the material... but that there didn't seem to be any end to it. The weeks started to bleed into each other, five days of new techniques, then two days of review. Five days of new material, two days of review.

The schedule and pace was more tiring than the actual effort involved, a cumulative fatigue of mind and body, to the point that her eyes opened to the morning light, then immediately slapped shut, groaning and wishing she had the power to turn the sun back.

Taima knocked on her door, and had to knock again because Pirogoeth really didn't want the day to start. But that wasn't Taima's fault, and Pirogoeth bid the servant girl enter before a third knock.

The aspiring chef was *far* too happy for Pirogoeth's sensibilities. "Pirogoeth! Are you still in bed?" she chirped.

"No," Pirogoeth snarked back, throwing her right arm over her eyes, "I've mastered the art of illusions. I've actually already woken, dressed, and even took a morning bath in the spring, and am waiting for you outside Socrato's private dining room, laughing while you speak to something that isn't really there."

Perhaps it was a sign of Pirogoeth's improving ethereal magic that Taima needed a moment's thought to dismiss the idea. She then yanked Pirogoeth's thin summer blanket off, and warned, "I have a cold pitcher of water outside. Don't make me use it."

Pirogoeth snarled grumpily, but complied, crossing the room to her wardrobe, dropping her nightgown on the floor in front of it, picking out a set of training clothes, and preparing herself for another day of hectic learning.

"Goodness... you *do* look terrible." Taima sounded concerned as she gathered up the thin gown to deposit it outside the door for the laundry servant.

"Then I look as I feel," the apprentice said testily as she finished wrapping up her chest, then stepped into her underwear.

"It's no wonder!" Taima said with sympathy. "The way the Dominus has been pushing you. Even I spare myself a day of rest a week." She then cheered right back up and said, "But, we do what we must, no?"

Pirogoeth sighed softly, adjusting her shirt so that the padded sections fit properly. "I suppose. Lead on."

"Oh, I'm afraid I can't this time," Taima said with a bright smile. "Things to do."

Pirogoeth's eyes narrowed suspiciously. "What is my master up to this time?"

She grinned. "Can't tell you."

The apprentice grunted in annoyance. "Of course not." Pirogoeth pulled the laces of her boots tight, gave another warning glare at Taima, stepped outside her chambers, noted there actually *was* a pitcher filled with water sitting next to her gown, and took her time reporting to her master. Not entirely due to reluctance, as the stairs were grueling even under ideal energy... much less when in a state that was only loosely described as "alive."

Upon reaching her destination, she put on the best face she could. Socrato was pushing her for a reason. The Void wasn't going to care if she was tired. The Void wasn't going to stop just because she had a tight schedule. She pushed open the door, quite pleased that she was able to do so without grunting from exertion, and bowed respectfully. "Good morning, master," she said with as bright a voice as she could muster.

Socrato leveled an appraising glare at her, and forced the air out of his lungs. "That was almost convincing, girl. Sit down. Eat. I have something that might help you wake up."

The sage saw right through her act. She shouldn't have been surprised. "I'm tired, but otherwise fine."

"No you're not," Socrato corrected dourly, even as his face turned regretful. "You've been dragging ever so slightly more every day, and it's my fault. I'm pushing you too hard. You should not suffer due to my impatience."

"But master..."

He held up his hand to silence her, a servant appearing with a metal carafe, pouring a deep black liquid into a ceramic mug in front of her as another servant followed with their breakfast. As the servants retreated, Socrato spoke before she could. "Your entire summer shouldn't be spent with your nose buried in studies and practice. As important as those things are... you need your rest time as well.

"Captain Daneid will accompany you and Taima to the Gold Coast, merely a couple of hours west of here by horse. I have a summer cabin on the beachfront that I rarely use, as I've had little reason to do so since Mila passed away. I will expect you back in three days."

"Then maybe you should join us!" Pirogoeth offered happily, her spirits immediately bolstered by the idea of a short vacation.

Socrato shook his head. "Oh, this break *is* as much for me as it is for you. It will give me time to prepare my next lessons for you and attend to keep matters that I had been neglecting. The world continues to move, after all. You'll leave as soon as you are packed... I suspect your two escorts have already done so. Although, I think you should take Taima for one more stop."

The sage handed over a brown leather pouch, tied at the top with tanned leather cord. From the weight, Pirogoeth figured there was more than a small handful of coins.

As she began to open it, Socrato chided her. "No, no, no... You are to give that to Lanka, and she will know if you've tampered with it beforehand. Tell her where you are going, and she will do the rest. Once she has taken her share, *then* you can have the rest." Pirogoeth knew why Socrato issued that stipulation. The coins were no doubt gold, and Pirogoeth would feel horribly guilty if she knew just how much was about to be spent on her and Taima.

She finished breakfast quickly, because she didn't want to keep anyone waiting. With a reserve of energy she didn't think lingered in her, she scampered down the stairs, and dashed to her chambers. She took out a small pack, as three days wasn't going to require terribly much, and hastily gathered the lightest clothes she had and three sets of undergarments.

Folding them tightly, she managed to wedge all the articles of clothing into the pack just as Taima came knocking. "Gold Coast!" She squealed in delight. "Oh, Pirogoeth, my friend, you are in for a delight! Sun, sand, the ocean breeze..."

"I take it you've been there?" Pirogoeth asked.

Taima's grinned. "Oh yes. At least once a summer, though staying more than one day was out of the question with my stipend. To have *three* days? Bliss!"

"So, how long did you know about this?" Pirogoeth asked curtly.

Taima winced. "Only since last night. Socrato ordered me not to tell you. He wanted it to be a surprise."

Pirogoeth forced herself not to grin. Well, two could play that game, and Pirogoeth knew exactly how. "Socrato wants me to stop by Lanka's before we leave. I think I need proper swim wear."

Taima didn't even try to hide her jealousy. "Oh, lucky little minx. I stole a peep at some of Lanka's summer wear before she could catch me. It's exquisite."

Pirogoeth hurried past her friend, if only because she couldn't keep her grin from cracking any longer, and didn't want Taima to see it. "Best not to keep the Captain waiting. I doubt it's going to be a vacation for *him*."

At first glance, that seemed to be the case, as the Phalanx captain was waiting just outside the inner keep doors in full armor. "Our horses are ready to depart when you give the word, my ladies. We can either go to the stables or have them delivered to us, on your word."

"We won't trouble anyone to bring them to us." Pirogoeth's tone said it was not up for debate. "Besides, I have one stop to make at Lanka's Clothiers before we go."

"Understood, my lady. Do you wish to take the lead?" Daneid said respectfully with a bow.

"Yes," Pirogoeth answered, doing exactly that and allowing Taima and the captain to fall in behind her.

"So, you're going to be on duty the entire time as our escort?" Taima asked, genuinely saddened by the idea.

Daneid laughed softly. "For the trip? Yes. I will serve as your official Phalanx escort. But the Gold Coast has its own Phalanx unit that keeps the peace. Once we arrive, I will be as free to enjoy myself as the two of you."

"Oh! That's a relief!" Taima said with one of her pleasant smiles. "One does not simply go to the Gold Coast and not have fun!"

"The people who live there do," Daneid corrected.

Pirogoeth's eyebrow rose, and she turned her head in her companion's direction. "People live on the beach?"

Taima amended, "Not *on* the beach directly, but there *is* a settlement just north of the coast, it's a very popular trading post with goods from all over the continent. There's a strong settlement of people who hail from Pallentia, another continent that fell into the Void many years ago. The cuisine there is so very unique... I'd love to learn more about it, but it can be so very expensive!"

"It's not cheap even on a Captain's salary," Daneid noted. "I rarely spend more than one night because I know if I did I'd lose half my savings. Fortunately, it's so close to us that short visits are tenable."

They both stopped cold several feet away from Lanka's shop. Even the Phalanx captain, a man trained for *war*, dared not cross that threshold. Pirogoeth rolled her eyes. "Coders take you both, she's not going to tear you asunder walking into her shop." The apprentice stepped inside, glaring at her two companions, who had only inched forward warily.

And initially, Pirogoeth's assessment appeared correct. The famed master tailor appeared on the sales floor with a pleasant smile. "Ah! If it isn't little Pirogoeth, come back again. Oh, how wonderful it is to see you, my dear! I trust that Dominus of ours hasn't been pounding your brain to mash in his dogged pursuit of whatever he seeks at any given time."

That assessment changed once Taima crossed the threshold. Instantly, the sales floor dropped ten degrees, and Lanka's eyes narrowed. She pointed at Taima, and said icily, "Oh, I remember you. You hover outside once a week, salivating like a dog staring at a chop. I don't suppose you plan to drool on my carpeting now."

Pirogoeth tugged on the hem of Lanka's skirt. "I am here to buy something." She jingled the coin pouch Socrato gave her. In a quieter tone that only Lanka could hear she added, "For the *both* of us... but don't tell her yet."

Lanka clenched her eyes shut tightly; whether trying to compose herself or playing along with the ruse wasn't entirely clear. "Yes. Business is business, as your master likes to say. Very well. What is it you need?"

"We are heading to the Gold Coast for three days. I need something suitable for beach and swimming wear."

Lanka clapped her hands excitedly. "Oh! The Gold Coast! Splendid! Don't you worry, child. Come with me! I think I have just the thing that will suit you!" She then stole a withering, baleful glare at Pirogoeth's companions. "I have a log of every single thing in my store and where it is. If even *one* thing is missing or out of place..." She then made a swift slashing motion across her throat to emphasize the threat.

"You *could* be nicer to potential customers." Pirogoeth said once they pushed through the curtain separating the back from the sales floor, trying very hard to keep her voice as pleasant as possible to avoid raising the master tailor's ire.

Lanka huffed. "So I am told. But you start treating the customer too nicely, then they start to think you exist for them. With their silly demands and requests that are either not plausible, horribly impractical, or vomitously ugly..." She shuddered. "My master was a complacent toy. I will not be. Even if it means my business is limited to those who have earned my respect."

With a snap of her fingers, her mood flashed to happy again. "Swimming clothes! Yes! The Pallentians had developed a wonderful material that proved to be fabulous for watery adventures. Fortunately, that knowledge did not die with their continent, and the rubber material is now grown and extracted in the marshes near the Gold Coast, in fact." She was rustling through racks and shelves, "It truly is an amazing material. It is very elastic, which allows for a snug fit over many different body shapes and sizes, very breathable, which is handy in hot, humid air like you'll find on the coast, and takes to color astonishingly well."

She then whirled about with the articles she had been looking for and cheered, "Like this!"

Pirogoeth wasn't sure she'd call them "clothes." She wasn't even sure "undergarments" were a suitable description. One was what amounted to a narrow tube colored in a jagged blend of rainbow colors seemingly at random, maybe six inches wide if she was being generous, and a matching bottom that she wouldn't have wanted to wear in the privacy of her own chambers, much less in public. "No," she said simply, aghast. "Absolutely not. You could try to force that onto my dead body, and I would come back to life and kill you."

Lanka clicked her tongue distastefully. "We simply *must* break you of those western sensibilities. But sadly, that cannot be done in one day. Very well... let's see if I can't find something more modest for you."

More modest turned out to be a very relative thing. Pirogoeth was used to swimwear made of cotton or linen that doubled her weight upon contact with water. There was *nothing* in Lanka's collection that came close to matching that.

She eventually chose a single piece suit of the rubber material Lanka was so enthusiastic about, though "distressingly unflattering" by her estimation. Pirogoeth figured having her arms and all but the top quarter of her legs bare was daring enough, and it wasn't like she had anything to flatter, anyway. It was dark blue with a random clutter of bright green streaks, which at least complimented her skin tone well enough.

Lanka sighed. "If that is as far as you will go, it will have to suit. Change and I'll have it packaged for you."

Pirogoeth complied, and emerged with the swimwear wrapped in paper and tucked under her arm. Lanka followed shortly after, and gave a scrutinizing look towards her merchandise on the sales floor. "Very good," she eventually said with reluctant approval. She then lowered her eyes on Taima, who cringed frightfully. The clothier then pointing authoritatively at the back room. "You. Follow me."

Taima gulped. "W... why?"

"Because I am to supply you with some swimwear as well, and I doubt you wish to disrobe here."

Taima's eyes flew open. "Me? Getting... swimwear?" The servant girl asked with timid awe.

"Yes." Lanka reiterated with a roll of her eyes. "The apprentice mage here purchased something well below her budget, and there is money for something for you. Now march unless you want those funds wasted."

Pirogoeth swore in the time it took her to blink, Taima was gone through the curtain. Seconds later, Lanka audibly shared Taima's enthusiasm. "Oh! A lady with taste! Brilliant!" the clothier squealed delightfully before both voices lowered below what Pirogoeth could clearly hear.

Pirogoeth noticed Daneid standing "guard" outside, and stepped into the front doorway. "She's probably not going to bite you, especially when you're armored."

"Proper duty, my lady," Daneid said simply. "And I *am* on duty for the time being." He then admitted sheepishly, "Besides, that woman is scary. Rumor has it she was the Dominus's mistress at one time. I wouldn't dare cross her if I can avoid it."

Pirogoeth smirked, partly because she knew it was more than rumor, and partly because it amused her to see a powerfully built and highly trained fighting machine terrified of a tailor. Then she decided his fear was actually of Socrato rather than Lanka, and found herself a bit annoyed by that.

She decided to bore herself looking around the sales floor rather than potentially get angry at their armed escort for reasons that not even she could really fault him for instead. Why wouldn't Daneid be intimidated by no doubt the most powerful mage on this side of the world?

The voices from the back room began to escalate again, but in the form of squeals and croons rather than anything coherent. At least Taima and Lanka were getting along...

The servant girl emerged several minutes later, grinning from ear to ear. Lanka was equally pleased. "Oh, how rare it is to find people with such good taste!" the clothier crooned happily. "If only you could share some of that gift with the apprentice mage here..."

Pirogoeth bit her tongue grumpily as Lanka jerked a thumb in her direction.

The tailor gave partings with a happy wave. "Enjoy the Gold

Coast, girlies. It is breathtaking. I tend to take a few days in the spring and fall, when the tourists aren't as numerous and the air is a little cooler. Tell your Dominus that he should suffer some free time himself once in a while."

"We will!" Taima said with an animated wave farewell. "And I promise I'll order all sorts of dresses when I have the money!"

Lanka laughed. "Oh, I think we can come to an arrangement, indeed." She handed the coin pouch back to Pirogoeth, which the apprentice noticed wasn't nearly as light as she was expecting it to be.

She looked up at Lanka questioningly, and the clothier nodded in confirmation. "I've taken my rightful share. Don't you even question that. Scurry along now, children. There's fun to be had, and the longer you're here, the less you're there."

The pair were quickly shooed out of the shop, and Daneid led them at a brisk pace to the north stables. It was a sturdy construct of gray stone bricks with tiled ceilings over the horse stalls and a canopy over the various wagons and carts stored there.

Pirogoeth had been expecting a most unholy stench as they approached, as that had been her experience with stables in the past, but Kartage maintained theirs well. It certainly wasn't meadow fresh by any measure, but the smell was remarkably tolerable.

She had expected horses to be brought out, and even Daneid seemed to think that had been the case, as he stepped out to the street where the girls were waiting. "Apparently, we're getting one of the Dominus's wagons."

The wagon followed, but as far as Pirogoeth could determine, it was exactly the same one that she had taken on the trip to Grand Aramathea. "How many wagons does Dominus Socrato *have*?"

"Four." A woman's voice from the driver's seat declared. She was a young woman of large stature, and no doubt needed to be in order to handle the reins of the three horses that led the wagon. Yet for that size, she seemed to have a pleasant personality. "I am Bittiri, and I'll be your driver." Bittiri held out a hand that seemed to devour Pirogoeth's, even if the grip was light enough to not cause any pain. Bittiri was at least six feet tall, and about as many feet wide, literally casting a shadow over the mage apprentice.

"Well, folks, load up! I'd rather like to make the Gold Coast before evening," the driver barked after making acquaintance with all three passengers and taking their luggage to load into the back compartment of the wagon. "Would you like the front seat, Captain?"

"I would, yes," Daneid answered, climbing into the driver's

bench. Though having such a lookout position was very unlikely to be necessary, he was going to follow proper protocol. Pirogoeth allowed Taima to climb into the wagon interior first, then the moment they were both settled, the wagon jerked forward, and the trip began in earnest.

The road was as much north as it was west, which matched what she knew about the general geography of the continent, and compared to the other journeys she had taken while under Socrato's tutelage this one indeed was very short. Afternoon had barely set in by the time that the wagon pulled to a stop. "We have reached our destination!" Bittiri bellowed, signaling two the women inside the cabin that it was safe to disembark. Daneid opened the door for them, and helped both girls down to ground level.

Pirogoeth was surprised by their surroundings. There didn't seem to be a beach in sight, the dense forest in all directions blocking any sort of view of anything past a hundred feet or so. There was a graveled path to the south that seemed to lead to a bright dot at the end, but that was the only other exit than the road to the east.

"The beachfront is that way," Daneid confirmed, "but I figure today could be best spent settling in. We'll have two more days to enjoy the sand and the town."

Pirogoeth nodded. "Surprised to see a forest here, is all."

"This is about as close to the border of the Free Provinces and eventually Avalon as you can go and still see civilization," Daneid explained. "Much of this area is undeveloped and more temperate than the rest of the Empire. You see similar landscapes as you go to the northern and eastern parts of the empire as well."

"It's the Dominus's vacation home, as I recall," Taima added. "It wouldn't surprise me that he'd desire a more secluded place." Pirogoeth acknowledged that made sense, and that brought her attention to the cabin itself.

There we actually two distinct parts to the cabin in front of her, one that was quite obviously older than the other. That part, made of very obviously aged dark pine logs, was in stark contrast to the section behind it, which was of a lighter and less weathered wood. Socrato had clearly added to the original cabin, most likely for more space, as the older section had not been very large.

The front door was to that older section, and while it definitely looked age beaten, the interior did not. It was not lavish, but certainly comfortable, with leather furniture in the form of chairs and futons; a diamond patterned carpet in stripes of red and orange decorated the polished wood floor, and a red brick fireplace. A kitchen and dining room formed the remainder of the original cabin, which Pirogoeth knew from experience would not have been their original purpose.

Taima pointed to above the fireplace. "Look! That must be the Dominus when he was younger!"

Pirogoeth followed Taima's gesture, to a portrait of indeed a younger man, with very thick brown hair and smooth facial features, the crooked smile betraying the man's identity. Pirogoeth could see why Socrato had earned unwanted favor from the women of his day. He had been rather handsome in an unassuming way. "It's hard to imagine the Dominus as someone younger, even though he must have been, huh?" Taima remarked.

Pirogoeth shrugged. It wasn't hard for her at all. People start young, they age, and eventually die. The details might vary, but it was a constant of life.

She turned towards the renovated wall that separated the older from newer section, when an abnormality caught her eye. One of the planks that formed the doorway was actually from the older section. It was so out of place that it must have been intentional.

She approached it slowly, trying to piece together what must have been special about this particular piece of wood, and she finally figured it out once she got close enough to see the notches carved into it, at increasing heights, with the letter "S" and increasing numbers.

"This isn't just Dominus Socrato's vacation home," Pirogoeth deduced. "This was his birthplace."

Taima and Daneid examined Pirogoeth's discovery. "It very well could be," Daneid acknowledged. "I had heard that he had grown up in the outskirts of the empire, unlike most venerated citizens that had their upbringings in major cities. It would make sense."

Pirogoeth found a new appreciation and kinship for her master with that discovery. She liked the idea that he could have had simple origins like hers: growing up off the beaten path, with an exceptional gift that granted them a greater destiny. Maybe he knew that... and had seen a little bit of himself in her.

It was a warm and fuzzy thought that she decided to cling to.

She led the other two into the addition to the cabin. The bedrooms and washrooms were there, six of the former and two of the latter. Most of the bedrooms were largely void of any individual decoration and plainly furnished, though two carried notches in their door frames very similar to Socrato's growth marks from earlier, marked with an "X" and a "C."

"Xavier and Corinth, Dominus Socrato's sons, no doubt,"

Daneid informed. "I served under Corinth during my early training. Very much like his father: stern and demanding when on duty, friendly and playful when off."

The two bedrooms to the end of the hall, however, still had some personality. The one to the left, like the others, hadn't been used in some time, judging from the dust in the corners that missed cleaning efforts. The burgundy blankets, sheets, and pillowcases were far different from the white on the previous four beds, and was at least double the size. A large wardrobe covered nearly the entirety of the west wall, and a panoramic window that opened onto a covered deck filled the south.

On the east wall, over the bed, was another painting, this of Socrato in a formal toga with a silver sash, and an Aramathean woman with long chestnut hair and dressed similarly. A chain of laurels wrapped around their arms and where there hands were linked. They were both visibly happy; the woman's smile could have lit the room itself.

"That has to be Mila," Taima said. "The older staff only had the kindest words to describe her. The Dominus didn't allow any visitors, unless on strict official business, for a month after she died, I'm told. I wish I could have met her."

Pirogoeth looked across the hall to the final room. She had a couple suspicions that she didn't want to air publicly to the other two out of respect for Socrato's wishes. She pointed across the way and said, "I'll take that one. Could one of you be a dear and bring my luggage to the doorway?"

Daneid complied as Taima decided to claim her room. "This is obviously where the Dominus stays, so I won't be here. Time to make a choice myself." Taima picked one of the unmarked plain white rooms. Daneid chose the one across from her, the one with Corinth's growth notches.

After that, Daneid led Taima to the market that was nearby so that she could purchase food for their stay. That allowed Pirogoeth to enter the final bedroom on her own. Both of her suspicions were immediately confirmed upon opening the door. Unlike the others, the hinges barely creaked as the door swung open, suggesting it had been used much more recently. And like Socrato's bedroom, it had a personalized flair, violet colors on the bed and the curtains, with a massive wardrobe on the west wall.

This was where Lanka went on her vacations as well.

Pirogoeth still wasn't entirely certain what to think about the relationship Socrato and Lanka had, one that his wife supposedly approved of to the point that Lanka bore both sons that Socrato and Mila raised as their own.

But Pirogoeth found enlightenment at the sight of a small painting, leaning against the wall on top of the wardrobe, and the empty hook above the bed where it normally would have rested. Pirogoeth recognized both subjects right away, Lanka and Mila, embracing and grinning playfully towards the viewer.

She picked it up off the wardrobe to give it a closer look, curiosity as to why it wasn't hanging taking control of her actions. Lanka took it off for a reason, and that reason was found on the back. There, written carefully in faded blank ink, was a message:

> *My dearest Lanka. Thank you for everything. You have been a friend, a lover, and the closest thing to family I have ever had. Every joy I experienced, every smile and every tear of happiness, is because of you. And when the end finally comes, I will meet you across the Void at the land of the Gold Sunrise. You are, and always will be, my first love.*
>
> *Love and blessings from Mila.*

Pirogoeth smiled at the sentiment, and the deep emotions they invoked. They were all a family of their own, no matter how unconventional it may seem. That's why it worked, she supposed, despite all the pitfalls it could have created, all the jealousy it could have spawned. Three people who all loved each other in their own ways, and accepted them for what they were.

There was a beauty in that, Pirogoeth decided. She set the painting back where she had found it, and left the bedroom, closing the door behind her. She then picked up her luggage with a grunt and slid it one door down to the room next to Taima's. If they asked, she'd just say she didn't like being that far away from everyone else... or maybe didn't like the color or the way the sun shone through the window. Even if Socrato claimed it wasn't much of a secret, that didn't mean Pirogoeth shouldn't keep it.

Day 98: Golden Sand

As Pirogoeth expected, her abrupt room change hadn't even raised an eyebrow. She hadn't even needed to provide a reason. This was a time for relaxation, not nosing around, after all. The morning was spent with a "simple" breakfast, at least by Taima's reckoning. This meant a king's feast for a normal person. Hashed potatoes with sausage, peppers and onion, thick strips of bacon, porridge with mashed banana, and coconut milk.

"Now I see why the people of the tower look so well fed," Daneid remarked candidly as he wiped his mouth clean with his forearm. "I might just have to assign myself tower detail once in a while." Taima visibly blushed at the compliment, and turned away so that the captain couldn't see her reaction. She then stole Pirogoeth an apologetic look that confused the apprentice mage. Was Pirogoeth supposed to feel insulted for some reason?

She decided to shift the topic towards their plans for the day. "So... are we going to the beach or the town first?"

"Oh, most certainly the beach!" Taima declared. "You simply *must* see it as soon as possible!"

"I concur," Daneid agreed. "The Town of Gold Coast isn't all that much different than other trading outposts within the empire. The coast itself, however, is fairly unique."

Pirogoeth decided to follow their suggestion. "Very well. I suppose we should change?"

"Best to do that at the beach," Daneid suggested. "They have dressing halls there so that you don't have to walk the entire way there and back in your swimwear." Pirogoeth acknowledged that was handy. And had the added benefit of minimizing her time spent in that horrific rubber sleeve.

"So, anyone want more to eat?" Taima asked. "Or should we go?"

The consensus from the other two was "go." They went their separate ways to gather their necessities, swimsuits and towels in satchels, and Taima even brought some oil, for tanning presumably. Pirogoeth honestly had no idea how the bronze servant girl could get much darker.

"For *you*, silly!" Taima replied when Pirogoeth had posed that question. "We're gonna try and get some color to your skin!"

Pirogoeth doubted that very much. She could spend hours in the summer sun of Bakkra, and unless she had a proper hat for shade, the only thing she got was a nasty red sunburn. Fortunately, she had anticipated such, and had packed a wide brimmed straw hat precisely to avoid that scenario.

The apprentice didn't have much experience swimming. There was a moderately sized pond near Bakkra that children occasionally dipped in, but that was while wearing linens and wool that effectively doubled in weight after just a few minutes, making long term swimming parties tiring. It didn't help that it was a dingy, muddy watering hole with clumpy brown clay and dirt that smeared your clothes and made them near impossible to clean.

So the sight of the Gold Coast as the forest gave way to the beach was indeed a new experience for her.

She had never seen a coastline like this... and she quickly understood how it got its name. The sand in front of them was a vibrant and almost metallic yellow, glimmering in the sunlight. The water was crystal clear to the point that by the horizon it was near impossible to tell where the water ended and the sky began.

"Breathtaking, isn't it?" Daneid teased, as Pirogoeth's jaw dropped animatedly.

The only problem with the beach was the number of people present. Pirogoeth estimated at least a hundred others lounging, swimming, or walking across the sands. "Awfully busy, isn't it?" Pirogoeth asked.

Daneid scoffed. "Hardly. At the height of summer, you're lucky to find a patch of empty sand to sit down on."

"Still no reason to waste time claiming our territory!" Taima cheered, grabbing Pirogoeth's wrist. "Let's go change! Quickly!"

Daneid laughed and declared, "I'll likely be waiting for you outside the changing cabin."

The changing cabin rested just off the beach front, on sturdier ground. It only resembled its namesake in that it was four walls of logs stacked like a cabin, with a door facing away from the beach. It didn't even have a roof, and the entire structure was open air. Pirogoeth figured it made sense; if you were going to the beach in the rain, it really didn't matter when you got drenched.

Inside, the cabin was split into stalls separated by thinner wood planks that could be closed with a sliding curtain. Pirogoeth entered one and did so, then dropped her satchel onto the ground at her feet and stepped out of her shoes. She knelt down, grabbed the edges of the bag and pulled, releasing the tension in the draw strings and revealing her towel and swimsuit inside.

It also contained one of her tomes, Pirogoeth having taken her master's advice to heart and making sure she had at least one of the books on her person at all times.

She reluctantly lifted the form fitting garment, eying it with distaste. She hastily undressed and tugged the damned thing on, grabbed her towel, crammed her clothes into the satchel, then dashed out of the cabin before embarrassment could catch up to her... only to slam headlong into Daneid, who didn't even have to take a step back to absorb the impact *and* catch her from falling over.

"Easy, my lady," he said with a smile. "I understand you're eager to experience the beach, but let's wait for our other friend, shall we?"

The captain's words were only the second thing that settled in Pirogoeth's mind. The first was a memory of the statue in the Diplomatic Suite made flesh. True, Daneid was wearing thin red trousers that covered the essential bits, but they left little to the imagination, and he was wearing precious little else. Pirogoeth's cheeks went bright red, and she had to swiftly turn away before he looked more closely. She straightened the brim of her hat as much to square it on her head as to hide. She just *had* to make a fool of herself at least once on this trip, didn't she?

"Oh! Am I interrupting something?" Taima teased, drawing Pirogoeth's attention, and restoring the pink glow to the apprentice's cheeks.

Pirogoeth should have expected something like this, considering how Lanka had been so pleased with herself after Taima had been provided for. Taima's swimsuit was in two separate pieces, a black and purple jagged pattern top with strap that went over her left shoulder, a band around the back, and joining in a v-shape that somehow managed to stay on while covering the barest minimum for modesty. The bottom half was no better, with leg holes that went from the crotch to the hip, leaving the full extent of Taima's legs bare. True, the servant girl was also wearing a sarong... but Pirogoeth saw little purpose for a skirt that was practically *transparent*, simply coloring Taima's legs with a hint of violet hue.

Daneid coughed in surprise, but regained his composure quickly. "Not at all, my lady."

Taima offered a skeptical smile. "Could you go on ahead and secure us a good spot, Captain?"

"Absolutely," he replied, taking the lead as the two ladies hung back.

Taima eyed Pirogoeth's choice in swimsuit, and shook her head. "*That* is what you chose?"

Pirogoeth cast an angry glare back and growled defensively. "What about it?"

"You're not going to get *any* attention from the fine men here wearing that."

Pirogoeth again blushed brightly. "Good!" she said forcefully. "I'm not looking for that attention anyway!"

Taima shook her head again, and sighed. "Sometimes I forget the age difference between us."

"It has nothing to do with that!" Pirogoeth protested. Although it was true that Taima being five years older than her rarely was brought up, and that Pirogoeth herself never particularly gave it any thought. "I don't... I don't like people looking at me."

Taima didn't say anything, but she stopped, and Pirogoeth could feel her friend's gaze. "My... peers... liked to tease me about looking like a boy," Pirogoeth explained. "During the summer, the girls would steal my blouse and force me to chase them around the school, saying that a boy like me shouldn't be wearing girl's clothes. It was... humiliating."

Taima hugged Pirogoeth at the shoulders. "Well, no one is going to confuse you for a boy here. I promise you. Do you want to go back?"

Pirogoeth shook her head. "We're supposed to be relaxing. I'm... going to relax, even I have to force myself to do so."

Taima gave Pirogoeth's shoulders a squeeze, and led her the rest of the way where Daneid had claimed them some prime real estate about twenty feet from the water line. There, they set down their towels and Pirogoeth took a seat on top of hers.

Taima flicked off her sarong with a flourish, and said, "I'm going to take a quick dip to test the water. I'll let you two know what I discover!"

"You don't want me to join you?" Daneid asked.

Taima shook her head. "Keep the lady company for the time being, will you?" Taima then flashed Pirogoeth a conspiratorial wink and a smile before she took off in a light jog towards the water line. Pirogoeth still had no idea what her friend was trying to imply until she noticed Daneid slide over to her side.

Oh.

Oh no.

Taima actually thought she fancied the Phalanx captain? Sure... the man was *hardly* unattractive, but he was at least in his mid-twenties if she had been informed correctly. Surely there were *far* more Aramathean prospects that caught his eye.

Daneid himself looked anxious, his head whipping about in all directions, his upper body contorting to look behind him several times. For a moment, Pirogoeth wondered what was wrong, until she remembered the last time that he had been in such close proximity.

"I don't think any fox-girl chimeras are going to charge you from behind, Captain," Pirogoeth said teasingly. "She'd be far too easily seen."

Daneid sighed, silently acknowledging he was being silly. "I know..."

"If anything, she'd burrow from the sand below to get you."

The captain stiffened, and glanced downward towards his feet. "I wouldn't put it past her," he growled warily. Another tired sigh followed. "Damn girl shouldn't have a quarrel with me. If she should be harassing anyone, it's my brother."

Pirogoeth's right eyebrow lifted in silent question, and Daneid surrendered further details. "My brother is a news writer for the town criers in Grand Aramathea. He told me that he had an excellent lead on pirate activity in the city. At the time, I was a Line Lieutenant for the First Army, and he convinced me that helping him expose said activity would be a quick road to a promotion."

He growled from the memory. "Story goes that he had gotten on the good side of this chimera... I don't even remember her name at this point. It was seven years ago, and I was far more interested in revealing the pirate haven that my brother suspected was somewhere in the city.

"He gives me a location, and tells me to apprehend her just after nightfall. I guess just after nightfall means something a wee bit different from my brother, because when I burst in... I caught them being... 'intimate'.

"After a great amount of embarrassment, I apprehend the girl, and drag her to the stockade. He didn't tell me she was a damned Gold Pirate. One day later, she was freed, and I was 'promoted' and reassigned to the Second Army guard post in Kartage." The bitter emphasis he put on "promoted" suggested to her that he didn't consider it so, even if it was technically a jump in rank.

"I take it being in the First Army carries more prestige?"

"It's the best and the brightest soldiers of the empire, trusted to guard the First Capital," Daneid explained. "My promotion to Captain here in terms of prestige was a lateral move at best. In addition, Grand Aramathea had been my home. I took great pride in defending my home town."

Pirogoeth frowned in sympathy. "I'm sorry. That's horribly unfair."

The captain exhaled once more, though this one was a much more pleasant sound. He dropped his head on his hands, eyes out to sea. "Oh... I've realized it's not *that* bad."

Pirogoeth followed his line of sight, just as Taima surfaced from a dive, swishing her hair to fling water away and her hands wiped over her eyes. She noticed the attention she was getting, and waved enthusiastically.

Pirogoeth's jaw dropped while smiling, and her eyes twinkled delightfully. "*You* like *Taima!*"

Daneid dropped his head. "I had been trying to pick your brain the night of the Lunar Eclipse to see if you could put in a good word for me when that damned chimera interrupted. But... perhaps it's for the best you don't."

Pirogoeth's eyebrows furrowed in confusion. "Why on earth would...?"

Daneid gestured out into the water. "While she may have another ten years in Kartage, there's no guarantee *I* will be stationed anywhere near the keep any given year. While I haven't been reassigned in years, that doesn't mean I won't *ever* be."

Pirogoeth punched him in the side, and the meager blow at least got his attention. "How about you don't put the cart before the horse? Maybe you'll get reassigned and you'll be unhappy. But if you do nothing, you'll *always* be unhappy."

Daneid didn't answer, his head lifting again to see Taima frolicking in the water, determined to give him and Pirogoeth space. The silly, unwitting girl... Pirogoeth slapped Daneid on the shoulder, and pointed out to sea. "March!"

Daneid cracked a smile, and snapped a lazy salute. "Yes, my lady."

Taima was confused to see Daneid stand and start walking towards the water, she rushed out to meet him, and while Pirogoeth couldn't hear exactly what was being said, the facial expressions were sufficient translation. Taima's look of surprise, Daneid's nervousness, followed by a warm smile that Taima returned. She pecked him on the cheek, and they returned with arms around each others' waists.

Pirogoeth was smiling more broadly than either of them. "So, did you two sort out some things?" she asked sweetly.

Taima dropped down to Pirogoeth's left as Daneid settled down next to Taima. "I'm still not certain how he was able to get such an infatuation considering how little our paths crossed... but we'll see where it goes. I'll be honest, I thought he was interested in *you*."

Pirogoeth shook her head. "Look at you. Then look at me. You actually look like an adult. I don't even look like I should be out alone."

Taima rolled her eyes. "For the last time. You do *not* look like you're twelve."

A voice interrupted them sweetly, coming from behind. "Excuse us?" All three turned to address the source: an Aramathean couple, probably in their forties, dressed "suitably" for their culture in swimsuits quite possibly wrought from Lanka's hand. The woman had been the one to speak first, but the man was the one to take over.

"We didn't mean to intrude," he said nervously, overlooking Pirogoeth to focus on Taima and Daneid. "But when we saw you both..."

The woman cut in to save her partner from talking further. "We just thought it was so wonderful to see young people adopting a foreign child. We hear so much about how children in Avalon are in need, so to see the younger generation taking one in warmed our heart."

Taima and Daneid's eyes bulged, then they both turned in fear towards Pirogoeth. The apprentice's eyes went unfocused, her expression wholly unreadable. However, below the surface, fire began to stir, amplified as she reached into her satchel, and found the tome she had tucked into an interior pocket.

A ball of fire ignited on her left palm, and that compelled her friends to action, Daneid putting on a friendly face as he gently led the pair away with an improvised tale on his "adoption" of the apprentice mage while Taima frantically shook Pirogoeth's shoulders and whispered soothingly in the younger girl's ear, desperate to calm her before she smelted the golden sands into golden glass.

Pirogoeth had at last dispelled the fireball harmlessly by the time Daneid returned. Taima looked up at him, then worriedly at Pirogoeth. "So... shall we... cool off? The water *is* wonderful."

Pirogoeth didn't verbally agree, but didn't need to be dragged out into the water either. Not being a particularly strong swimmer, she didn't dare go much farther than chest deep, but it was enough to experiment with some shallow dives.

Kids didn't dive at the watering hole outside Bakkra. There was nothing to see but mud. The Gold Coast, however, was an entirely different world under the water level. The sand was just as vibrant, and mussels, clams, and even smaller fish shared the shallows with her. She emerged, gasping for breath, and again caught sight of an immaculate blue horizon, not even flecked with the slightest bit of cloud cover.

In the back of her mind, she knew the Void slowly crept forward, but for the first time, it felt as far away as it really was. She had time... the world had time... she wasn't going to do *anyone* any good burning the candle to nothing before she was ready to do anything.

Pirogoeth needed that reminder.

They were able to avoid the worst of the sun that way, settling back on their towels for lounging as it waned into the afternoon. Taima presented some jerky and some light wine from her satchel that served as a quick mid-day meal.

Taima then went to work covering Pirogoeth in tanning oil. The apprentice would not have called the experience pleasant. She felt filthy, like covered in a thin grime, that didn't go away even as it dried. She tried her best to hide her discomfort, but wasn't successful.

"You'll thank me later," Taima said as she leaned back then closed her eyes like she was taking a nap. Pirogoeth somehow doubted that, but leaned back, closed her eyes, and found yet another world she hadn't noticed.

There were other sensations that she had overlooked with all the sights. The hiss of the breeze coming off the ocean, and the feeling of it against her skin. The background chatter from other beach goers. The calls of various birds overhead. The crashing of the waves as they hit the coastline. The salty smell of the sea air. Pirogoeth found them all strangely relaxing, a massage for her senses. Tension she didn't realize she had started uncoiling and leaving her body. She felt like she was about ready to fall asleep...

Then Taima nudged Pirogoeth in the side. "You might want to turn over. Don't want to look uneven." With a grunt of exertion, Pirogoeth rolled over onto her stomach, resting her head on her arms.

From this position, she became more aware of the sand underneath her towel, a surface that felt something between solid and fluid. With a bit of wriggling, it conformed to her body shape comfortably. So very... comfortably...

Taima nudged her again, and the apprentice mage growled angrily.

"Pirogoeth... we should be getting back to the cabin for dinner," Taima said, gently shaking her friend by the shoulders.

Dinner? It was barely past... Pirogoeth's eyes flashed open, and found that the sun was much lower in the sky than it should be. She had fallen asleep. The apprentice pushed herself up, then slid her knees out from under her, rubbing her eyes and yawning.

"I hadn't wanted to wake you, I've never seen you so relaxed," Taima said in apology. "But I was worried you might burn, and we do need to be heading back. Daneid's no doubt waiting for us at the changing cabins."

Pirogoeth was disappointed she had dozed off, losing several hours of beach time. Taima bumped her playfully and said, "You didn't miss much. Merely Daneid clumsily trying to lay out what we should do in town tomorrow. It was fairly useless planning, as I already know." Pirogoeth's eyebrows rose questioningly, but Taima refused to let her in on the secret. "You'll learn when he does. Not before!"

The apprentice mage frowned angrily, but knew that Taima wouldn't be intimidated by any theatrics. So she resigned herself to being surprised, and spent dinner and the rest of the evening in pleasant company before retiring to her room for the night.

As she laid down into her bed, she only hoped the oil had worked as Taima claimed... otherwise, her two companions would have to deal with a very sore and reddened mage for the rest of their stay on the Gold Coast.

Day 99: Chance Meetings and Curry

The first thing Pirogoeth did upon waking was dash to the bathroom, and the mirror mounted on the west wall. The apprentice sighed in relief when she was distinctly not sun-scoured, though Taima would no doubt be disappointed that the oil and the sun had only managed to apply a barely visible kiss of bronze to Pirogoeth's skin.

Personally, Pirogoeth considered that a success.

She returned to her room to dress, then took the hall to the original section of the cabin. Daneid was already at the dining room table when Pirogoeth emerged, and waved in greeting. Taima stuck her head around the corner of the kitchen, and frowned, not impressed by her friend's skin tone. "Hmm. Maybe I used too much oil."

Pirogoeth shook her head. "This is about as dark as I get. I'm never going to pass for a good Aramathean."

"I tried, at the very least," Taima replied with comic dismay before she laughed and pointed at the dining room table. "Sit. I'm almost done."

Breakfast was not particularly robust that morning, porridge, two slices of toast fried in beaten eggs and dusted with sugar and cinnamon, and orange juice. Pirogoeth then felt horribly guilty that she now considered that meager, when she would have considered that a morning feast less than a year ago.

Neither her nor Daneid dared ask, though their faces must have given them away, because Taima answered with a coy smile, "Don't want you to get too full. You're going to want a healthy appetite for lunch!"

Well, that was a clue at least. Daneid confirmed, leaning in to say quietly, "there is an abundance of diners and restaurants open during the summer in the Town of Gold Coast. Which one was so good that it impressed Taima... *that* I couldn't say."

"She could be doing some scouting," Pirogoeth replied, smiling innocently as Taima gathered the dishes with a warning eye. "Perhaps something she hasn't had before or wants to try and replicate."

Daneid nodded. "That's a very strong possibility."

Taima rolled her eyes at the not-so-secretive discussion. "You'll find out. Now make sure you're all dressed and ready, because I'm leaving within the hour with or without you."

Pirogoeth only needed to go back to her room to get her

satchel, making sure she had put her tome back in there after a late night's study before returning to the front of the cabin.

Taima took up the rear, holding her satchel over her right shoulder, completely empty. When Pirogoeth attempted to ask why, the cook cut in before Pirogoeth could even speak. "A girl *always* needs an empty bag for when she goes shopping," Taima said defensively. "Surely even northern girls know *that*."

Pirogoeth tapped her satchel, and said, "I think Socrato would sear the skin off my bones if I left my book behind."

Taima nodded in acceptance. "That is true enough." She then said to Daneid, "I hope you are ready to be bored to tears, good Captain."

He shrugged indifferently. "It's something I'm no doubt going to have to get used to. Might as well start now."

Pirogoeth winked. "I think he's a keeper, Taima."

Taima shook her head, and flipped her wrist to beckon her friends. "Let's go. There's much to see in town, and I want to have time to see it all."

The path to town started in the same way as the path to the beach, only once the forest broke, they walked northwest parallel to the coast until the dirt road branched away and turned to cobblestone. It was another half hour and up a steady incline to the outskirts of the Town of Gold Coast.

It was nothing like Kartage, with merely a single wooden barricade that didn't even look like it could withstand a stiff breeze, much less anything of consequence. Like the other Aramathean cities she had experienced, it was divided into distinct sections, in this case, a bazaar, residences, and permanent shops.

"Due to the relative warmth year round, and the presence of the Northwest Great Trade Line nearby, the Town of Gold Coast is pretty well frequented and a lot of trade occurs all year, mostly from Avalon, but occasionally traders from the Free Provinces as well," Daneid said as they entered the city proper, presenting identification to the Phalanx on guard at the gate.

"We'll go to the bazaar first," Taima declared, turning to the east with little warning, causing Pirogoeth and Daneid to lose a stride and having to jog to catch up.

The bazaar didn't look too much different than what she had seen in Kartage, but that wasn't much of a surprise. While the area had been settled by refugees from Pallentia and Tanzibar, they were the ones that mostly held permanent shops rather than temporary booths in the bazaar. There was definitely more of a western feel here, judging from all the pale and lightly tanned faces that littered the roadside.

But as Taima admired some silver Avalon jewelry, one face in particular stood out from the rest... mostly because it pushed its way into Pirogoeth's line of sight. "Hey!" a female voice shouted over the ambient noise of the bazaar, though Pirogoeth paid it no mind until it followed up with, "Blond haired boy!"

That got Pirogoeth to stiffen, then a hand grabbed Pirogoeth by the shoulder and pulled her violently full about, turning Pirogoeth face to face with a girl she never thought she'd see for some time. Her name was Patilla, one of the cadre from Bakkra that had not exactly taken Pirogoeth's existence kindly.

"Coders, it *is* you!" Patilla said, both surprised and angry. "I was wondering where you had run off to months ago. I was telling the others that Aramathean witch ate you." Pirogoeth didn't respond to the obvious jab. "Nothing to say?" Patilla snarled, shoving Pirogoeth down to ground. "Cicia *still* doesn't have shoulder length hair because of you!"

Daneid stepped in between them as Taima tried to help Pirogoeth to her feet. "Get out of my way!" Patilla shouted at Daneid, trying to force herself around him with another shove.

He instead stopped her cold with a firm grip on Patilla's arm. "Man or woman, if you assault a Phalanx Captain, you will *not* like the consequences. Guards!"

Pirogoeth brushed off Taima's assistance. "Stand down, Captain. It's all right." She then turned her head to where three armored Phalanx were rapidly approaching. "Guards, you may return to your posts."

Pirogoeth should have been surprised that all four military men complied without resistance, and Daneid even released Patilla. But she was far too annoyed even to wonder why Patilla did not take advantage of her freedom, instead slowly backing away from Pirogoeth with what looked like confused terror. All that mattered to Pirogoeth was that she made her message clear, and she did it as menacingly as she could muster.

"If you *dare* touch me again, I will do *far* more than sear your hair," she hissed quietly, the background chatter muting as she did so. "I suspect you are with your uncle to help him with his booth. I'd suggest you get back to it and leave me in peace. As far as you are concerned, the two of us never crossed paths. Understood?" Patilla nodded vigorously, her knees visibly trembling.

Even Daneid and Taima seemed spooked by the aura Pirogoeth was projecting. No wonder it was rattling someone who would consider herself Pirogoeth's enemy.

"Go," Pirogoeth ordered flatly, and Patilla took that as permission, scrambling and stumbling across the street and two booths east before literally diving behind the booth counter and peeking over the blood red tapestry in fright.

It was only then that Pirogoeth noticed the fear in her companion's eyes. "What?" she asked crossly.

That startled them from their collective haze, and they shook themselves. "Nothing," Taima said. "Just remind me never to get on your bad side."

Pirogoeth smiled, and chuckled warmly, which served to dispel the remaining tension. "I don't think you have anything to worry about that."

"I don't understand why you didn't want that girl to get what was coming to her," Daneid said, throwing a cold glare in the direction of Patilla's booth. "She attacked you and got aggressive with me. That should have earned her a few days in the stockade."

"It wasn't worth it," Pirogoeth replied, her expression and voice haughty. "She's a bully, and a pretty pathetic one at that. She can't hurt me, either physically or emotionally, and I know that now. I've dined with a general and been a guest of an emperor. I've realized how insignificant she really is. Dragging her off to the stockade would mean she still had some impact on me, even if small."

Pirogoeth hoped they believed that. While sending Patilla fleeing in terror had felt like a triumph, it had been a fleeting one. In truth, she just wanted to get as far away from the bazaar as possible. All those memories of her childhood were bubbling up, and it was all she could do to keep from crying. In truth, she hadn't wanted Patilla arrested because it reminded her of all the times she *would* tattle on her tormentors, only to have them treat her *worse* for it.

Fortunately, the event soured Taima as well. "I think now is as good of a time as any for lunch, then we can shop in the storefront."

"I agree," Pirogoeth said confidently. She was impressed at how well she was keeping her composure.

"Then lead on, my lady," Daneid said to Taima with an extended arm down the road. "As you seem to know what we are doing and where we are going."

That Taima did, as she walked with purpose, weaving through streets of the residential district, and to the storefront where the citizens of the town did their business. Pirogoeth noticed that, unlike Kartage, which had a rather uniform style, the Town of Gold Coast had a myriad of architecture and design unlike anywhere she had ever seen. There were the usual stucco houses that Pirogoeth recognized, but she also saw more wooden frames and vibrant colors like red and orange, with sharply steeped roofs made from straw and tar and trimmed with black. Others had domed ceilings and columns, trimmed with silver and gold.

"Pretty, isn't it?" Taima said, as she followed Pirogoeth's eyes. "The cultures in this area have remained very distinct, rather than melting together like you see in the rest of the empire. I rather like seeing such individuality remain."

"Some would say that those who cling to old ways stubbornly weaken the empire, and that they should accept that they are in a new place and should adapt," Daneid added.

Taima shot him a cross look. "And some would say that just because you are part of an empire doesn't mean you should be required to abandon everything that makes you unique."

They then both appealed to Pirogoeth with their eyes, as if she had a tie-breaking vote. The apprentice mage refused to cater to either of them. "Leave me out of this," she said with a swift shake of her head.

Any comment Taima might have had was interrupted by her squeal of delight. "We're here!"

"Here" was a wood panel building, the planks stained so dark as to be near black. Lighter wood, painted red, formed the trim along the exterior, and as Pirogoeth gave them a closer look, the trim was actually carved in a serpentine form, along the corners, up to the arched roof. She and Daneid took several steps backward so that they could see where the tails led... to the very top of the roof, where a copper colored coiled dragon with emeralds for eyes lifted its head with a tongue of sculpted fire.

"Well... *that's* certainly elaborate," Pirogoeth commented.

Taima beckoned them forward again. "This is Radi's House," Taima explained. "Chef Vargat would recommend this place to me frequently, but when it costs a month's stipend for one meal here... well... I think you can guess how many times I've been here. If you let him, Vargat will talk your ear off about their curry!"

Pirogoeth felt stupid asking, but she had to. "What's... curry?" When Taima looked astonished, the apprentice added angrily, "I'm not the most worldly person! You already know this!"

Taima grabbed her by the wrist. "Well you are about to learn!

Come!"

She was pulled through the main doors and into a kaleidoscope of color. The wall were *mostly* purple, but arches of yellow and red occasionally flared around pieces of wall art and were accentuated by hanging lamps casting the surroundings in a warm yellow hue. Golden statues of dragons and finely sculpted men, thankfully clothed, served as the columns that held up the ceiling of the truly large dining room. It had to be nearly the size of the main dining hall in Kartage. It was certainly garish, yet... it really seemed to work.

A young woman, who couldn't have been much older than Pirogoeth, approached them, with a dress that shimmered like it was encrusted with emeralds, and gold trim that looped over her left shoulder and under her right, and tied with a bronze sash around her waist. Her black hair was pulled up into a bun and held there with a single thick, long hairpin, and chocolate brown eyes that complimented her copper skin tone very well.

"Good afternoon, sir and madams," the girl said cheerfully. "Welcome to Radi's House. I am Patri, and I will serve you today. Will it just be the three of you?"

Taima nodded. "Yes, dear. Would you happen to have any window seating available?"

"We do, if that would be your preference."

"It is."

Patri nodded amiably, then bowed in respect. "Then follow me." The windows of Radi's House were open air, but with broad awnings off the exterior to keep out rain. The table itself was as colorfully decorated as the rest of the establishment, large red diamond patterns splayed on the cream background, and even the chairs were painted a dark red.

Their waitress brought a large clear carafe, filled with what looked like tea... but with crushed ice pieces visibly floating on the surface. Three crystal glasses were set down in front of them, and Patri dutifully filled them with the liquid that should not be. "I can't say I've ever had ice cold tea before." Pirogoeth said, eying her glass warily.

"It's not popular in Kartage, no," Taima admitted. "Chef Vargat finds it not suitable for his palette, but for me, on a hot summer day like this one, it's a blessing." She punctuated that statement by promptly drinking half her glass in one go.

Pirogoeth took an experimental sip, and winced at the unexpected sweetness that hit her tongue. It wasn't *bad*... it just wasn't much like the hot tea that she had gotten accustomed to. A second sip went down easier, and she began to taste the tea itself despite the sweet. It *was* refreshing, Pirogoeth gave it that, but it certainly wasn't something she was going to want to drink every day.

"Do you know what you wish to order?" Patri asked.

Taima seemed to know what she was doing, so Daneid and Pirogoeth deferred to her. The aspiring cook didn't disappoint. "We'd like your red duck curry, if we could."

Patri bowed in acknowledgment. "Excellent choice, my lady. Would you like any appetizers?"

"Shrimp rolls, if we could."

Again, their waitress bowed. "It will be as you desire."

Patri took her leave, and Taima's composure abandoned her, the servant girl giggling animatedly and drumming her fingers against the table in anticipation. "Oh, you are both in for a treat. Actually, Captain, have you had curry before?"

Daneid nodded. "Not often, and certainly not from here, but what I've had was tasty enough." He asked Pirogoeth, "How do you and spicy foods get along? Sometimes curry can have an impressive bite."

Pirogoeth shrugged. "We'll find out."

Taima rolled her eyes. "I can assure you that she's had food with just as much kick before. What Vargat makes in the tower can be just as eye watering as any Pallentian dish."

Daneid held up his hands in surrender. "I do beg your pardon. I just know that exploding out of both ends isn't a pleasant experience."

Pirogoeth clenched her eyes shut, her lips curled in disgust, "Nor does it make for a pleasant mental image, thank you."

Taima was also revolted by the thought. "Yes. I agree. On... both counts. Can we change the subject, please?"

Daneid attempted to, though wound up stepping in something more dire. "So... I bet you were surprised to see someone you knew here in town."

Taima's eyes flared in fright, silently warning Daneid not to press any further. He seemed confused by Taima's body language, and rightfully so, as Pirogoeth was determined to brush it off without showing her nerves.

She said with a dismissive shrug, "Bakkra often collects its tradable goods as sells them at market as a collective. Her uncle is the one tasked with selling those goods. It's not a huge surprise that he would find himself here at the height of summer. This town *does* seem to be a large trading hub."

"She seemed awfully agitated. I take it you weren't friends?"

Pirogoeth clenched her teeth, and let the mask fall slightly with the annoyance in her voice. "No, we weren't. And I'd rather not discuss it further."

That was the hint Daneid needed to back off. "Understood."

There was a fairly uncomfortable silence until the appetizer arrived, at which point they were too busy eating to try and add awkward conversation. Pirogoeth found the shrimp rolls nothing short of delicious, the thin rice wrapping complimenting the vegetables and shrimp inside, along with a slight hint of chili spice to give it flavor.

Of course, she thought that Taima and Vargat did better, but that could very possibly been personal bias.

Within minutes of the trio finishing their appetizer, the main course arrived in the form of a broad bowl on a single tray, along with slightly smaller bowl of white rice that had a unique aroma, one that she hadn't smelled before.

"Jasmine." Taima said, noting Pirogoeth's nose hovering over the rice bowl as it was set down. "Pallentian cuisine adds oils from other plants like jasmine as they dry their rice. It *does* add to the flavor as well. But *this* is what we are here for!"

Pirogoeth examined the entree as an ivory plate was set in front of her, as well as a fork and spoon. To be perfectly honest, it did *not* look particularly appetizing. It looked more like a soup than anything, with a thick red sauce flecked with onion, red pepper, zucchini, and evenly sized cubes of roasted duck meat.

It would explain why the plates had a raised upper lip, at least.

Taima began parceling the rice as their drinks were refilled, then got to distributing the curry. Once on her plate, it somehow looked much more edible, as the sauce had been hiding the fact that it was much more robust than first looks suggested.

Taima was quick to start eating, having swallowed her first bite before Pirogoeth had even picked up her fork. The servant girl threw back her head and moaned happily. "I *wish* I could make this..."

Pirogoeth paused, fork in hand, and asked, "Why can't you?"

"The chefs here keep their recipes and their methods secret. Most elite chefs do, in fact. I can make curry... just nothing like this. Coders, Vargat was right, this is amazing."

Daneid exhaled sharply, having started himself. "Definitely has a nice kick, but not *too* much. Very good indeed. I guess you really do get what you pay for."

Pirogoeth finally got the opportunity to share the experience.

The fiery flash was immediate, and it certainly got her attention, putting some color to her cheeks, but as Taima said, it wasn't particularly hotter than what she had already gotten used to from the months in Kartage. And once that initial kick died, the other flavors began to shine: the vegetables, the duck, and what she identified as ginger, giving it an added tang at the end.

"*Wow*," the apprentice mage finally assessed. "That *is* good."

Taima enthusiastically agreed, "Isn't it?"

A fine dinner, with good company, helped Pirogoeth push aside the turmoil that the morning had stirred up. After paying their bill, Taima resumed shopping, this time in the brick and mortar shopping district. It was an enthusiasm Pirogoeth didn't particularly share, she discovered. Shopping bored her more than anything... which was apparently one of many ways she was not "normal."

She didn't want to *say* anything about it as the hours dragged on painfully slow, she *really* didn't want to look like she was complaining. Nonetheless, she no doubt looked incredibly relieved when Taima announced they were returning to the cabin for dinner.

The evening meal was a relatively simple affair, pork chops in gravy, a tossed spinach salad, stuffed pita with lamb and spinach, and a fortified red wine. It suited Pirogoeth just fine, a laid back dinner just before she settled in for some light studying.

So she was a bit surprised as evening waned to have Taima knocking on her door.

The servant girl wore a broad smile. "Get your shoes on. We're going back into town!"

Pirogoeth's eyebrows furrowed. "Whatever for? By the time we get there it'll be almost nighttime."

"I know! We don't want to be late!"

"Late for *what?*"

Taima's grin refused to crack. "You'll see! Just hurry, we're going to want to find a good spot!"

Taima turned full about and left as Pirogoeth stuck her head through the doorway and demanded loudly, "A good spot for *what?*"

"The fireworks show in town," Taima said. "The Town of Gold Coast holds one at the end of every week during the summer."

Pirogoeth knew what fireworks were. Traders would occasionally bring them in during the late summer, little knickknacks that didn't even impress child Pirogoeth, much less the adolescent Pirogoeth now. "I'll stay here. You and Daneid have fun."

Taima literally pushed her way in. "No. You're coming with.

Get your shoes on!"

"Why?" the apprentice mage said darkly. "Do you plan to annoy me until you get your way?" Taima's broad grin was all that was needed to answer that question. Pirogoeth grumbled in annoyance to herself as she forced her feet into her boots and tightened the laces. She had *just* gotten nice and comfortable.

She made no attempt to hide her frustration either as she stomped into the front of the cabin. Daneid had that same knowing grin as Taima, and that managed to irritate Pirogoeth *more*.

Pirogoeth willingly took the rear of the procession as they began the hike *back* into the town they had already left, getting increasingly dour as the sun dropped further to the horizon. But once they reached their destination, Taima led the party along the perimeter, off the road and onto the grass.

They weren't the only ones there either. A large throng of people were assembling at the top of a decline to the north of town, into a valley and a dried up, grassy flood plain that stretched for miles. In the center of that plain, along the banks of what remained of the water, Pirogoeth could barely make out tiny dots of people in the rapidly fading light.

"Is that where the fireworks are going to be lit?" Pirogoeth asked with an annoyed frown. "We're not going to be able to see anything from here."

Pirogoeth didn't like the knowing grin Taima and Daneid gave each other. "You obviously have never seen *real* fireworks," Taima said.

Pirogoeth was about to demand what that meant when a hissing roar reached her ears and drew her attention back to the flood plain. A single finger of fire rapidly cut a jagged path towards the stars, before it burst into a flower of purple sparks with a loud crack.

The mage's mouth opened in surprise, and Taima nudged her. "That was just the test rocket."

Dusk turned to night, followed by a symphony of color that nearly turned it back to day. Hundreds of fireworks were launched, in a bevy of colors to match the rainbow, sometimes individually, sometimes in clusters, some just small plumes others with bursts that nearly covered the whole of the visible sky.

It was such a delightful display that so exceeded her expectations that her earlier annoyance was forgotten. When the final barrage faded into the night, and the crowd began to disperse, Pirogoeth admitted it was a far better cap to their time on the Gold Coast than she had planned to spend it.

For tomorrow morning, Bittiri was scheduled to return, and take the three of them back to Kartage and to the normal daily grind.

Day 100: Black Arts; Black Book

There was one truth about vacations that Pirogoeth learned once hers was over. They don't actually revitalize a person. If anything Pirogoeth felt *more* exhausted over the prospect of returning to her studies, especially when the tower of Kartage appeared on the horizon. She knew she had to, she knew it was vital work, but it still wasn't easy to see the walls of the great keep coming closer after the days of rest that now felt far too short.

The sun was at its apex as the wagon pulled to a stop outside the doors of the inner keep. Taima and Pirogoeth offered partings to Daneid as he left to report to his unit quarters, and the two girls prepared to return to their duties in the tower.

At least... until the Phalanx guard stopped Pirogoeth at the front gate. "Orders from the Dominus, my lady. You are to use the side entrance to the lower keep." He anticipated her next question by adding, "I don't know why, Apprentice, nor is it my place to ask. Just that you are to use that entrance."

Pirogoeth knew *why* (it was the one that had a shifting portal), but not the reason for that why. Just what could the old man have planned for her *this* time? She was rather worried, considering he had three days to think about it.

Taima looked worried, probably for the same reason, but Pirogoeth waved off any concern. "I'll be fine. The coot hasn't killed me yet. Don't see any reason to think this will be any different." She bowed respectfully to the guard, and said, "I know the way, and I'll attend to the Dominus's order immediately."

Pirogoeth followed the perimeter of the tower to the side entrance that led to the lower keep. She nodded to the pair of Phalanx standing guard, expecting to see the black curtain of the shifting spell as they opened the door. Instead, there was just a stairway down. "The Dominus is waiting for you in the lower keep," the guard to the right of the door said, his features unreadable. "I do not know why."

Pirogoeth dismissed the grip of unease that was trying to clench her stomach. She had never actually *been* to the lower keep before; there were no stairs that connected it to the ground floor, and this was the only entrance she knew of that actually went there. If it was referenced at all, it was in hushed tones, and no one could ever say what exactly Socrato did in those depths. Pirogoeth never had the courage to ask, either. She knew the way of the mage occasionally went down some very dark roads, and had not been eager to pry.

It looked like she was going to find out regardless.

Unlike the other stairways within the tower, the steps to the lower keep were of old solid gray stone, and much more naturally spaced. The stones used to form the arched walls and ceiling were made of the same material, and certainly looked older than the rest of the tower. It was quite possible wherever this was existed even before Kartage did. The path was well lit at least, with magical candles every ten feet that burned with a clean and unnatural white light. That trend continued when the stairway ended into a long hall made from the same old stone.

Ten feet into the hall Socrato was waiting, his features grim. "I honestly had to think very long and very hard about what I am about to instruct you on," he said, "for this is a very dangerous field of study, very dark and very disturbing."

Pirogoeth didn't like the sound of that.

"But... I suppose it is something I must get out of the way, and I might as well do it now just so I can know if you are one that can be trusted with the deepest secrets I've learned of the magic ways." Socrato offered a tired, apologetic smile. "You've learned so very quickly... and honestly, if you do not pass this trial, you can consider my tutelage at an end."

"Master... I..." Pirogoeth stuttered.

"It would be no fault of yours. You would be a journeyman in your own right, much like Torma before you. She never even got this far." Socrato dropped his head, his voice ashamed. He obviously didn't want to do or say any of this. "I am... not a young man, Pirogoeth. I do not delude myself that I have too many more years left. I can't waste it on someone who isn't the one that can fulfill the dire task in these coming years."

Pirogoeth inhaled slowly and deeply. "I understand, master." And she did. If the Void was truly coming (and there was no doubt it was) and he had a theory on how to stop it, her personal feelings could not be taken into account if she wasn't up to the challenge. She fought back the clenching of her stomach. "Let's not waste time, present me this challenge, and I will do my best to meet it."

Socrato again gave her an apologetic smile. "Such a brave young lady. Very well... follow me." He turned about, waited for Pirogoeth to fall into step, then explained, "In case you were curious, this is what remains of a fort of Damathine, one of the ancient empires from days long gone. About forty years ago, it became the den of a particularly loathsome witch who pursued some very dark arts. I had Kartage constructed on top of it in the hopes that history would forget this place ever existed."

"And we're down here... why?"

Socrato's grim expression returned as he leveled his eyes in her direction. "Because you're about to show me what you know of the very dark art this witch pursued. It's something that can be very disquieting for anyone who might stumble upon it."

"Awfully unfair to test me on a school of magic I've never studied or practiced."

"Oh, you have, even if you don't realize it," Socrato corrected. "Twice at the very least in my very presence, and no doubt more."

There was a moment of confusion as Pirogoeth tried to think of what he could possibly be talking about. But she dropped the thought; having learned that once he started speaking in such a vague manner that her answer would soon be coming anyway.

"Pirogoeth!" a familiar voice screeched. "Is this your idea of revenge?" The pair had turned into a nondescript room with torches mounted along the walls for lighting. In the center of the room was a cage, like for a dog, holding Patillia prisoner.

Pirogoeth's eyes widened in shock, flabbergasted at what she was seeing. "What... is she doing here?"

"Regardless of your wish to not press charges, the law pertaining to assaulting a Phalanx officer, even off duty, is fairly strict," Socrato explained. "When I learned of it, I had her transferred here. She will be more than suitable for your test."

Patilla and Pirogoeth's response was identical and simultaneous. "Test for *what?*"

Socrato took a deep breath, and said sternly to Patilla, "Young lady, the crimes you have committed to my apprentice are beyond what I am willing to enumerate. You *will* be contrite and apologize for them."

"I most certainly will *not* apologize to that little monster!" Patilla screeched, shaking the case angrily. "And if I get the chance, I'll rip her hair out!"

Socrato's voice grew dark. "That was *not* a request, woman. You *will* be contrite, whether you like it or not. Preferably not, actually... as the test is for my apprentice to *make* you apologize."

"What?" Pirogoeth said. "How..."

Socrato scoffed. "This girl's mind is simple. Base. Barely

sentient..."

Patilla protested. "Hey!"

"Her will would be easily bent, dear girl," Socrato said, ignoring Patilla. "You more than have the power. Don't you *want* her to apologize for the pain she's caused?"

Pirogoeth gulped nervously. Of *course* she would love to see that.

"Then *make* her. Every tome has that ability buried deep within, though not expressed. Channel the raw, unfocused power of your tome, and use that power to amplify your will. I promise that it is something you have already done unwittingly."

The hand clenching her stomach was only tightening its grip. "I... can do that?"

"Absolutely," Socrato assured. "This meager minded sot will not offer much resistance."

"Like hell I will you wrinkled pervert!" Patilla howled. "I won't give you any pleasure, I'm a lot more distinguishing than the little boy here that you've no doubt gotten to excite you..."

"Silence!" Pirogoeth bellowed angrily at Patilla. "You will *not* disparage my master!" Patilla, surprisingly, complied, her mouth instantly snapping shut as she turned her head to face the now angered Pirogoeth. The apprentice approached the cage, building in power, as she snarled, "Forget apologizing to me. I don't *care* what you say about me. But you *will* apologize to my master for your slander!" Patilla cowered, stumbling backward to the opposite end of the cage. "*Now!*" Pirogoeth demanded.

Patilla gulped, stammered, lips flapping loosely, and managed to form enough words to say, "I... I am sorry, sir. I won't... behave that way again."

Socrato nodded. "While wonderful, apprentice, the purpose of this exercise *is* to bend her to *your* will, not *mine*. I must insist you proceed."

Pirogoeth really didn't want to escalate things further. "But..."

"It is imperative."

Socrato rarely ever was so coldly insistent. This was clearly very important to him, and it was apparently vital to her future training. And to be honest, being so assertive *had* felt good. Seeing Patilla *afraid* of her... it had been a rush.

"Try pulling back on the rage. It's an easy way to trigger your power, but it's not necessary. I want to see just your force of will. Know what you want, then take it," Socrato advised, his posture and eyes scrutinizing her.

She followed her master's instructions, drawing into her tome, feeling the power bubbling but without any expressed purpose. She gave it one. Pirogoeth snapped, "Patilla! Look at me!" Her old tormentor nervously turned her eyes on Pirogoeth. "Come here." With trembling knees, the girl stepped forward, more shambling then walking. The terror in her eyes honestly disturbed Pirogoeth.

The apprentice could remember that look; it was a look Pirogoeth knew had etched *her* face more than once. But that empathy was fleeting. The pain took over, the desire to subjugate Patilla taking over. "You *will* apologize to me for all you have done. Understand?"

Patilla nodded frantically. "Yes, Pirogoeth. I am *so* very sorry. I should *never* have participated in hurting you. You weren't the monster. I was. Whatever penance I need to undergo to earn your forgiveness, I will do it."

Pirogoeth had heard some pretty fake apologies before, most often after she had tattled on the antics of her abusers. This *should* have sounded fake as well. There was every reason to believe this was also a lie. But... it wasn't. It was certainly over the top, but it felt entirely earnest. Patilla meant every word.

Socrato also was convinced. He nodded approvingly, a grim expression on his face. "Yes... very good. Very well done indeed apprentice. But I think you can go further still."

"Further still?"

"Yes. You can do more than make her apologize. Now, make her *like* you."

"I can't do that!" Pirogoeth sputtered.

Socrato disagreed. "Of course you can. You've already shown the ability to manipulate her feelings."

"Making someone apologize for past slights is one thing," Pirogoeth replied. "Making someone like me is entirely another."

Socrato scoffed. "Why? What difference are the specific feelings involved?"

"Perhaps *can't* wasn't the right word. I *won't*."

Socrato became stern. "This is *not* the time for a values discussion. This test is the limit of your power, not the limit of your moral compass."

"This is *wrong*."

"Of course it is. That's why we are down here. Mages *must* occasionally do things that are wrong. We *have* to push the lines of what is acceptable. There is more at stake here than one pathetic whelp of a woman."

Pirogoeth stiffened, and her eyes broadened in shock at the casual disdain her master was showing. But the emotionless mask cracked in the process, and she could somewhat get a read on what was underneath. He was in turmoil. He didn't like this any more than she did... but he was desperate. Something about this entire test was of vital importance, it was a question that he needed an answer to, and quickly.

She closed her eyes, and fought back her own disgust. Her master needed an answer.

She would give him one.

"Patilla!" she barked, focusing her willpower on her target. "You *will* like me. I *will* be your only friend from now on. Am I clear?"

The young woman visibly jerked, like she had been unexpectedly jolted by an electric shock. If that hadn't been unsettling, when Patilla focused again, something... was off. She didn't look right. There was a glaze over her eyes, and her motions were slightly sluggish. Patilla's voice turned airy, and her lips curled in an unnatural smile. "Of course, Pirogoeth. To be honest, I never really hated you anyway. Mari was the ringleader, really. The rest of us followed her lead. Had I known how amazing you truly were, I would have never sided with her to begin with!"

Pirogoeth's skin literally crawled at the admission. Again, it sounded earnest. *Too* earnest. Whoever this woman was now, it *wasn't* Patilla. She looked at Socrato with increasing discomfort, and asked, "Master? What... have I done? What is going on here?"

Socrato's initial response was to open the cage, and allow Patilla freedom. The girl immediately raced to Pirogoeth, stopping and looking down on the apprentice mage with an unnerving smile of adoration.

Socrato had moved behind Pirogoeth, leaning forward to catch her ear. "Good. Very good. Now go further still. Make her *love* you. Make her a slave to your every word."

"*What?*" Pirogoeth yelped, aghast.

"You heard me. Push your power to its limit. She is already prepared to worship the ground you walk on. *Make* her. Make your wants and needs hers. Dominate her so completely that nothing else exists other than to please you."

"What? No! Absolutely not!"

"Do it!" Socrato hissed.

"I can't! I won't!" Pirogoeth bellowed back. She spun around to face her master and screamed, "If this is what I must do in order to continue as your apprentice, then I *refuse!*"

Socrato grabbed her by the shoulders, and shook her violently. The mask had finally fallen to reveal the frenzy in his face and voice. "This is *not* an option, Pirogoeth! I *must* know your limits!"

He stopped himself, as if he himself realized what he was doing. He released her, took several steps back, and gathered up his rampant emotions. With a deep breath, he tried to explain himself better. "The Art of Domination is a very rare, very sinister skill. Those few who have that power are extraordinarily dangerous. Pirogoeth... I need to know just how powerful you are. If you do not show me..." His hands ignited in magical fire, which highlighted the pools of moisture forming on his cheeks. "If you do not show me, I will have to assume the worst. I... I will have to kill you here."

Pirogoeth recoiled, the hand around her stomach at full clench. The tension in the chamber was so high that she could almost drown in it. She turned back to Patilla, who seemed oblivious to the environment, still smiling with that distant expression. "Will... will I hurt her?"

Socrato shook his head, "No. Your tormentor is beyond pain."

Patilla looked beyond a good many things. "How can I?" Pirogoeth asked. "I... I don't want this. I'm sorry, master. But I can't do what you want me to do."

Socrato heaved a massive sigh of relief. "And that... is what I wanted to hear." His entire body was shaking as he approached Patilla, and said warmly, "Young lady, do you remember the way you came in?"

The girl blinked slowly twice, and nodded.

"Then leave the same way. Tell the nice men standing guard that they are to watch you until I retrieve you."

Patilla turned her head to Pirogoeth, as if waiting for permission, which Pirogoeth provided with a nod. Without further word of any sort, Patilla walked through the doorway with an empty smile.

Socrato offered a nervous explanation. "I am deeply sorry. One of my colleagues had an apprentice who turned a great number of her tower against her and tried to take her life. I had to know not just the depth of your power, but how far you were willing to take it. I will be able to restore her to normal after our business is concluded."

Pirogoeth wasn't entirely certain, but she thought she heard her master add under his breath, "Mostly."

The venerated sage took a slow, deliberate breath. "Magic, at its core, is the power of denial. Material, the denial of natural law. Ethereal, the denial of reality. Decay and Restoration, the denial of life and death, respectively." He then leveled solemn eyes in her direction. "And Domination, the denial of free will. The darkest of magical arts. To take not just a life, but the utter annihilation of the self. And as loathsome as it is, it is *also* an art you will learn."

Pirogoeth shuddered, "I'd rather not."

"I'm sure. But it is through knowledge that you defeat the evil that lies in the hearts of man, not ignorance," Socrato advised. "Don't worry, *that* is a skill we will refine at a later date. For now... I think you are ready to learn the whole purpose I have for you."

Pirogoeth's eyes widened in anticipation. She knew the overall goal of her training, but that had only been through some ill-advised eavesdropping. He had never openly discussed the details, and she was eager to finally be privy to the elder mage's endgame.

"Come with me," he said, taking his leave of the chamber. "We'll take a shift... even if there *was* another way to get up there, I wouldn't be keen on a hike to the top of the tower from all the way down here."

The top of the tower? Socrato *never* let anyone up there.

The black curtain of a shifting spell dropped right where she expected it to. Socrato crossed first, disappearing into the inky ether, and Pirogoeth followed. The somewhat familiar moment of total blackness was followed by her first look at Socrato's inner sanctum.

This was the very top of the tower, judging from the open air deck all around her in a circle. It was both remarkable and plain, while the chessboard pattern of granite and onyx stone was lovely, there were few furnishings along the perimeter, couches and chairs of drab brown leather, and a single desk strewn with books along with what looked to be charts of some sort that she couldn't clearly see from her position.

The bronze ceiling was also retractable, as a full third of it had been drawn on itself, no doubt so that the large silver telescope could peer out into the sky, though she wondered what her master had hoped to see in the middle of the day. "I had been stargazing last night," Socrato explained, noticing his apprentice's line of sight. "Forgot to pull the top back down. My mind was... lost on other things, as I'm sure you could guess."

Pirogoeth nodded. She had figured that reaching the decision to do what he had done today had not been an easy one. "How many of

your students have you... needed to... deal with before?"
"Socrato smiled wanly. "Mercifully, none. You're the first I've ever deemed worthy of reaching that point. What I need is over here. Come along." The floor was actually a series of four descending steps that circled the observatory, and at the bottom, the telescope raised off the ground by iron chains, and the floor literally opened up into a six foot wide porthole with a plain metal staircase descending into a lower chamber. "I... have a lot of secret hideaways here," he said simply. "For good reason, I may add."

"I don't doubt you," Pirogoeth replied, accepting his gesture for her to go first.

The lower chamber actually wasn't poorly lit, only seeming so from outside it in the observatory. Though the light wasn't coming from any candle or torch or even electrical source, but from wisps of pale white energy dancing in the air like fireflies. "What... is this?" She asked in awe, reaching out her hand to touch one of the wisps, the ghostly thread winding through her fingers playfully before fluttering away.

"You may have already guessed that Kartage rests on one of the primary gathering points of ley energy in the world. As a result this entire region is already rich with magic. And it gathers even more densely in the presence of *that*."

"That" was a magical tome, sitting on a marble podium ten feet away; near entirely black save for blood red trim and an image on the front cover that resembled an eye. But even from the distance, Pirogoeth could *feel* it wasn't a typical tome. There was something very different about it.

"It is an ancient relic, predating even the oldest of civilizations," Socrato said. "I believe it, and others like it, are artifacts from the Coders' very creation of this world."

Pirogoeth was surprised by Socrato's close presence, jolting as the older mage displayed a book similar to the one on the pedestal, of the same color and eye-shaped image, but in green as opposed to red. Socrato tucked his tome into a pocket inside his toga, and turned her attention back to the red trimmed one. "It was serendipity that I learned of this particular item in the gallery of a fellow venerated citizen several months ago."

The admission clicked several pieces together in her head. "*This* was the item you had those two merchants acquire."

"Indeed," the venerated sage nodded.

More pieces fell into place. "And you dominated your peer

when he came to you demanding its return."

Socrato paused before reluctantly admitting, "I am not proud of it, but it had to be done."

"Why? Don't you already have one?"

"It wasn't for me," Socrato corrected, "but for the one that I found worthy of my task. For you."

Pirogoeth's skin went clammy at the idea of possessing that overwhelmingly powerful tome. "I think that thing would vaporize me."

"This isn't a tome in the way you think of it," Socrato said. "Not even I have to power to demand the power of one of these artifacts. But one thing I have discovered I can do with it is scry, and very effectively. It was scrying through my artifact that allowed me to sense the weakening of the ley lines within the South Gibraltar Islands."

He put a hand on Pirogoeth's back, and gently applied enough pressure to coax her forward, guiding his apprentice towards the podium despite her reservations. "Come now... just give it the attempt. I won't even ask you to offer blood for it," Socrato encouraged. "At the very worst, you'll have no success. I assure you."

Pirogoeth shot him a glare. "Pardon me if I don't immediately take the word of a master illusionist at face value anymore." It was an unfair shot, and she knew it. Socrato had done a good many things that irritated her, but he had never lied to her about the dangers of something.

At least her master didn't take offense. He grinned playfully instead, and quipped, "No, you really shouldn't. But fortunately for you, I am not a master of anything."

"Is that right?" Pirogoeth said flatly.

"Of course," he replied. "For to master something is to have nothing else to learn, and I can assure you I learn more every day."

Pirogoeth *really* didn't need wordplay right now.

"Now come on... quit dawdling," Socrato prodded, both verbally and physically with a poke to her upper back between the shoulder blades. "After what you've gone through, *this* is the *easy* part."

Pirogoeth exhaled sharply. "We're not going anywhere until I give it a shot, aren't we?"

"The day's still young, and I don't eat all that much lately, so I'm good until late evening. How about you?"

"How many of your students have wanted to paint the walls

with your intestines?" she grumbled as she stomped one step forward.

"Oh, all of them at some point," Socrato replied candidly. "That's how I know I'm a good teacher."

Pirogoeth paused to offer one more irritated glare, before finally grasping both sides of the podium and staring down intently at the ancient tome in front of her. Inhaling slowly, she let it out at the same time she pushed her will onto the tome...

Only to *literally* be thrown backwards five feet by what felt like a concussive force, and saved from a nasty fall by Socrato catching her.

"Well... *that's* a reaction I wasn't expecting," Socrato quipped, the humor in his voice gone. "Perhaps we should rethink this."

Pirogoeth pushed herself away, angrily focused on the tome, and a Scryer's Mark burning in her retinas. She blinked repeatedly to clear it away, and snarled. She had felt something in the tome, a sense of disdain. It didn't respect her, and made its dismissal clear.

"No," Pirogoeth retorted, this time taking deliberate strides to the tome and grabbing the podium. It was *personal* now.

"Stand back, master... just in case it tries to throw me further this time." This time, Pirogoeth was ready for the wall of force, and she refused to let it blow her back. She pushed forward mentally, though with no discernible success. She hadn't even felt herself leave her body. The wall of power was dense, imposing, and unyielding.

Exhaustion finally set in, and Pirogoeth had to give up the fight. She staggered backward, panting heavily from her exertions, brushing off Socrato's concern. "I'm just tired. That is not a very cooperative tome."

Socrato pointed up, and said, "I beg to differ."

Pirogoeth followed the gesture, to where the black book was levitating off the podium, the pages flipping as if by an unseen hand. The wisps of energy floating about was drawn into a ball above the tome, forming a Scryer's Mark above.

"Fascinating," Socrato said thoughtfully.

Pirogoeth guessed, "This sort of thing has never happened to you, I take it?"

"No, that it has not. The artifact is reacting to you in ways I have never seen before." The sage nodded to himself, and said, "Yes, I do believe the task of unlocking its secrets is yours. Now take it and follow me. There's still more to discuss."

The book didn't resist being picked up, at least. Pirogoeth was able to tuck it under her arm without incident and fall in step behind her master again as they continued down the lower section of the inner sanctum and into a hallway.

She quickly decided this hall was far too long to be directly underneath the observatory. "Okay, we can't possibly be in the tower. Where is this place?"

"Underneath the observatory," Socrato confirmed. "You are dealing with a skilled illusionist after all."

With a snap, Pirogoeth discovered that there was now light, and that she hadn't moved much more than ten feet, now inside a circular room with a mahogany desk flanked by bookshelves. A large globe was in the center of the room on a silver axis and stand, clearly made during an age where there was more than one continent, as Tanzibar and Pallentia were still in their old glory.

"Nothing is ever simple with you, is it?" Pirogoeth asked.

The old mage was unrepentant, his smile broad and playful. "I find constant practice keeps my skills sharp." He quickly turned serious, stopping in front of the globe and setting into a slow spin on its axis. "As you know, the Void has been a creeping, unstoppable, insatiable blight on this world. It has consumed most of the world already, and has begun encroaching on this last sanctuary as well. The South Gibraltar Islands are just the start, you know it as well as I."

Pirogoeth nodded in silent confirmation.

Socrato allowed himself to sound hopeful. "But... what if there was a way to stop it? What if artifacts like the ones you and I hold are the key to discovering the knowledge of the Coders themselves, and with that knowledge, stopping this collapse?"

The apprentice said nothing, but her interest was definitely piqued further.

"My fellow great sages and I believe that could be the case, and we have pooled our efforts towards a study that spans a continent and crosses political bounds to that one task. Kartage wasn't constructed here on accident, as I already told you. It is a major convergence point for the ley lines, as is Tortuga in the Northwest of Avalon, and in Damask, the keep maintained by the Dominus Augustus on the Island of Donne under the auspices of Reaht.

While we have learned much, there is one place missing, and we feel that if we had someone working there as well, that our efforts could yield more and greater fruit."

He stopped the globe's rotation with a finger, and traced his finger upward and to the right towards his target, a tiny finger of land jutting out into the Eastern Forever Sea. "The Northeast, the peninsula of Kuith, where it is my hope you will eventually set court and join us in our research."

He looked at her with the reluctance of a man on his last hope. "I cannot force your cooperation even if I wanted to, but I must insist as strongly as I can that this duty is beyond the highest importance. Greater than any war or empire... or any life."

Pirogoeth crossed her arms as the entirety of what he was suggesting began to sink in. A Domina... her... a veritable ruler of a keep like Kartage. But it was on damn near the other side of the continent. She'd likely never go home again...

"Say I agree to this insane idea," she said with far less emotion than she was really feeling. "What then?"

"For now? You learn under my tutelage. I will be as swift as you are able to learn and retain. Once you are ready, I will supply you with as much money and resources as I can. Fortunately for you, Kuith is in the Free Provinces, unlike the other three, and you should be able to integrate your keep into the sparsely populated region easily enough." He paused only to breathe. "You will need to learn more than magic as a result. Management of a keep is not easy, even if it is your only task. That too, I will teach you as best as I am able."

"'It's an honor,' Torma said," the apprentice grumbled quietly. "'A true blessing,' she said. 'To have drawn the interest of someone so grand and wise,' she said."

"Oh, all lies, to be sure. This will not be an easy road. The purpose I have for you is one that even the most gifted of mages would find daunting. It will push your will and your mind as far as it can go, then beyond."

Pirogoeth knew she couldn't wrestle with the offer very long, mostly because she really already knew her answer. It had to be done. "You're lucky, Dominus. For I accept this challenge."

The tension in her master's frame melted away, and he clapped once happily. "Splendid! Then tomorrow we will get right back to work. Time is not necessarily our friend, and the sooner you are prepared for your new position, the better the continent will be for it."

Pirogoeth nodded, accepting the tiring study that would be in her future. For the sake of the people she cared for, and even those she didn't, she had to.

Other works by Thomas Knapp

The Broken Prophecy

The Sixth Prophet

For more information, visit http://www.tkocreations.com

Other works by Fred Gallagher

MegaTokyo: Volumes 1-3

MegaTokyo Omnibus Vol. 1

Available from Dark Horse Comics

MegaTokyo: Volumes 4-6

Available from DC Comics

For more information, visit http://www.megatokyo.com or http://www.megagear.com

Made in the USA
San Bernardino, CA
26 March 2016